Wanderers

Knut Hamsun

Wanderers

The present edition is a reproduction of previous publication of this classic work. Minor typographical errors may have been corrected without note; however, for an authentic reading experience the spelling, punctuation, and capitalization have been retained from the original text.

ISBN: 978-1-63637-743-8

CONTENTS

WANDERERS

A WANDERER PLAYS ON MUTED STRINGS

WANDERERS

INTRODUCTION

An autobiographical element is evident in practically everything that Hamsun has written. But it is particularly marked in the two volumes now published under the common title of "Wanderers," as well as in the sequel named "The Last Joy." These three works must be considered together. They have more in common than the central figure of "Knut Pedersen from the Northlands" through whose vision the fates of Captain Falkenberg and his wife are gradually unfolded to us. Not only do they refer undisguisedly to events known to be taken out of Hamsun's own life, but they mirror his moods and thoughts and feelings during a certain period so closely that they may well be regarded as diaries of an unusually intimate character. It is as psychological documents of the utmost importance to the understanding of Hamsun himself that they have their chief significance. As a by-product, one might almost say, the reader gets the art which reveals the story of the Falkenbergs by a process of indirect approach equalled in its ingenuity and verisimilitude only by Conrad's best efforts.

The line of Hamsun's artistic evolution is easily traceable through certain stages which, however, are not separated by sharp breaks. It is impossible to say that one stage ended and the next one began in a certain year. Instead they overlap like tiles on a roof. Their respective characters are strikingly symbolized by the titles of the dramatic trilogy which Hamsun produced between 1895 and 1898—"At the Gate of the Kingdom," "The Game of Life," and "Sunset Glow."

"Hunger" opened the first period and "Pan" marked its climax, but it came to an end only with the eight-act drama of "Vendt the Monk" in 1902, and traces of it are to be found in everything that Hamsun ever wrote. Lieutenant Glahn might survive the passions and defiances of his youth and lapse into the more or less wistful resignation of Knut Pedersen from the Northlands, but the cautious, puzzled Knut has moments when he shows not only the Glahn limp but the Glahn fire.

Just when the second stage found clear expression is a little hard to tell, but its most characteristic products are undoubtedly the two volumes now offered to the American public, and it persists more or less until 1912, when "The Last Joy" appeared, although the first signs of Hamsun's final and greatest development showed themselves as early as 1904, when "Dreamers" was published. The difference between the second and the third stages lies chiefly in a maturity and tolerance of vision that restores the narrator's sense of humour and eliminates his own personality from the story he has to tell.

Hamsun was twenty-nine when he finished "Hunger," and that was the age given to one after another of his central figures. Glahn is twenty-nine, of course, and so is the Monk Vendt. With Hamsun that age seemed to stand principally for the high water mark of passion. Because of the fire burning within themselves, his heroes had the supreme courage of being themselves in utter defiance of codes and customs. Because of that fire they were capable of rising above everything that life might bring—above everything but the passing of the life-giving passion itself. A Glahn dies, but does not grow old.

Life insists on its due course, however, and in reality passion may sink into neurasthenia without producing suicides. Ivar Kareno discovers it in "Sunset Glow," when, at the age of fifty, he turns renegade in more senses than one. But even then his realization could not be fully accepted by the author himself, still only thirty-eight, and so Kareno steps down into the respectable and honoured sloth of age only to be succeeded, by another hero who has not yet passed the climacteric twenty-ninth year. Even Telegraph-Rolandsen in "Dreamers" retains the youthful glow and charm and irresponsibility that used to be thought inseparable from the true Hamsun character.

It is therefore with something of a shock one encounters the enigmatic Knut Pedersen from the Northlands, who has turned from literature to tramping, who speaks of old age as if he had reached the proverbial three-score and ten, and who time and again slips into something like actual whining, as when he says of himself: "Time has worn me out so that I have grown stupid and sterile and indifferent; now I look upon a woman merely as literature." The two volumes named "Under the Autumn Star" and "A Wanderer Plays on Muted Strings" form an unbroken cry of regret, and the object of that regret is the hey-day of youth—that golden age of twenty-nine—when every woman regardless of age and colour and caste was a challenging fragment of life.

Something more than the passing of years must have characterized the period immediately proceeding the production of the two volumes just mentioned. They mark some sort of crisis reaching to the innermost depths of the soul it wracked with anguish and pain. Perhaps a clue to this crisis may be found in the all too brief paragraph devoted to Hamsun in the Norwegian "Who's who." There is a line that reads as follows: "Married, 1898, Bergljot Bassöe Bech (marriage dissolved); 1908, Marie Andersen." The man that wrote "Under the Autumn Star" was unhappy. But he was also an artist. In that book the artist within him is struggling for his existence. In "A Wanderer Plays with Muted Strings" the artist is beginning to assert himself more and more, and that he had conquered in the meantime we know by "Benoni" and "Rosa" which appeared in 1908. The crisis was past, but echoes of it were heard as late as 1912, the year of "Last Joy," which well may be called Hamsun's most melancholy book. Yet that is the book which seems to have paved the way and laid the foundation for "The Growth of the Soil"—just as "Dreamers" was a sketch out of which in due time grew "Children of the Time" and "Segelfoss Town."

Hamsun's form is always fluid. In the two works now published it approaches formlessness. "Under the Autumn Star" is a mere sketch, seemingly lacking both plan and plot. Much of the time Knut Pedersen is merely thinking aloud. But out of his devious musings a purpose finally shapes itself, and gradually we find ourselves the spectator of a marital drama that becomes the dominant note in the sequel. The development of this main theme is, as I have already suggested, distinctly Conradian in its method, and looking back from the ironical epilogue that closes "A Wanderer Plays on Muted Strings," one marvels at the art that could work such a compelling totality out of such a miscellany of unrelated fragments.

There is a weakness common to both these works which cannot be passed up in silence. More than once the narrator falls out of his part as a tramp worker to rail journalistically at various things that have aroused his particular wrath, such as the tourist traffic, the city worker and everything relating to Switzerland. It is done very naively, too, but it is well to remember how frequently in the past this very kind of naiveté has associated with great genius. And whatever there be of such shortcomings is more than balanced by the wonderful feeling for and understanding of nature that most frequently tempt Hamsun into straying from the straight and narrow path of conventional story telling. What cannot be forgiven to the man who writes of "faint whisperings that come from forest and river as if millions of nothingnesses kept streaming and streaming," and who finds in those whisperings "one eternity coming to an understanding with another eternity about something"?

EDWIN BJORKMAN

UNDER THE AUTUMN STAR

I

Smooth as glass the water was yesterday, and smooth as glass it is again today. Indian summer on the island, mild and warm—ah! But there is no sun.

It is many years now since I knew such peace. Twenty or thirty years, maybe; or maybe it was in another life. But I have felt it some time, surely, since I go about now humming a little tune; go about rejoicing, loving every straw and every stone, and feeling as if they cared for me in return.

When I go by the overgrown path, in through the woods, my heart quivers with an unearthly joy. I call to mind a spot on the eastern shores of the Caspian, where I once stood. All just as it is here, with the water still and heavy and iron-grey as now. I walked through the woods, touched to the heart, and verging on tears for sheer happiness' sake, and saying to myself all the time: God in heaven. To be here again....

As if I had been there before.

Ah well, I may have been there once before, perhaps, coming from another time and another land, where the woods and the woodland paths were the same. Perhaps I was a flower then, in the woods, or perhaps a beetle, with its home in some acacia tree.

And now I have come to this place. Perhaps I was a bird and flew all that long way. Or the kernel in some fruit sent by a Persian trader.

See, now I am well away from the rush and crowd of the city, from people and newspapers; I have fled away from it all, because of the calling that came to me once more from the quiet, lonely tracts where I belong. "It will all come right this time," I tell myself, and am full of hope. Alas, I have fled from the city like this before, and afterwards returned. And fled away again.

But this time I am resolved. Peace I will have, at any cost. And for the present I have taken a room in a cottage here, with Old Gunhild to look after me.

Here and there among the pines are rowans, with ripe coral berries; now the berries are falling, heavy clusters striking the earth. So they reap themselves and sow themselves again, an inconceivable abundance to be squandered every single year. Over three hundred clusters I can count on a single tree. And here and there about are flowers still in bloom, obstinate things that will not die, though their time is really past.

1

But Old Gunhild's time is past as well—and think you she will die? She goes about as if death were a thing did not concern her. When the fishermen are down on the beach, painting their boats or darning nets, comes Gunhild with her vacant eyes, but with a mind as keen as any to a bargain.

"And what is the price of mackerel today?" she asks.

"The same as yesterday."

"Then you can keep it, for all I care."

And Gunhild goes back home.

But the fishermen know that Gunhild is not one of those that only pretend to go away; she has gone off like that before now, up to her cottage, without once looking back. So, "Hey" they call to her, and say they'll make it seven to the half-dozen today, seeing she is an old customer.

And Gunhild buys her fish.

Washing hangs on the lines to dry; red petticoats and blue shirts, and under-things of preposterous thickness, all spun and woven on the island by the old women still left alive. But there is washing, too, of another sort: those fine chemises without sleeves, the very thing to make a body blue with cold, and mauve woollen undervests that pull out to no more than the thickness of a string. And how did these abominations get there? Why, 'tis the daughters, to be sure, the young girls of the present day, who've been in service in the towns, and earned such finery that way. Wash them carefully, and not too often, and the things will last for just a month. And then there is a lovely naked feeling when the holes begin to spread.

But there is none of that sort of nonsense, now, about Gunhild's shoes, for instance. At suitable intervals, she goes round to one of the fishermen, her like in age and mind, and gets the uppers and the soles done in thoroughly with a powerful mess of stuff that leaves the water simply helpless. I've seen that dubbin boiling on the beach; there's tallow in it, and tar and resin as well.

Wandering idly along the beach yesterday, looking at driftwood and scales and stones, I came upon a tiny bit of plate glass. How it ever got there, is more than I can make out; but the thing seems a mistake, a very lie, to look at. Would any fisherman, now, have rowed out here with it and laid it down and rowed away again? I left it where it lay; it was thick and common and vulgar; perhaps a bit of a tramcar window. Once on a time glass was rare, and bottle-green. God's blessing on the old days, when something could be rare!

Smoke rising now from the fisher-huts on the southern point of the island. Evening time, and porridge cooking for supper. And when supper's done, decent folk go to their beds, to be up again with

2

the dawn. Only young and foolish creatures still go trapesing round from house to house, putting off their bedtime, not knowing what is best for themselves.

II

A man landed here this morning—come to paint the house. But Old Gunhild, being very old indeed, and perishing with gout most times, gets him to cut up a few days' firewood for her cooking before he starts. I've offered many a time to cut that wood myself, but she thinks my clothes too fine, and would not let me have the ax on any account.

This painter, now, is a short, thick-set fellow with red hair and no beard. I watch him from behind a window as he works, to see how he handles the ax. Then, noticing that he is talking to himself, I steal out of the house to listen. If he makes a false stroke, he takes it patiently, and does not trouble himself; but whenever he knocks his knuckles, he turns irritable and says: "Fan! Fansmagt!"[1] —and then looks round suddenly and starts humming a tune to cover his words.

Yes; I recognize that painter man. Only, he's not a painter at all, the rascal, but Grindhusen, one of the men I worked with when I was roadmaking at Skreia.

I go up to him, and ask if he remembers me, and we talk a bit.

Many, many years it is now since we were roadmenders together, Grindhusen and I; we were youngsters then, and danced along the roads in the sorriest of shoes, and ate what we could get as long as we had money enough for that. But when we'd money to spare, then there would be dancing with the girls all Saturday night, and a crowd of our fellow-workers would come along, and the old woman in the house sold us coffee till she must have made a little fortune. Then we worked on heart and soul another week through, looking forward to the Saturday again. But Grindhusen, he was as a red-headed wolf after the girls.

Did he remember the old days at Skreia?

He looks at me, taking stock of me, with something of reserve; it is quite a while before I can draw him out to remember it at all.

Yes, he remembers Skreia well enough.

"And Anders Fila and 'Spiralen' and Petra?"

---

[1] "The Devil! Power of the Devil!"

3

"Which one?"

"Petra—the one that was your girl."

"Ay, I remember her. I got tied up with her at last." Grindhusen falls to chopping wood again.

"Got tied up with her, did you?"

"Ay, that was the end of it. Had to be, I suppose. What was I going to say, now? You've turned out something fine, by the look of things."

"Why? Is it these clothes you're thinking of? You've Sunday clothes yourself, now, haven't you?"

"What d'you give for those you've got on?"

"I can't remember, but it was nothing very much. Couldn't say exactly what it was."

Grindhusen looks at me in astonishment and bursts out laughing.

"What? Can't remember what you paid for them?"

Then he turns serious, shakes his head, and says: "No, I dare say you wouldn't. No. That's the way when you've money enough and beyond."

Old Gunhild comes out from the house, and seeing us standing there by the chopping-block wasting time in idle talk, she tells Grindhusen he'd better start on the painting.

"So you've turned painter now?" said I.

Grindhusen made no answer, and I saw I had said a thing that should not have been said in others' hearing.

III

Grindhusen works away a couple of hours with his putty and paint, and soon one side of the little house, the north side, facing the sea, is done all gaily in red. At the mid-day rest, I go out and join him, with something to drink, and we lie on the ground awhile, chatting and smoking.

"Painter? Not much of a one, and that's the truth," says he. "But if any one comes along and asks if I can paint a bit of a wall, why, of course I can. First-rate Brændevin this you've got."

His wife and two children lived some four miles off, and he went home to them every Saturday. There were two daughters besides, both grown up, and one of them married. Grindhusen was a grandfather already. As soon as he'd done painting Gunhild's cottage—two coats it was to have—he was going off to the vicarage to dig a well. There was always work of some sort to be had about

4

the villages. And when winter set in, and the frost began to bind, he would either take a turn of woodcutting in the forests or lie idle for a spell, till something else turned up. He'd no big family to look after now, and the morrow, no doubt, would look after itself just as today.

"If I could only manage it," said Grindhusen, "I know what I'd do. I'd get myself some bricklayer's tools."

"So you're a bricklayer, too?"

"Well, not much of a one, and that's the truth. But when that well's dug, why, it'll need to be lined, that's clear...."

I sauntered about the island as usual, thinking of this and that. Peace, peace, a heavenly peace comes to me in a voice of silence from every tree in the wood. And now, look you, there are but few of the small birds left; only some crows flying mutely from place to place and settling. And the clusters from the rowans drop with a sullen thud and bury themselves in the moss.

Grindhusen is right, perhaps: tomorrow will surely look after itself, just as today. I have not seen a paper now these last two weeks, and, for all that, here I am, alive and well, making great progress in respect of inward calm; I sing, and square my shoulders, and stand bareheaded watching the stars at night.

For eighteen years past I have sat in cafés, calling for the waiter if a fork was not clean: I never call for Gunhild in the matter of forks clean or not! There's Grindhusen, now, I say to myself; did you mark when he lit his pipe, how he used the match to the very last of it, and never burned his horny fingers? I saw a fly crawling over his hand, but he simply let it crawl; perhaps he never noticed it was there. That is the way a man should feel towards flies....

In the evening, Grindhusen takes the boat and rows off. I wander along the beach, singing to myself a little, throwing stones at the water, and hauling bits of driftwood ashore. The stars are out, and there is a moon. In a couple of hours Grindhusen comes back, with a good set of bricklayer's tools in the boat. Stolen them somewhere, I think to myself. We shoulder each our load, and hide away the tools among the trees.

Then it is night, and we go each our separate way.

Grindhusen finishes his painting the following afternoon, but agrees to go on cutting wood till six o'clock to make up a full day's work. I get out Gunhild's boat and go off fishing, so as not to be there when he leaves. I catch no fish, and it is cold sitting in the boat; I look at my watch again and again. At last, about seven o'clock: he must be gone by now, I say to myself, and I row home. Grindhusen has got over to the mainland, and calls across to me from there: "Farvel!"

5

Something thrilled me warmly at the word; it was like a calling from my youth, from Skreia, from days a generation gone.

I row across to him and ask:

"Can you dig that well all alone?"

"No. I'll have to take another man along."

"Take me," I said. "Wait for me here, while I go up and settle at the house."

Half-way up I heard Grindhusen calling again:

"I can't wait here all night. And I don't believe you meant it, anyway."

"Wait just a minute. I'll be down again directly."

And Grindhusen sets himself down on the beach to wait. He knows I've some of that first-rate Brændevin still left.

IV

We came to the vicarage on a Saturday. After much doubting, Grindhusen had at last agreed to take me as his mate. I had bought provisions and some working clothes, and stood there now, in blouse and high boots, ready to start work. I was free and unknown; I learned to walk with a long, slouching stride, and for the look of a laboring man, I had that already both in face and hands. We were to put up at the vicarage itself, and cook our food in the brew-house across the yard.

And so we started on our digging.

I did my share of the work, and Grindhusen had no fault to find with me as a work-mate. "You'll turn out a first-rate hand at this, after all," he said.

Then after we'd been working a bit, the priest came out to look, and we took off our hats. He was an oldish man, quiet and gentle in his ways and speech; tiny wrinkles spread out fanwise from the corners of his eyes, like the traces of a thousand kindly smiles. He was sorry to interrupt, and hoped we wouldn't mind—but they'd so much trouble every year with the fowls slipping through into the garden. Could we leave the well just for a little, and come round and look at the garden wall? There was one place in particular....

Grindhusen answered: surely; we'd manage that for him all right.

So we went up and set the crumbling wall to rights. While we were busy there a young lady came out and stood looking on. We greeted her politely, and I thought her a beautiful creature to see.

6

Then a half-grown lad came out to look, and asked all sorts of questions. The two were brother and sister, no doubt. And the work went on easily enough with the young folk there looking on.

Then evening came. Grindhusen went off home, leaving me behind. I slept in the hayloft for the night.

Next day was Sunday. I dared not put on my town clothes lest they should seem above my station, but cleaned up my working things as neatly as I could, and idled about the place in the quiet of Sunday morning. I chatted to the farm-hands and joined them in talking nonsense to the maids; when the bell began ringing for church, I sent in to ask if I might borrow a Prayer Book, and the priest's son brought me one himself. One of the men lent me a coat; it wasn't big enough, really, but, taking off my blouse and vest, I made it do. And so I went to church.

That inward calm I had been at such pains to build up on the island proved all too little yet; at the first thrill of the organ I was torn from my setting and came near to sobbing aloud. "Keep quiet, you fool," I said to myself, "it's only neurasthenia." I had chosen a seat well apart from the rest, and hid my emotion as best I could. I was glad when that service was over.

When I had boiled my meat and had some dinner, I was invited into the kitchen for a cup of coffee. And while I sat there, in came Frøkenen, the young lady I had seen the day before; I stood up and bowed a greeting, and she nodded in return. She was charming, with her youth and her pretty hands. When I got up to go, I forgot myself and said:

"Most kind of you, I'm sure, my dear young lady!"

She glanced at me in astonishment, frowned, and the colour spread in her cheeks till they burned. Then with a toss of her head she turned and left the room. She was very young.

Well, I had done a nice thing now!

Miserable at heart, I sneaked up into the woods to hide. Impertinent fool, why hadn't I held my tongue! Of all the ridiculous things to say....

The vicarage buildings lay on the slope of a small hill; from the top, the land stretched away flat and level, with alternating timber and clearing. It struck me that here would be the proper place to dig the well, and then run a pipe-line down the slope to the house. Judging the height as nearly as I can, it seems more than enough to give the pressure needed; on the way back I pace out the approximate length: two hundred and fifty feet.

But what business was it of mine, after all? For Heaven's sake let me not go making the same mistake again, and insulting folk by talking above my station.

7

V

Grindhusen came out again on Monday morning, and we fell to digging as before. The old priest came out to look, and asked if we couldn't fix a post for him on the road up to the church. He needed it badly, that post; it had stood there before, but had got blown down; he used it for nailing up notices and announcements.

We set up a new post, and took pains to get it straight and upstanding as a candle in a stick. And by the way of thanks we hooded the top with zinc.

While I was at work on the hood, I got Grindhusen to suggest that the post should be painted red; he had still a trifle of red paint left over from the work at Gunhild's cottage. But the priest wanted it white, and Grindhusen was afraid to contradict, and carefully agreed to all he said, until at last I put in a word, and said that notices on white paper would show up better against red. At that the priest smiled, with the endless wrinkles round his eyes, and said: "Yes, yes, of course, you're quite right."

And that was enough; just that bit of a smile and saying I was right made me all glad and proud again within.

Then Frøkenen came up, and said a few words to Grindhusen; even jested with him, asking what that red cardinal was to be stuck up there for on the road. But to me she said nothing at all, and did not even look at me when I took off my hat.

Dinner was a sore trial to me that day, not that the food was bad, no, but Grindhusen, he ate his soup in a disgusting fashion, and his mouth was all greasy with fat.

"What'll he be like when it comes to eating porridge?" I thought to myself hysterically.

Then when he leaned back on the bench to rest after his meal in the same greasy state, I called to him straight out:

"For Heaven's sake, man, aren't you going to wipe your mouth?"

He stared at me, wiping his mouth with one hand. "Mouth?" he said.

I tried to turn it off then as a joke, and said: "Haha, I had you there!" But I was displeased with myself, for all that, and went out of the brewhouse directly after.

Then I fell to thinking of Frøkenen. "I'll make her answer when I give a greeting," I said to myself. "I'll let her see before very long that I'm not altogether a fool." There was that business of the well and the pipe-line, now; what if I were to work out a plan for the whole installation all complete! I had no instruments to take the height and fall of the hill ... well, I could make one that would serve.

And I set to work. A wooden tube, with two ordinary lamp-glasses fixed in with putty, and the whole filled with water.

Soon it was found there were many little things needed seeing to about the vicarage—odd matters here and there. A stone step to be set straight again, a wall to be repaired; the bridgeway to the barn had to be strengthened before the corn could be brought in. The priest liked to have everything sound and in order about the place—and it was all one to us, seeing we were paid by the day. But as time went on I grew more and more impatient of my work-mate's company. It was torture to me, for instance, to see him pick up a loaf from the table, hold it close in to his chest, and cut off a slice with a greasy pocket-knife that he was always putting in his mouth. And then, again, he would go all through the week, from Sunday to Sunday, without a wash. And in the morning, before the sun was up, and the evening, after it had gone, there was always a shiny drop hanging from the tip of his nose. And then his nails! And as for his ears, they were simply deformed.

Alas! I was an upstart creature, that had learned fine manners in the cafés in town. And since I could not keep myself from telling my companion now and then what I thought of his uncleanly ways, there grew up a certain ill-feeling between us, and I feared we should have to separate before long. As it was, we hardly spoke now beyond what was needed.

And there was the well, as undug as ever. Sunday came, and Grindhusen had gone home.

I had got my apparatus finished now, and in the afternoon I climbed up to the roof of the main building and set it up there. I saw at once that the sight cut the hillside several metres below the top. Good. Even reckoning a whole metre down to the water-level, there would still be pressure enough and to spare.

While I was busy up there the priest's son caught sight of me. Harald Meltzer was his name. And what was I doing up there? Measuring the hill; what for? What did I want to know the height for? Would I let him try?

Later on I got hold of a line ten metres long, and measured the hill from foot to summit, with Harald to help. When we came down to the house, I asked to see the priest himself, and told him of my plan.

VI

The priest listened patiently, and did not reject the idea at once.

"Really, now!" he said, with a smile. "Why, perhaps you're right. But it will cost a lot of money. And why should we trouble about it at all?"

"It's seventy paces from the house to the well we started to dig. Seventy steps for the maids to go through mud and snow and all sorts, summer and winter."

"That's true, yes. But this other way would cost a terrible lot of money."

"Not counting the well—that you'll have to have in any case; the whole installation, with work and material, ought not to come to more than a couple of hundred Kroner," said I.

The priest looked surprised.

"Is that all?"

"Yes."

I waited a little each time before answering, as if I were slow by nature, and born so. But, really, I had thought out the whole thing beforehand.

"It would be a great convenience, that's true," said the priest thoughtfully. "And that water tub in the kitchen does make a lot of mess."

"And it will save carrying water to the bedrooms as well."

"The bedrooms are all upstairs. It won't help us there, I'm afraid."

"We can run the pipes up to the first floor."

"Can we, though? Up to the bedrooms? Will there be pressure enough for that, do you think?"

Here I waited longer than usual before answering, as a stolid fellow, who did not undertake things lightly.

"I think I can answer for a jet the height of the roof," I said.

"Really, now!" exclaimed the priest. And then again: "Come and let us see where you think of digging the well."

We went up the hill, the priest, Harald, and I, and I let the priest look through my instrument, and showed him that there would be more than pressure enough.

"I must talk to the other man about it," he said.

But I cut out Grindhusen at once, and said: "Grindhusen? He's no idea of this work at all."

The priest looked at me.

"Really?" he said.

Then we went down again, the priest talking as if to himself.

10

"Quite right; yes. It's an endless business fetching water in the winter. And summer, too, for that matter. I must see what the women think about it."

And he went indoors.

After ten minutes or so, I was sent for round to the front steps; the whole family were there now.

"So you're the man who's going to give us water laid on to the house?" said Fruen kindly.

I took off my cap and bowed in a heavy, stolid fashion, and the priest answered for me: yes, this was the man.

Frøkenen gave me one curious glance, and then started talking in an undertone to her brother. Fruen went on with more questions—would it really be a proper water-supply like they had in town, just turn on a tap and there was the water all ready? And for upstairs as well? A couple of hundred Kroner? "Really, I think you ought to say yes," she said to her husband.

"You think so? Well, let's all go up to the top of the hill and look through the thing and see."

We went up the hill, and I set the instrument for them and let them look.

"Wonderful!" said Fruen.

But Frøkenen said never a word.

The priest asked:

"But are you sure there's water here?"

I answered carefully, as a man of sober judgment, that it was not a thing to swear to beforehand, but there was every sign of it.

"What sort of signs?" asked Fruen.

"The nature of the ground. And you'll notice there's willow and osiers growing about. And they like a wet soil."

The priest nodded, and said:

"He knows his business, Marie, you can see."

On the way back, Fruen had got so far as to argue quite unwarrantably that she could manage with one maid less once they'd water laid on. And not to fail her, I put in:

"In summer at least you might. You could water all the garden with a hose fixed to the tap and carried out through the cellar window."

"Splendid!" she exclaimed.

But I did not venture to speak of laying a pipe to the cow-shed. I had realized all the time that with a well twice the size, and a branch pipe across the yard, the dairymaid would be saved as much as the kitchen-maids in the house. But it would cost nearly twice as much. No, it was not wise to put forward so great a scheme.

11

Even as it was, I had to agree to wait till Grindhusen came back. The priest said he wanted to sleep on it.

VII

So now I had to tell Grindhusen myself, and prepare him for the new arrangement. And lest he should turn suspicious, I threw all the blame on the priest, saying it was his idea, but that I had backed him up. Grindhusen had no objection; he saw at once it meant more work for us since we should have the well to dig in any case, and the bed for the pipes besides.

As luck would have it, the priest came out on Monday morning, and said to Grindhusen half jestingly:

"Your mate here and I have decided to have the well up on the hill, and lay down a pipe-line to the house. What do you think of it? A mad idea?"

Grindhusen thought it was a first-rate idea.

But when we came to talk it over, and went up all three to look at the site of the well, Grindhusen began to suspect I'd had more to do with it than I had said. We should have to lay the pipes deep down, he said, on account of the frost....

"One metre thirty's plenty," I said.

... and that it would cost a great deal of money.

"Your mate here said about a couple of hundred Kroner in all," answered the priest.

Grindhusen had no idea of estimates at all, and could only say:

"Well, well, two hundred Kroner's a deal of money, anyway."

I said:

"It will mean so much less in Aabot when you move."

The priest looked at me in surprise.

"Aabot? But I'm not thinking of leaving the place," he said.

"Why, then, you'll have the full use of it. And may your reverence live to enjoy it for many a year," said I.

At this the priest stared at me, and asked:

"What is your name?"

"Knut Pedersen."

"Where are you from?"

"From Nordland."

But I understood why he had asked, and resolved not to talk in that bookish way any more.

Anyhow, the well and the pipe-line were decided on, and we set to work....

The days that followed were pleasant enough. I was not a little anxious at first as to whether we should find water on the site, and I slept badly for some nights. But once that fear was past, all that remained was simple and straightforward work. There was water enough; after a couple of days we had to bale it out with buckets every morning. It was clay lower down, and our clothes were soon in a sorry state from the work.

We dug for a week, and started the next getting out stones to line the well. This was work we were both used to from the old days at Skreia. Then we put in another week digging, and by that time we had carried it deep enough. The bottom was soon so soft that we had to begin on the stonework at once, lest the clay walls should cave in on top of us.

So week after week passed, with digging and mining and mason's work. It was a big well, and made a nice job; the priest was pleased with it. Grindhusen and I began to get on better together; and when he found that I asked no more than a fair labourer's wage, though much of the work was done under my directions, he was inclined to do something for me in return, and took more care about his table manners. Altogether, I could not have wished for a happier time; and nothing on earth should ever persuade me to go back to town life again!

In the evenings I wandered about the woods, or in the churchyard reading the inscriptions on the tombstones, and thinking of this and that. Also, I was looking about for a nail from some corpse. I wanted a nail; it was a fancy of mine, a little whim. I had found a nice piece of birch-root that I wanted to carve to a pipe-bowl in the shape of a clenched fist; the thumb was to act as a lid, and I wanted a nail to set in, to make it specially lifelike. The ring finger was to have a little gold ring bent round.

Thinking of such trifles kept my mind calm and at ease. There was no hurry now for me about anything in life. I could dream as I pleased, having nothing else to do; the evenings were my own. If possible, too, I would see and arrive at some feeling of respect for the sacredness of the church and terror of the dead; I had still a memory of that rich mysticism from days now far, far behind, and wished I could have some share in it again. Now, perhaps, when I found that nail, there would come a voice from the tombs: "That is mine!" and I would drop the thing in horror, and take to my heels and run.

"I wish that vane up there wouldn't creak so," Grindhusen would say at times.

13

"Are you afraid?"

"Well, not properly afraid; no. But it gives you a creeping feeling now and then to think of all the corpses lying there so near."

Happy man!

One day Harald showed me how to plant pine cones and little bushes. I'd no idea of that sort of work before; we didn't learn it in the days when I was at school. But now I'd seen the way of it, I went about planting busily on Sundays; and, in return, I taught Harald one or two little things that were new to him at his age, and got to be friends with him.

VIII

And all might have been well if it had not been for Frøkenen, the daughter of the house. I grew fonder of her every day. Her name was Elischeba, Elisabeth. No remarkable beauty, perhaps; but she had red lips, and a blue, girlish glance that made her pretty to see. Elischeba, Elisabeth—a child at the first dawn of life, with eyes looking out upon the world. She spoke one evening with young Erik from the neighbouring gaard, and her eyes were full of sweetness and of something ripening.

It was all very well for Grindhusen. He had gone ravening after the girls when he was young, and he still spanked about with his hat on one side, out of habit. But he was quiet and tame enough now, as well he might be—'tis nature's way. But some there are who would not follow nature's way, and be tamed; and how shall it fare with them at last? And then there was little Elisabeth; and she was none so little after all, but as tall as her mother. And she'd her mother's high breast.

Since that first Sunday they had not asked me in to coffee in the kitchen, and I took care myself they should not, but kept out of the way. I was still ashamed of the recollection. But then, at last, in the middle of the week, one of the maids came with a message that I was not to go running off into the woods every Sunday afternoon, but come to coffee with the rest. Fruen herself had said so.

Good!

Now, should I put on my best clothes or not? No harm, perhaps, in letting that young lady get into her head that I was one who had chosen to turn my back upon the life of cities, and taken upon myself the guise of a servant, for all I was a man of parts, that could lay on water to a house. But when I had dressed, I felt myself that my working clothes were better suited to me now; I took off my best things again, and hid them carefully in my bag.

But, as it happened, it was not Frøkenen at all who received me on that Sunday afternoon, but Fruen. She talked to me for quite a while, and she had spread a little white cloth under my cup.

"That trick of yours with the egg is likely to cost us something before we've done with it," said Fruen, with a kindly laugh. "The boy's used up half a dozen eggs already."

I had taught Harald the trick of passing a hard boiled egg with the shell off through the neck of a decanter, by thinning the air inside. It was about the only experiment in physics that I knew.

"But that one with breaking the stick in the two paper loops was really interesting," Fruen went on. "I don't understand that sort of thing myself, but.... When will the well be done?"

"The well is done. We're going to start on the trench tomorrow."

"And how long will that take to do?"

"About a week. Then the man can come and lay the pipes."

"No! really?"

I said my thanks and went out. Fruen had a way she had kept, no doubt, from earlier years; now and again she would glance at one sideways, though there was nothing the least bit artful in what she said....

Now the woods showed a yellowing leaf here and there, and earth and air began to smell of autumn. Only the fungus growths were now at their best, shooting up everywhere, and flourishing fine and thick on woolly stems—milk mushrooms, and the common sort, and the brown. Here and there a toadstool thrust up its speckled top, flaming its red all unashamed. A wonderful thing! Here it is growing on the same spot as the edible sorts, fed by the same soil, given sun and rain from heaven the same as they; rich and strong it is, and good to eat, save, only, that it is full of impertinent muscarin. I once thought of making up a fine old story about the toadstool, and saying I had read it in a book.

It has always been a pleasure to me to watch the flowers and insects in their struggle to keep alive. When the sun was hot they would come to life again, and give themselves up for an hour or so to the old delight; the big, strong flies were just as much alive as in midsummer. There was a peculiar sort of earth-bug here that I had not seen before—little yellow things, no bigger than a small-type comma, yet they could jump several thousand times their own length. Think of the strength of such a body in proportion to its size! There is a tiny spider here with its hinder part like a pale yellow pearl. And the pearl is so heavy that the creature has to clamber up

15

a stalk of grass back downwards. When it comes upon an obstacle the pearl cannot pass, it simply drops straight down and starts to climb another. Now, a little pearl-spider like that is not just a spider and no more. If I hold out a leaf towards it to help it to its footing on a floor, it fumbles about for a while on the leaf, and thinks to itself: "H'm, something wrong about this!" and backs away again, refusing to be in any way entrapped on to a floor....

Some one calls me by name from down in the wood. It is Harald; he has started a Sunday school with me. He gave me a lesson out of Pontoppidan to learn, and now I'm to be heard. It is touching to be taught religion now as I should have taught it myself when I was a child.

IX

The well was finished, the trench was dug, and the man had come to lay the pipes. He chose Grindhusen to help him with the work, and I was set to cutting a way for the pipes up from the cellar through the two floors of the house.

Fruen came down one day when I was busy in the cellar. I called out to her to mind the hole in the floor; but she took it very calmly.

"There's no hole there now, is there?" she asked, pointing one way. "Or there?" But at last she missed her footing after all, and slipped down into the hole where I was. And there we stood. It was not light there anyway; and for her, coming straight in from the daylight outside, it must have seemed quite dark. She felt about the edge, and said:

"Now, how am I to get up again?"

I lifted her up. It was no matter to speak of; she was slight of figure, for all she had a big girl of her own.

"Well, I must say...." She stood shaking the earth from her dress. "One, two, three, and up!—as neatly as could be.... Look here, I'd like you to help me with something upstairs one day, will you? I want to move some things. Only we must wait till a day when my husband's over at the annexe; he doesn't like my changing things about. How long will it be before you've finished all there is to do here?"

I mentioned a time, a week or thereabout.

"And where are you going then?"

"To the farm just by. Grindhusen's fixed it up for us to go and dig potatoes there...."

16

Then came the work in the kitchen; I had to saw through the floor there. Frøken Elisabeth came in once or twice while I was there; it could hardly have been otherwise, seeing it was the kitchen. And for all her dislike of me, she managed to say a word or two, and stand looking at the work a little.

"Only fancy, Oline," she said to the maid, "when it's all done, and you'll only have to turn on a tap."

But Oline, who was old, did not look anyways delighted. It was like going against Providence, she said, to go sending water through a pipe right into the house. She'd carried all the water she'd a use for these twenty years; what was she to do now?

"Take a rest," said I.

"Rest, indeed! We're made to work, I take it, not to rest."

"And sew things against the time you get married," said Frøken Elisabeth, with a smile.

It was only girlish talk, but I was grateful to her for taking a little part in the talk with us, and staying there for a while. And heavens, how I did try to behave, and talk smartly and sensibly, showing off like a boy. I remember it still. Then suddenly Frøken Elisabeth seemed to remember it wasn't proper for her to stay out here with us any longer, and so she went.

That evening I went up to the churchyard, as I had done so many times before, but seeing Frøkenen already there, I turned away, and took myself off into the woods. And afterwards I thought: now she will surely be touched by my humility, and think: poor fellow, he showed real delicacy in that. And the next thing, of course, was to imagine her coming after me. I would get up from the stone where I was sitting, and give a greeting. Then she would be a little embarrassed, and say: "I was just going for a walk—it's such a lovely evening—what are you doing here?" "Just sitting here," say I, with innocent eyes, as if my thoughts had been far away. And when she hears that I was just sitting there in the late of the evening, she must realize that I am a dreamer and a soul of unknown depth, and then she falls in love with me....

She was in the churchyard again the following evening, and a thought of high conceit flew suddenly into my mind: it was myself she came to see! But, watching her more closely, I saw that she was busy, doing something about a grave, so it was not me she had come for. I stole away up to the big ant-heap in the wood and watched the insects as long as I could see; afterwards, I sat listening to the falling cones and clusters of rowan berries. I hummed a tune, and whispered to myself and thought; now and again I had to get up and walk a little to get warm. The hours passed, the night came on, and I

17

was so in love I walked there bare-headed, letting myself be stared out of all countenance by the stars.

"How's the time?" Grindhusen might ask when I came back to the barn.

"Just gone eleven," I would say, though it might be two or three in the morning.

"Huh! And a nice time to be coming to bed. Fansmagt! Waking folk up when they've been sleeping decently!"

And Grindhusen turns over on the other side, to fall asleep again in a moment. There was no trouble with Grindhusen.

Eyah, it's over-foolish of a man to fall in love when he's getting on in years. And who was it set out to show there was a way to quiet and peace of mind?

X

A man came out for his bricklayer's tools; he wanted them back. What? Then Grindhusen had not stolen them at all! But it was always the same with Grindhusen: commonplace, dull, and ordinary, never great in anything, never a lofty mind.

I said:

"You, Grindhusen, there's nothing in you but eat and sleep and work. Here's a man come for those tools now. So you only borrowed them; that's all you're good for. I wouldn't be you for anything."

"Don't be a fool," said Grindhusen.

He was offended now, but I got him round again, as I had done so many times before, by pretending I had only spoken in jest.

"What are we to do now?" he asked.

"You'll manage it all right," said I.

"Manage it—will I?"

"Yes, or I am much mistaken."

And Grindhusen was pacified once more.

But at the midday rest, when I was cutting his hair, I put him out of temper once again by suggesting he should wash his head.

"A man of your age ought to know better than to talk such stuff," he said.

And Heaven knows but he may have been right. His red thatch of hair was thick as ever, for all he'd grandchildren of his own....

Now what was coming to that barn of ours? Were spirits about? Who had been in there one day suddenly and cleaned the place and made all comfortable and neat? Grindhusen and I had each our own bedplace; I had bought a couple of rugs, but he turned in every night fully dressed, with all he stood up in, and curled himself up in the hay all anyhow. And now here were my two rugs laid neatly, looking for all the world like a bed. I'd nothing against it; 'twas one of the maids, no doubt, setting to teach me neat and orderly ways. 'Twas all one to me.

I was ready now to start cutting through the floor upstairs, but Fruen begged me to leave it to next day; her husband would be going over to the annexe, and that way I shouldn't disturb him. But next morning we had to put it off again; Frøken Elisabeth was going in to the store to buy no end of things, and I was to go with her and carry them.

"Good," said I, "I'll come on after."

Strange girl! had she thought to put up with my company on the way? She said:

"But do you think you can find the way alone?"

"Surely; I've been there before. It's where we buy our things."

Now, I couldn't well walk through all the village in my working things all messed up with clay: I put on my best trousers, but kept my blouse on over. So I walked on behind. It was a couple of miles or more; the last part of the way I caught sight of Frøken Elisabeth on ahead now and again, but I took care not to come up close. Once she looked round, and at that I made myself utterly small, and kept to the fringe of the wood.

Frøken Elisabeth stayed behind with some girl friend after she had done her shopping; I carried the things back to the vicarage, getting in about noon, and was asked in to dinner in the kitchen. The house seemed deserted. Harald was away, the maids were wringing clothes, only Oline was busy in the kitchen.

After dinner, I went upstairs, and started sawing in the passage.

"Come and lend me a hand here, will you?" said Fruen, walking on in front of me.

We passed by her husband's study and into the bedroom.

"I want my bed moved," said Fruen. "It's too near the stove in winter, and I can't stand the heat."

We moved the bed over to the window.

"It'll be nicer here, don't you think? Cooler," said she.

And, happening to glance at her, I saw she was watching me with that queer, sideways look.... Ey.... And in a moment I was all flesh and blood and foolishness. I heard her say:

"Are you mad?—Oh no, dear, please ... the door...."

Then I heard my name whispered again and again....

19

I sawed through the floor in the passage, and got everything done. Fruen was there all the time. She was so eager to talk, to explain, and laughing and crying all the time.

I said:

"That picture that was hanging over your bed—wouldn't it be as well to move that too?"

"Ye—es, perhaps it would," said Fruen.

XI

Now all the pipes were laid, and the taps fixed; the water spurted out in the sink in a fine, powerful jet. Grindhusen had borrowed the tools we needed from somewhere else, so we could plaster up a few holes left here and there; a couple of days more, and we had filled in the trench down the hillside, and our work at the vicarage was done. The priest was pleased with us; he offered to stick up a notice on the red post saying we were experts in the business of wells and pipes and water-supply, but, seeing it was so late in the year, and the frost might set in any time, it wouldn't have helped us much. We begged him instead to bear us in mind next spring.

Then we went over to the neighbouring farm to dig potatoes, promising to look in at the vicarage again some time.

There were many hands at work on the new place; we divided up into gangs and were merry enough. But the work would barely last over a week; after that we should have to shift again.

One evening the priest came over and offered to take me on as an outdoor hand at the vicarage. It was a nice offer, and I thought about it for a while, but ended by saying no. I would rather wander about and be my own master, doing such work as I could find here and there, sleeping in the open, and finding a trifle to wonder at in myself. I had come across a man here in the potato fields that I might join company with when Grindhusen was gone. This new man was a fellow after my own mind, and from what I had heard and seen of him a good worker; Lars Falkberget was his name, wherefore he called himself Falkenberg.[2]

Young Erik was foreman and overseer in charge of the potato diggers, and carted in the crop. He was a handsome lad of twenty, steady and sound for his age, and a proper son of the house. There

---

[2] The latter name has a more distinguished sound than the native and rustic "Falkberget."

was something no doubt between him and Frøken Elisabeth from the vicarage, seeing she came over one day and stood talking with him out in the fields for quite a while. When she was leaving, she found a few words for me as well, saying Oline was beginning to get used to the new contrivances of water-pipes and tap.

"And yourself?" I asked.

Out of politeness, she made some little answer to this also, but I could see she had no wish to stay talking to me.

So prettily dressed she was, with a new light cloak that went so well with her blue eyes....

Next day Erik met with an accident; his horse bolted, dragging him across the fields and throwing him up against a fence at last. He was badly mauled, and spitting blood; a few hours later, when he had come to himself a little, he was still spitting blood. Falkenberg was now set to drive.

I feigned to be distressed at what had happened, and went about silent and gloomy as the rest, but I did not feel so. I had no hope of Frøken Elisabeth for myself, indeed; still, I was rid of one that stood above me in her favour.

That evening I went over to the churchyard and sat there a while. If only she would come, I thought to myself. And after a quarter of an hour she came. I got up suddenly, entirely as I had planned, made as if to slip away and hide, then I stopped, stood helplessly and surrendered. But here all my schemes and plans forsook me, and I was all weakness at having her so near; I began to speak of something.

"Erik—to think it should have happened—and that, yesterday...."

"I know about it," she answered.

"He was badly hurt."

"Yes, yes, of course, he was badly hurt—why do you talk to me about him?"

"I thought.... No, I don't know. But, anyhow, he'll get better. And then it will be all right again, surely."

"Yes, yes...."

Pause.

It sounded as if she had been making fun of me. Then suddenly she said with a smile:

"What a strange fellow you are! What makes you walk all that way to come and sit here of an evening?"

"It's just a little habit I've got lately. For something to do till bedtime."

"Then you're not afraid?"

Her jesting tone gave me courage; I felt myself on surer ground, and answered:

"No, that's just the trouble. I wanted to learn to shiver and shake."

"Learn to shiver and shake? Like the boy in the fairy tale. Now where did you read about that, I wonder?"

"I don't know. In some book or other, I suppose."

Pause.

"Why wouldn't you come and work for us when Father asked you?"

"I'd be no good at that sort of work. I'm going out on the roads now with another man."

"Which way are you going?"

"That I cannot say. East or west. We are just wanderers."

Pause.

"I'm sorry," she said. "I mean, I don't think it's wise of you.... Oh, but what was it you said about Erik? I only came to ask about him...."

"He's in a baddish way now, but still."

"Does the doctor think he will get better?"

"Yes, as far as I know. I've not heard otherwise."

"Well—good-night."

Oh to be young and rich and handsome, and famous and learned in sciences!... There she goes....

Before leaving the churchyard I found a serviceable thumbnail and put it in my pocket. I waited a little, peering this way and that, and listening, but all was still. No voice came saying, "That's mine!"

XII

Falkenberg and I set out. It is evening; cool air and a lofty sky with stars lighting up. I persuaded him to go round by way of the churchyard; in my foolishness I wished to go that way, to see if there should be light in one little window down at the vicarage. Oh to be young and rich and....

We walked some hours, having but little weight to carry, and, moreover, we were two wanderers still a bit strange each to the other, so we could talk a little. We passed by the first trading station, and came to another; we could see the tower of the annexe church in the evening light.

From sheer habit I would have gone into the churchyard here as well. I said:

22

"What do you think? We might find a place here for the night?"

"No sense on earth in that," said Falkenberg, "when there's hay in every barn along the road. And if we're turned out, there'll be shelter in the woods."

And we went on again, Falkenberg leading.

He was a man of something over thirty. Tall and well-built, but with a slight stoop; his long moustaches rounded downwards. He was short of speech for the most, quick-witted and kindly; also he had a splendid voice for songs; a different sort from Grindhusen in every way. And when he spoke he used odd words from different local dialects, with a touch of Swedish here and there; no one could tell what part he came from.

We came to a farmstead where the dogs barked, and folk were still about. Falkenberg asked to see the man. A lad came out.

Had he any work for us?

No.

But the fence there along by the road was all to pieces, if we couldn't mend that, now?

No. Man himself had nothing else to do this time of the year.

Could they give us shelter for the night?

Very sorry, but....

Not in the barn?

No, the girls were still sleeping there.

"Swine," muttered Falkenberg, as we moved away. We turned in through a little wood, keeping a look out now for a likely place to sleep.

"Suppose we went back to the farm now to the girls in the barn? Like as not they wouldn't turn us out."

Falkenberg thought for a moment.

"The dogs will make a row," he said.

We came out into a field where two horses were loose. One had a bell at its neck.

"Nice fellow this," said Falkenberg, "with his horses still out and his womenfolk still sleeping in the barn. It'd be doing these poor beasts a good turn to ride them a bit."

He caught the belled horse, stuffed its bell with grass and moss, and got on its back. My beast was shy, and I had a deal of trouble to get hold of it.

We rode across the field, found a gate, and came out on to the road. We each had one of my rugs to sit on, but neither had a bridle.

Still, we managed well enough, managed excellently well; we rode close on five miles, and came to another village. Suddenly we heard some one ahead along the road.

"Better take it at a gallop," said Falkenberg over his shoulder. "Come along."

But Falkenberg was no marvel of a horseman, for all his leg; he clutched the bell-strap first, then slithered forward and hung on with both arms round the horse's neck. I caught a glimpse of one of his legs against the sky as he fell off.

Fortunately, there was no great danger waiting us after all; only a young couple out sweethearting.

Another half-hour's riding, and we were both of us stiff and sore. We got down, turned the horses' faces to home, and drove them off. And now we were foot-passengers once more.

Gakgak, gakgak—the sound came from somewhere far off. I knew it well; it was the grey goose. When we were children, we were taught to clasp our hands and stand quite still, lest we should frighten the grey goose as it passed. No harm in that; no harm in doing so now. And so I do. A quiet sense of mystery steals through me; I hold my breath and gaze. There it comes, the sky trailing behind it like the wake of a ship. Gakgak, high overhead. And the splendid ploughshare glides along beneath the stars....

We found a barn at last, at a farmstead where all was still, and there we slept some hours. They found us next morning sound asleep.

Falkenberg went up to the farmer at once and offered to pay for our lodging. We had come in late the night before, he explained, and didn't like to wake folk out of their beds, but we were no runaways for all that. The man would not take our money; instead he gave us coffee in the kitchen. But he had no work for us; the harvest was in, and he and his lad had nothing to do themselves now but mend their fences here and there.

XIII

We tramped three days and found no work, but had to pay for our food and drink, getting poorer every day.

"How much have you got left, and how much have I got left? We'll never get any great way at this rate," said Falkenberg. And he threw out a hint that we'd soon have to try a little stealing.

We talked it over a bit, and agreed to wait and see how things turned out. Food was no difficulty, we could always get hold of a fowl or so at a pinch. But ready money was the thing we really

24

needed, and that we'd have to get. If we couldn't manage it one way, we'd have to manage another. We didn't set up to be angels.

"I'm no angel out of heaven alive," said Falkenberg. "Here am I now, sitting around in my best clothes, and they no better than another man's workaday things. I can give them a wash in a stream, and sit and wait till they're dry; if there's a hole I mend it, and if I chance to earn a bit extra some day, I can get some more. And that's the end of it."

"But young Erik said you were a beggar to drink."

"That young cock. Drink—well, of course I do. No sense in only eating.... Let's look about for a place where there's a piano," said Falkenberg.

I thought to myself: a piano on a place means well-to-do folk; that's where he is going to start stealing.

In the afternoon we came to just such a place. Falkenberg had put on my town clothes beforehand, and given me his sack to carry so he could walk in easily, with an air. He went straight up to the front steps, and I lost sight of him for a bit, then he came out again and said yes, he was going to tune their piano.

"Going to what?"

"You be quiet," said Falkenberg. "I've done it before, though I don't go bragging about it everywhere."

He fished out a piano-tuner's key from his sack, and I saw he was in earnest.

I was ordered to keep near the place while he was tuning.

Well, I wandered about to pass the time; every now and then coming round to the south side of the house, I could hear Falkenberg at work on the piano in the parlour, and forcibly he dealt with it. He could not strike a decent chord, but he had a good ear; whenever he screwed up a string, he was careful to screw it back again exactly where it was before, so the instrument at any rate was none the worse.

I got into talk with one of the farm-hands, a young fellow. He got two hundred Kroner a year, he said, besides his board. Up at half-past six in the morning to feed the horses, or half-past five in the busy season. Work all day, till eight in the evening. But he was healthily content with his life in that little world. I remember his fine, strong set of teeth, and his pleasant smile as he spoke of his girl. He had given her a silver ring with a gold heart on the front.

"And what did she say to that?"

"Well, she was all of a wonder, you may be sure."

"And what did you say?"

"What I said? Why, I don't know. Said I hoped she'd like it

25

and welcome. I'd like to have given her stuff for a dress as well, but...."

"Is she young?"

"Why, yes. Talk away like a little jews' harp. Young—I should think so."

"And where does she live?"

"Ah, that I won't say. They'd know it all over the village if I did."

And there I stood like another Alexander, so sure of the world, and half contemptuous of this boy and his poor little life. When we went away, I gave him one of my rugs; it was too much of a weight to go carrying two. He said at once he would give it to his girl; she would be glad of a nice warm rug.

And Alexander said: If I were not myself I would be you....

When Falkenberg had finished and came out, he was grown so elegant in his manners all at once, and talked in such a delicate fashion, I could hardly understand him. The daughter of the house came out with him. We were to pass on without delay, he said, to the farm adjacent; there was a piano there which needed some slight attention. And so "Farvel, Frøken, Farvel."

"Six Kroner, my boy," he whispered in my ear. "And another six at the next place, that's twelve."

So off we went, and I carried our things.

XIV

Falkenberg was right; the people at the next farm would not be outdone by their neighbours; their piano must be seen to as well. The daughter of the house was away for the moment, but the work could be done in her absence as a little surprise for her when she came home. She had often complained that the piano was so dreadfully out of tune it was impossible to play on it at all. So now I was left to myself again as before, while Falkenberg was busy in the parlour. When it got dark he had lights brought in and went on tuning. He had his supper in there too, and when he had finished, he came out and asked me for his pipe.

"Which pipe?"

"You fool! the one with the clenched fist, of course."

Somewhat unwillingly I handed him my neatly carved pipe; I had just got it finished; with the nail set in and a gold ring, and a long stem.

"Don't let the nail get too hot," I whispered, "or it might curl up."

Falkenberg lit the pipe and went swaggering up with it indoors. But he put in a word for me too, and got them to give me supper and coffee in the kitchen.

I found a place to sleep in the barn.

I woke up in the night, and there was Falkenberg standing close by, and calling me by name. The full moon shone right in, and I could see his face.

"What's the matter now?"

"Here's your pipe. Here you are, man, take it."

"Pipe?"

"Yes, your pipe. I won't have the thing about me another minute. Look at it—the nail's all coming loose."

I took the pipe, and saw the nail had begun to curl away from the wood. Said Falkenberg:

"The beastly thing was looking at me with a sort of nasty grin in the moonlight. And then when I remembered where you'd got that nail...."

Happy Falkenberg!

Next morning when we were ready to start off again, the daughter of the house had come home. We heard her thumping out a waltz on the piano, and a little after she came out and said:

"It's made no end of difference with the piano. Thank you very much."

"I hope you may find it satisfactory," said the piano-tuner grandly.

"Yes, indeed. There's quite a different tone in it now."

"And is there anywhere else Frøkenen could recommend...?"

"Ask the people at Øvrebø; Falkenberg's the name."

"What name?"

"Falkenberg. Go straight on from here, and you'll come to a post on the right-hand side about a mile and a half along. Turn off there and that'll take you to it."

At that Falkenberg sat down plump at the steps and began asking all sorts of questions about the Falkenbergs at Øvrebø. Only to think he should come across his kinsmen here, and find himself, as it were, at home again. He was profusely grateful for the information. "Thanks most sincerely, Frøken."

Then we went on our way again, and I carried the things.

Once in the wood we sat down to talk over what was to be done. Was it advisable, after all, for a Falkenberg of the rank of piano-tuner to go walking up to the Captain at Øvrebø and claim relationship? I was the more timid, and ended by making

27

Falkenberg himself a little shy of it. On the other hand, it might be a merry jest.

Hadn't he any papers with his name on? Certificates of some sort?

"Yes, but for Fan, there's nothing in them except saying I'm a reliable workman."

We cast about for some way of altering the papers a little, but finally agreed it could be better to make a new one altogether. We might do one for unsurpassed proficiency in piano-tuning and put in the Christian name as Leopold instead of Lars.[3] There was no limit to what we could do in that way.

"Think that you can write out that certificate?" he asked.

"Yes, that I can."

But now that wretched brain of mine began playing tricks, and making the whole thing ridiculous. A piano-tuner wasn't enough, I thought; no, make him a mechanical genius, a man who had solved most intricate problems, an inventor with a factory of his own....

"Then I wouldn't need to go about waving certificates," said Falkenberg, and refused to listen any more. No, the whole thing looked like coming to nothing after all.

Downcast and discouraged both, we tramped on till we came to the post.

"You're not going up, are you?" I asked.

"You can go yourself," said Falkenberg sourly. "Here, take your rags of things."

But a little way farther on he slackened his pace, and muttered:

"It's a wicked shame to throw away a chance like that. Why, it's just cut out for us as it is."

"Well, then, why don't you go up and pay them a call? Who knows, you might be some relation after all."

"I wish I'd thought to ask if he'd a nephew in America."

"What then? Could you talk English to them if he had?"

"You mind your own business, and don't talk so much," said Falkenberg. "I don't see what you've got to brag about, anyway."

He was nervous and out of temper, and began stepping out. Then suddenly he stopped and said:

"I'll do it. Lend me that pipe of yours again. I won't light it."

We walked up the hill, Falkenberg putting on mighty airs, pointing this way and that with the pipe and criticizing the place. It annoyed me somewhat to see him stalking along in that vainglorious fashion while I carried the load. I said:

---

[3] Again substituting an aristocratic for a rustic name.

"Going to be a piano-tuner this time?"

"I think I've shown I can tune a piano," he said shortly. "I am good for that at any rate."

"But suppose there's some one in the house knows all about it—Fruen, for instance—and tries the piano after you've done?"

Falkenberg was silent. I could see he was growing doubtful again. Little by little his lordly gait sank to a slouching walk.

"Perhaps we'd better not," he said. "Here, take your pipe. We'll just go up and simply ask for work."

XV

As it happened, there was a chance for us to make ourselves useful the moment we came on the place. They were getting up a new flagstaff, and were short of hands. We set to work and got it up in fine style. There was a crowd of women looking on from the window.

Was Captain Falkenberg at home?

No.

Or Fruen?

Fruen came out. She was tall and fair, and friendly as a young foal; and she answered our greeting in the kindliest way.

Had she any work for us now?

"Well, I don't know. I don't think so really, not while my husband's away."

I had an idea she found it hard to say no, and touched my cap and was turning away, not to trouble her any more. But she must have found something strange about Falkenberg, coming up like that wearing decent clothes, and with a man to carry his things; she looked at him inquisitively and asked:

"What sort of work?"

"Any kind of outdoor work," said Falkenberg. "We can take on hedging and ditching, bricklayer's work...."

"Getting late in the year for that sort," put in one of the men by the flagstaff.

"Yes, I suppose it is," Fruen agreed. "I don't know.... Anyhow, it's just dinner-time; if you'd like to go in and get something to eat meanwhile. Such as it is."

"Thank you kindly," answered Falkenberg.

Now, that seemed to my mind a poor and vulgar way to speak; I felt he shamed us both in answering so, and it distressed me. So I must put in a word myself.

29

"Mille grâces, Madame; vous êtes trop aimable," I said gallantly, and took off my cap.

Fruen turned round and stared at me in astonishment; the look on her face was comical to see.

We were shown into the kitchen and given an excellent meal. Fruen went indoors. When we had finished, and were starting off, she came out again; Falkenberg had got back his courage now, and, taking advantage of her kindness offered to tune the piano.

"Can you tune pianos too?" she asked, in surprise.

"Yes, indeed; I tuned the one on the farm down below."

"Mine's a grand piano, and a good one. I shouldn't like it...."

"Fruen can be easy about that."

"Have you any sort of...."

"I've no certificate, no. It's not my way to ask for such. But Fruen can come and hear me."

"Well, perhaps—yes, come this way."

She went into the house, and he followed. I looked through the doorway as they went in, and saw a room with many pictures on the walls.

The maids fussed about in and out of the kitchen, casting curious glances at me, stranger as I was; one of the girls was quite nice-looking. I was thankful I had shaved that morning.

Some ten minutes passed; Falkenberg had begun. Fruen came out into the kitchen again and said:

"And to think you speak French! It's more than I do."

Now, Heaven be thanked for that. I had no wish to go farther with it myself. If I had, it would have been mostly hackneyed stuff, about returning to our muttons and looking for the lady in the case, and the State, that's me, and so on.

"Your friend showed me his papers," said Fruen. "You seem to be decent folk. I don't know.... I might telegraph to my husband and ask if he's any work for you."

I would have thanked her, but could not get a word out for swallowing at something in my throat.

Neurasthenia!

Afterwards I went out across the yard and walked about the fields a bit; all was in good order everywhere, and the crops in under cover. Even the potato stalks had been carted away though there's many places where they're left out till the snow comes. I could see nothing for us to do at all. Evidently these people were well-to-do.

When it was getting towards evening, and Falkenberg was still tuning, I took a bit of something to eat in my pocket and went off for a walk, to be out of the way so they should not ask me in to supper. There was a moon, and the stars were out, but I liked best to grope my way into the dense part of the wood and sit down in the dark. It was more sheltered there, too. How quiet the earth and air seemed now! The cold is beginning, there is rime on the ground; now and again a stalk of grass creaks faintly, a little mouse squeaks, a rook comes soaring over the treetops, then all is quiet again. Was there ever such fair hair as hers? Surely never. Born a wonder, from top to toe, her lips a ripened loveliness, and the play of dragonflies in her hair. If only one could draw out a diadem from a sack of clothes and give it her. I'll find a pink shell somewhere and carve it to a thumbnail, and offer her the pipe to give her husband for a present ... yes....

Falkenberg comes across the yard to meet me, and whispers hurriedly:

"She's got an answer from the Captain; he says we can set to work felling timber in the woods. Are you any good at that?"

"Yes."

"Well, then, go inside, into the kitchen. She's been asking for you."

I went in and Fruen said:

"I wondered where you'd got to. Sit down and have something to eat. Had your supper? Where?"

"We've food with us in the sack."

"Well, there was no need to do that. Won't you have a cup of tea, then? Nothing?... I've had an answer from my husband. Can you fell trees? Well, that's all right. Look, here it is: 'Want couple of men felling timber, Petter will show trees marked.'...."

Heaven—she stood there beside me, pointing to the message. And the scent of a young girl in her breath....

XVI

In the woods. Petter is one of the farm-hands; he showed us the way here.

When we talked together, Falkenberg was not by any means so grateful to Fruen for giving us work. "Nothing to bow and scrape for in that," he said. "It's none so easy to get workmen these days." Falkenberg, by the way, was nothing out of the ordinary in the woodcutting line, while I'd had some experience of the work in another part of the world, and so could take a lead in this at a finish. And he agreed I was to be leader.

Just now I began working in my mind on an invention.

With the ordinary sort of saw now in use, the men have to lie

31

down crookedwise on the ground and pull sideways. And that's why there's not so much gets done in a day, and a deal of ugly stumps left after in the woods. Now, with a conical transmission apparatus that could be screwed on to the root, it should be possible to work the saw with a straight back-and-forward movement, but the blade cutting horizontally all the time. I set to work designing parts of a machine of this sort. The thing that puzzled me most was how to get the little touch of pressure on the blade that's needed. It might be done by means of a spring that could be wound up by clockwork, or perhaps a weight would do it. The weight would be easier, but uniform, and, as the saw went deeper, it would be getting harder all the time, and the same pressure would not do. A steel spring, on the other hand, would slacken down as the cut grew deeper, and always give the right amount of pressure. I decided on the spring system. "You can manage it," I told myself. And the credit for it would be the greatest thing in my life.

The days passed, one like another; we felled our nine-inch timber, and cut off twigs and tops. We lived in plenty, taking food and coffee with us when we started for the woods, and getting a hot meal in the evening when we came home. Then we washed and tidied ourselves—to be nicer-mannered than the farm-hands—and sat in the kitchen, with a big lamp alight, and three girls. Falkenberg had become Emma's sweetheart.

And every now and then there would come a wave of music from the piano in the parlour; sometimes Fruen herself would come out to us with her girlish youth and her blessed kindly ways. "And how did you get on today?" she would ask. "Did you meet a bear in the woods?" But one evening she thanked Falkenberg for doing her piano so nicely. What? did she mean it? Falkenberg's weather-beaten face grew quite handsome with pleasure; I felt proud of him when he answered modestly that he thought himself it was a little better now.

Either he had gained by his experience in tuning already, or Fruen was grateful to him for not having spoiled the grand piano.

Falkenberg dressed up in my town clothes every evening. It wouldn't do for me to take them back now and wear them myself; every one would believe I'd borrowed them from him.

"Let me have Emma, and you can keep the clothes," I said in jest.

"All right, you can take her," he answered.

I began to see then that Falkenberg was growing cooler towards his girl. Oh, but Falkenberg had fallen in love too, the same as I. What simple boys we were!

32

"Wonder if she will give us a look in this evening again?" Falkenberg would say while we were out at work.

And I would answer that I didn't care how long the Captain stayed away.

"No, you're right," said Falkenberg. "And I say, if I find he isn't decent to her, there'll be trouble."

Then one evening Falkenberg gave us a song. And I was proud of him as ever. Fruen came out, and he had to sing it over again, and another one after; his fine voice filled the room, and Fruen was delighted, and said she had never heard anything like it.

And then it was I began to be envious.

"Have you learnt singing?" asked Fruen. "Can you read music at all?"

"Yes, indeed," said Falkenberg. "I used to sing in a club."

Now that was where he should have said: no, worse luck, he'd never learned, so I thought to myself.

"Have you ever sung to any one? Has any one ever heard you?"

"I've sung at dances and parties now and again. And once at a wedding."

"But I mean for any one that knew: has any one tried your voice?"

"No, not that I know of—or yes, I think so, yes."

"Well, won't you sing some more now? Do."

And Falkenberg sang.

The end of it'll be he'll be asked right into the parlour one evening, I thought to myself, with Fruen—to play for him. I said:

"Beg pardon, but won't the Captain be coming home soon?"

"Yes, soon," answered Fruen. "Why do you ask?'

"I was only thinking about the work."

"Have you felled all the trees that were marked?"

"No, not yet—no, not by a long way. But...."

"Oh...." said Fruen suddenly, as if she had just thought of something. "You must have some money. Yes, of course...."

I grasped at that to save myself, and answered:

"Thank you very much."

Falkenberg said nothing.

"Well, you've only to ask, you know. Varsaagod" and she handed me the money I had asked for. "And what about you?"

"Nothing, thank you all the same," answered Falkenberg.

Heavens, how I had lost again—fallen to earth again! And Falkenberg, that shameless imposter, who sat there playing the man of property who didn't need anything in advance. I would tear my clothes off him that very night, and leave him naked.

Only, of course, I did nothing of the sort.

XVII

And two days went by.

"If she comes out again this evening," Falkenberg would say up in the woods, "I'll sing that one about the poppy. I'd forgotten that."

"You've forgotten Emma, too, haven't you?" I ask.

"Emma? Look here, I'll tell you what it is: you're just the same as ever, that's what you are."

"Ho, am I?"

"Yes; inside, I mean. You wouldn't mind taking Emma right there, with Fruen looking on. But I couldn't do that."

"That's a lie!" I answered angrily. "You won't see me tangled up in any foolery with the girls as long as I am here."

"Ah, and I shan't be out at nights with any one after. Think she'll come this evening? I'd forgotten that one about the poppy till now. Just listen."

Falkenberg sang the Poppy Song.

"You're lucky, being able to sing like that," I said. "But there's neither of us'll get her, for all that."

"Get her! Why, whoever thought.... What a fool you are!"

"Ah, if I were young and rich and handsome, I'd win her all the same," I said.

"If—and if.... So could I, for the matter of that. But there's the Captain."

"Yes, and then there's you. And then there's me. And then there's herself and everybody else in the world. And we're a couple of brutes to be talking about her like this at all," said I, furious now with myself for my own part. "A nice thing, indeed, for two old woodcutters to speak of their mistress so."

We grew pale and thin the pair of us, and the wrinkles showed up in Falkenberg's drawn face; neither of us could eat as we used. And by way of trying to hide our troubles from each other, I went about talking all sorts of cheerful nonsense, while Falkenberg bragged loudly at every meal of how he'd got to eating too much of late, and was getting slack and out of form.

"Why, you don't seem to eat anything at all," Fruen would say when we came home with too much left of the food we had taken with us. "Nice woodcutters, indeed."

"It's Falkenberg that won't eat," said I.

34

"Ho, indeed!" said Falkenberg; "I like that. He's given up eating altogether."

Now and again when she asked us to do her a favour, some little service or other, we would both hurry to do it; at last we got to bringing in water and firewood of our own accord. But one day Falkenberg played me a mean trick: he came home with a bunch of hazel twigs for a carpet-beater, that Fruen had asked me expressly to cut for her.

And he sang every evening now.

Then it was I resolved to make Fruen jealous—ey, ey, my good man, are you mad now, or merely foolish? As if Fruen would ever give it as much as a thought, whatever you did.

But so it was. I would try to make her jealous.

Of the three girls on the place, there was only one that could possibly be used for the experiment, and that was Emma. So I started talking nonsense to Emma.

"Emma, I know of some one that is sighing for you."

"And where did you get to know of that, pray?"

"From the stars above."

"I'd rather hear of it from some one here on earth."

"I can tell you that, too. At first hand."

"It's himself he means," put in Falkenberg, anxious to keep well out of it.

"Well, and I don't mind saying it is. Paratum cor meum."

But Emma was ungracious, and didn't care to talk to me, for all I was better at languages than Falkenberg. What—could I not even master Emma? Well ... I turned proud and silent after that, and went my own ways, making drawings for that machine of mine and little models. And when Falkenberg was singing of an evening, and Fruen listening, I went across to the men's quarters and stayed there with them. Which, of course, was much more dignified. The only trouble about it was that Petter was ill in bed, and couldn't stand the noise of ax and hammer, so I had to go outside every time I'd any heavy piece of work to do.

Still, now and again I fancied Fruen might perhaps be sorry, after all, at missing my company in the kitchen. It looked so, to me. One evening, when we were at supper, she turned to me and said:

"What's that the men were saying about a new machine you're making?"

"It's a new kind of saw he's messing about with," said Falkenberg. "But it's too heavy to be any good."

I made no answer to that, but craftily preferred to be wronged. Was it not the fate of all inventors to be so misjudged? Only wait: my time was not yet come. There were moments when I could

35

hardly keep from bursting out with a revelation to the girls, of how I was really a man of good family, led astray by desperation over an unhappy love affair, and now taking to drink. Alas, yes, man proposes, God disposes.... And then, perhaps, Fruen herself might come to hear of it....

"I think I'll take to going over with the men in the evenings," said Falkenberg, "the same as you."

And I knew well enough why Falkenberg had suddenly taken it into his head to spend his evenings there; he was not asked to sing now as often as before; some way or other, he was less in demand of late.

XVIII

The Captain had returned.

A big man, with a full beard, came out to us one day while we were at work, and said:

"I'm Captain Falkenberg. Well, lads, how goes it?"

We greeted him respectfully, and answered: "Well enough."

Then there was some talk of what we had done and what remained to do. The Captain was pleased with our work—all clean cut and close to the root. Then he reckoned out how much we had got through per day, and said it came to a good average.

"Captain's forgetting Sundays." said I.

"That's true," said he. "Well, that makes it over the average. Had any trouble at all with the tools? Is the saw all right?"

"Quite all right."

"And nobody hurt?"

"No."

Pause.

"You ought by rights to provide your own food," he said, "but if you would rather have it the other way, we can square it when we come to settle up."

"We'll be glad to have it as Captain thinks best."

"Yes," agreed Falkenberg as well.

The Captain took a turn up through the wood and came back again.

"Couldn't have better weather," he said. "No snow to shovel away."

"No, there's no snow—that's true; but a little more frost'd do no harm."

"Why? Cooler to work in d'you mean?"

"That, too, perhaps; yes. But the saw cuts easier when timber's frozen."

"You're an old hand at this work, then?"

"Yes."

"And are you the one that sings?"

"No, more's the pity. He is the one that sings."

"Oh, so you are the singer, are you? We're namesakes, I believe?"

"Why, yes, in a way," said Falkenberg, a little awkwardly, "My name is Lars Falkenberg, and I've my certificate to show for that."

"What part d'you come from?"

"From Trøndelagen."

The Captain went home. He was friendly enough, but spoke in a short, decisive way, with never a smile or a jesting word. A good face, something ordinary.

From that day onwards Falkenberg never sang but in the men's quarters, or out in the open; no more singing in the kitchen now the Captain had come home. Falkenberg was irritable and gloomy; he would swear at times and say life wasn't worth living these days; a man might as well go and hang himself and have done with it. But his fit of despair soon came to an end. One Sunday he went back to the two farms where he had tuned the pianos, and asked for a recommendation from each. When he came back he showed me the papers, and said:

"They'll do to keep going with for a bit."

"Then you're not going to hang yourself, after all?"

"You've better cause to go that way, if you ask me," said Falkenberg.

But I, too, was less despairing now. When the Captain heard about my machine idea, he wanted to know more about it at once. He saw at the first glance that my drawings were far from perfect, being made on small pieces of paper, and without so much as a pair of dividers to work with. He lent me a set of drawing instruments, and gave me some useful hints about how such things were done. He, too, was afraid my saw would prove too cumbersome. "But keep on with it, anyway," he said. "Get the whole thing drawn to a definite scale, then we can see."

I realized, however, that a decently constructed model of the thing would give a better idea of it, and as soon as I was through with the drawings I set to work carving a model in wood. I had no lathe, and had to whittle out the two rollers and several wheels and screws by hand. I was working at this on the Sunday, and so taken up with it I never heard the dinner-bell. The Captain came out and called, "Dinner!" Then, when he saw what I was doing, he offered to

37

drive over himself to the smithy the very next day, and get the parts I needed cut on the lathe. "All you need do is to give me the measurements," he said. "And you must want some tools, surely? Saw and drills; right! Screws, yes, and a fine chisel ... is that all?"

He made a note of the things on the spot. A first-rate man to work under.

But in the evening, when I had finished supper and was crossing the courtyard to the men's room, Fruen called me. She was standing between the kitchen windows, in the shadow, but slipped forward now.

"My husband said ... he ... said ... you can't be warm enough in these thin clothes," she said. "And would you ... here, take these."

She bundled a whole suit into my arms.

I thanked her, stammering foolishly. I was going to get myself some new things soon. There was no hurry; I didn't need....

"Of course, I know you can get things yourself. But when your friend is so ... so ... oh, take these."

And she ran away indoors again, the very fashion of a young girl fearing to be caught doing something over-kind. I had to call my last thanks after her.

When the Captain came out next evening with my wheels and rollers, I took the opportunity of thanking him for the clothes.

"Oh—er—yes," he answered. "It was my wife that.... Do they fit you all right?"

"Yes; many thanks."

"That's all right, then. Yes; it was my wife that ... well, here are the things for your machine, and the tools. Good-night."

It seemed, then, as if the two of them were equally ready to do an act of kindness. And when it was done, each would lay the blame on the other. Surely this must be the perfect wedded life, that dreamers dreamed of here on earth....

XIX

The woods are stripped of leaf now, and the bird sounds are gone; only the crows rasp out their screeching note at five in the morning, when they spread out over the fields. We see them, Falkenberg and I, as we go to our work; the yearling birds, that have not yet learned fear of the world, hop along the path before our feet.

Then we meet the finch, the sparrow of the timbered lands. He has been out in the woods already, and is coming back now to humankind, that he likes to live with and study from all sides. Queer little finch. A bird of passage, really, but his parents have taught him that one can spend a winter in the north; and now he will teach his children that the north's the only place to spend the winter in at all. But there is still a touch of emigrant blood in him, and he remains a wanderer. One day he and his will gather together and set off for somewhere else, many parishes away, to study a new collection of humans there—and in the aspen grove never a finch to be seen. And it may be a whole week before a new flock of this winged life appears and settles in the same place.... Herregud! how many a time have I watched the finches in their doings, and found pleasure in all.

One day Falkenberg declares he is all right again now. Going to save up and put aside a hundred Kroner this winter, out of tuning pianos and felling trees, and then make up again with Emma. I, too, he suggests, would be better advised to give over sighing for ladies of high degree, and go back to my own rank and station.

Falkenberg was right.

On Saturday evening we stopped work a trifle earlier than usual to go up and get some things from the store. We wanted shirts, tobacco and wine.

While we were in the store I caught sight of a little work-box, ornamented with shells, of the kind seafaring men used to buy in the old days at Amsterdam, and bring home to their girls; now the Germans make them by the thousand. I bought the workbox, with the idea of taking out one of the shells to serve as a thumbnail for my pipe.

"What d'you want with a workbox?" asked Falkenberg. "Is it for Emma, what?" He grew jealous at the thought, and not to be outdone, he bought a silk handkerchief to give her himself.

On the way back we sampled the wine, and got talking. Falkenberg was still jealous, so I took out the workbox, chose the shell I wanted, and picked it off and gave him the box. After that we were friends again.

It was getting dark now, and there was no moon. Suddenly we heard the sound of a concertina from a house up on a hillside; we could see there was dancing within, from the way the light came and went like a lighthouse beam.

"Let's go up and look," said Falkenberg.

Coming up to the house, we found a little group of lads and girls outside taking the air. Emma was there as well.

"Why, there's Emma!" cried Falkenberg cheerily, not in the least put out to find she had gone without him. "Emma, here, I've got something for you!"

He reckoned to make all good with a word, but Emma turned away from him and went indoors. Then, when he moved to go after

39

her, others barred his way, hinting pretty plainly that he wasn't wanted there.

"But Emma is there. Ask her to come out."

"Emma's not coming out. She's here with Markus Shoemaker."

Falkenberg stood there helpless. He had been cold to Emma now for so long that she had given him up. And, seeing him stand there stupidly agape, some of the girls began to make game of him: had she left him all alone, then, and what would he ever do now, poor fellow?

Falkenberg set his bottle to his lips and drank before the eyes of all, then wiped his mouth with the back of his hand and passed to the nearest man. There was a better feeling now towards us; we were good fellows, with bottles in our pockets, and willing to pass them round; moreover, we were strangers in the place, and that was always something new. Also, Falkenberg said many humorous things of Markus Shoemaker, whom he persisted in calling Lukas.

The dance was still going on inside, but none of the girls left us to go in and join.

"I'll bet you now," said Falkenberg, with a swagger, "that Emma'd be only too glad to be out here with us."

Helene and Rønnaug and Sara were there; every time they drank, they gave their hands prettily by way of thanks, as the custom is, but some of the others that had learned a trifle of town manners said only, "Tak for Skjænken," and no more. Helene was to be Falkenberg's girl, it seemed; he put his arm round her waist and said she was his for tonight. And when they moved off farther and farther away from the rest of us, none called to them to come back; we paired off, all of us, after a while, and went our separate ways into the woods. I went with Sara.

When we came out from the wood again, there stood Rønnaug still taking the air. Strange girl, had she been standing there alone all the time? I took her hand and talked to her a little, but she only smiled to all I said and made no answer. We went off towards the wood, and Sara called after us in the darkness: "Rønnaug, come now and let's go home." But Rønnaug made no answer; it was little she said at all. Soft, white as milk, and tall, and still.

XX

The first snow is come; it thaws again at once, but winter is not far off, and we are nearing the end of our woodcutting now at

Øvrebø—another week or so, perhaps, no more. What then? There was work on the railway line up on the hills, or perhaps more woodcutting at some other place we might come to. Falkenberg was for trying the railway.

But I couldn't get done with my machine in so short a time. We'd each our own affairs to take our time; apart from the machine, there was that thumbnail for the pipe I wanted to finish, and the evenings came out all too short. As for Falkenberg, he had made it up with Emma again. And that was a difficult matter and took time. She had been going about with Markus Shoemaker, 'twas true, but Falkenberg for his part could not deny having given Helene presents—a silk handkerchief and a work box set with shells.

Falkenberg was troubled, and said:

"Everything is wrong, somehow. Nothing but bother and worry and foolery."

"Why, as to that..."

"That's what I call it, anyway, if you want to know. She won't come up in the hills as we said."

"It'll be Markus Shoemaker, then, that's keeping her back?"

Falkenberg was gloomily silent. Then, after a pause:

"They wouldn't even have me go on singing."

We got to talking of the Captain and his wife. Falkenberg had an ill-forboding all was not as it might be between them.

Gossiping fool! I put in a word:

"You'll excuse me, but you don't know what you are talking about."

"Ho!" said he angrily. And, growing more and more excited, he went on: "Have you ever seen them, now, hanging about after each other? I've never heard them say so much as a word."

The fool!—the churl!

"Don't know what is the matter with you to-day the way you're sawing. Look—what do you think of that for a cut?"

"Me? We're two of us in it, anyway, so there."

"Good! Then we'll say it's the thaw. Let's get back to the ax again."

We went on working each by himself for a while, angered and out of humour both. What was the lie he had dared to say of them, that they never so much as spoke to each other? But, Heaven, he was right! Falkenberg had a keen scent for such things. He knew something of men and women.

"At any rate, they speak nicely of each other to us," I said.

Falkenberg went on with his work.

I thought over the whole thing again.

41

"Well, perhaps you may be right as far as that goes, that it's not the wedded life dreamers have dreamed of, still...."

But it was no good talking to Falkenberg in that style; he understood never a word.

When we stopped work at noon, I took up the talk again.

"Didn't you say once if he wasn't decent to her there'd be trouble?"

"Yes, I did."

"Well, there hasn't been trouble."

"Did I ever say he wasn't decent to her?" said Falkenberg irritably. "No, but they're sick and wearied of each other—that's what it is. When one comes in, the other goes out. Whenever he starts talking of anything out in the kitchen, her eyes go all dead and dull, and she doesn't listen."

We got to work again with the ax, each thinking his own ways.

"I doubt but I'll need to give him a thrashing," said Falkenberg.

"Who?"

"Lukas...."

I got my pipe done, and sent Emma in with it to the Captain. The nail had turned out fine and natural this time, and with the fine tools I had now, I was able to cut well down into the thumb and fasten it on the underside, so that the two little copper pins would not show. I was pleased enough with the work.

The Captain came out while we were at supper that evening, to thank me for the pipe. At the same time, I noticed that Falkenberg was right; no sooner had the Captain come out than Fruen went in.

The Captain praised my pipe, and asked how I had managed to fix the nail; he said I was an artist and a master. All the others were standing by and heard his words—and it counted for something to be called an artist by the Captain himself. I believe I could have won Emma at that moment.

That night I learned to shiver and shake.

The corpse of a woman came up to me where I lay in the loft, and stretched out its left hand to show me: the thumbnail was missing. I shook my head, to say I had had a thumbnail once, but I had thrown it away, and used a shell instead. But the corpse stood there all the same, and there I lay, shivering, cold with fear. Then I managed to say I couldn't help it now; in God's name, go away! And, Our Father which art in heaven.... The corpse came straight towards me; I thrust out two clenched fists and gave an icy shriek—and there I was, crushing Falkenberg flat against the wall.

"What is it?" cried Falkenberg. "In Heaven's name...."

I woke, dripping with sweat, and lay there with open eyes, watching the corpse as it vanished quite slowly in the dark of the room.

"It's the corpse," I groaned. "Come to ask for her thumbnail." Falkenberg sat straight up in bed, wide awake all at once.

"I saw her," he said.

"Did you see her, too? Did you see her thumb? Ugh!"

"I wouldn't be in your shoes now for anything."

"Let me lie inside, against the wall," I begged.

"And what about me?"

"It won't hurt you; you can lie outside all right."

"And let her come and take me first? Not if I know it."

And at that Falkenberg lay down again and pulled the rug over his eyes.

I thought for a moment of going down to sleep with Petter; he was getting better now, and there was no fear of infection. But I was afraid to go down the stairs.

It was a terrible night.

Next morning I searched high and low for the nail, and found it on the floor at last, among the shavings and sawdust. I took it out and buried it on the way to the wood.

"It's a question if you oughtn't to carry it back where you took it from," said Falkenberg.

"Why, that's miles away—a whole long journey...."

"They won't ask about that if you're called to do it. Maybe she won't care about having a thumb one place and a thumbnail in another."

But I was brave enough now; a very desperado in the daylight. I laughed at Falkenberg for his superstition, and told him science had disposed of all such nonsense long ago.

XXI

One evening there came visitors to the place, and as Petter was still poorly, and the other lad was only a youngster, I had to go and take out the horses. A lady got out of the carriage.

"Is any one at home?" she asked.

The sound of wheels had brought faces to the windows; lamps were lit in the rooms and passages. Fruen came out, calling:

"Is that you, Elisabeth? I'm so glad you've come."

It was Frøken Elisabeth from the vicarage.

"Is he here?" she asked in surprise.

"Who?"

It was myself she meant. So she had recognized me....

Next day the two young ladies came out to us in the wood. At first I was afraid lest some rumour of a certain nightly ride on borrowed horses should have reached the vicarage, but calmed myself when nothing was said of it.

"The water-pipes are doing nicely," said Frøken Elisabeth.

I was pleased to hear it.

"Water-pipes?" said Fruen inquiringly.

"He laid on a water-supply to the house for us. Pipes in the kitchen and upstairs as well. Just turn a tap and there it is. You ought to have it done here."

"Really, though? Could it be done here, do you think?"

I answered: yes; it ought to be easy enough.

"Why didn't you speak to my husband about it?"

"I did speak of it. He said he would see what Fruen thought about it."

Awkward pause. So he would not speak to her even of a thing that so nearly concerned herself. I hastened to break the silence, and said at random.

"Anyhow, it's too late to start this year; the winter would be on us before we could get it done. But next spring...."

Fruen seemed to come back to attention from somewhere far away.

"Oh yes, I remember now, he did say something about it," she said. "We talked it over. But it was too late this year.... Elisabeth, don't you like watching them felling trees?"

We used a rope now and then to guide the tree in its fall. Falkenberg had just fixed this rope high up, and the tree stood swaying.

"What's that for?"

"To make it fall the right way," I began. But Fruen did not care to listen to me any more; she turned to Falkenberg and put the question to him directly:

"Does it matter which way it falls?"

Falkenberg had to answer her.

"Why, no, we'll need to guide it a bit, so it doesn't break down too much of the young growth when it falls."

"Did you notice," said Fruen to her friend, "what a voice he has? He's the one that sings."

How I hated myself now for having talked so much, instead of reading her wish! But at least I would show her that I understood the hint. And, moreover, it was Frøken Elisabeth and no other I was in love with; she was not full of changing humours, and was just as

44

pretty as the other—ay, a thousand times prettier. I would go and take work at her father's place.... I took care now, whenever Fruen spoke, to look first at Falkenberg and then at her, keeping back my answer as if fearing to speak out of my turn. I think, too, she began to feel a little sorry when she noticed this, for once she said, with a little troubled smile: "Yes, yes, it was you I asked."

That smile with her words.... Then came a whirl of joy at my heart; I began swinging the ax with all the strength I had gained from long use, and made fine deep cuts, I heard only a word now and then of what they said.

"They want me to sing to them this evening," said Falkenberg, when they had gone.

Evening came.

I stood out in the courtyard, talking to the Captain. Three or four days more, and our work on the timber would be at an end.

"And where will you be going then?" asked the Captain.

"We were going to get work on the railway."

"I might find you something—to do here," said the Captain. "I want the drive down to the high road carried a different way; it's too steep as it is. Come and see what I mean."

He took me round to the south side of the house, and pointed this way and that, though it was already dark.

"And by the time that's done, and one or two other little things, we shall be well on to the spring," he said. "And then there'll be the water, as you said. And, besides, there's Petter laid up still; we can't get along like this. I must have another hand to help."

Suddenly we heard Falkenberg singing. There was a light in the parlour; Falkenberg was in there, singing to an accompaniment on the piano. The music welled out toward us—the man had a remarkable voice—and made me quiver against my will.

The Captain started, and glanced up at the windows.

"No," he said suddenly; "I think, after all, we'd better leave the drive till next spring as well. How soon did you say you'd be through with the timber?"

"Three or four days."

"Good! We'll say three or four days more for that, and then finish for this year."

A strangely sudden decision. I thought to myself. And aloud I said:

"There's no reason why we shouldn't do the road work in winter. It's better in some ways. There's the blasting, and getting up the loads...."

"Yes, I know ... but ... well, I think I must go in now and listen to this...."

45

The Captain went indoors.

It crossed my mind that he did so out of courtesy, wishing to make himself, as it were, responsible for having Falkenberg in the parlour. But I fancied he would rather have stayed talking with me.

Which was a coxcomb's thought, and altogether wrong.

XXII

I had got the biggest parts of my machine done, and could fix them together and try it. There was an old stump by the barn-bridge from an aspen that had been blown down; I fixed my apparatus to that, and found at once that the saw would cut all right. Aha, now, what have you got to say? Here's the problem solved! I had bought a huge saw-blade and cut teeth all down the back; these teeth fitted into a little cogwheel set to take the friction, and driven forward by the spring. The spring itself I had fashioned originally from a broad staybusk Emma had given me, but, when I came to test it; it proved too weak; so I made another from a saw-blade only six millimetres across, after I had first filed off the teeth. This new spring, however, was too strong; I had to manage as best I could by winding it only half-way up, and then, when it ran down, half-way up again.

I knew too little theory, worse luck; it was a case of feeling my way at every step, and this made it a slow proceeding. The conical gear, for instance, I found too heavy when I came to put it into practice, and had to devise a different system altogether.

It was on a Sunday that I fixed my apparatus to the stump; the new white woodwork and the shining saw-blade glittered in the sun. Soon faces appeared at the windows, and the Captain himself came. He did not answer my greeting, so intent was he on the machine.

"Well, how do you think it will work?"'

I set it going.

"Upon my soul, I believe it will...."

Fruen and Frøken Elisabeth came out, all the maids came out, Falkenberg came out, and I let them see it work. Aha, what did I say?

Said the Captain presently:

"Won't it take up too much time, fixing the apparatus to one tree after another?"

"Part of the time will be made up by easier work. No need to keep stopping for breath."

"Why not?"

"Because the lateral pressure's effected by the spring. It's just that pressure that makes the hardest work."

"And what about the rest of the time?"

"I'm going to discard this screw-on arrangement and have a clamp instead, that can be pressed down by the foot. A clamp with teeth to give a better grip, and adjustable to any sized timber."

I showed him a drawing of this clamp arrangement; I had not had time to make the thing itself.

The Captain took a turn at the saw himself, noticing carefully the amount of force required. He said:

"It's a question whether it won't be too heavy, pulling a saw twice the width of an ordinary woodcutting saw."

"Ay," agreed Falkenberg; "it looks that way."

All looked at Falkenberg, and then at me. It was my turn now.

"A single man can push a goods truck with full load on rails," I said. "And here there'll be two men to work a saw with the blade running on two rollers over oiled steel guides. It'll be easier to work than the old type of saw—a single man could work it, if it came to a pinch."

"It sounds almost impossible."

"Well, we shall see."

Frøken Elisabeth asked half in jest:

"But tell me—I don't understand these things a bit, you know—why wouldn't it be better to saw a tree across in the old way?"

"He's trying to get rid of the lateral pressure; that's a strain on the men working," explained the Captain. "With a saw like this you can, as he says, make a horizontal cut with the same sort of pressure you would use for an ordinary saw cutting down vertically. It's simply this: you press downwards, but the pressure's transmitted sideways. By the way," he went on, turning to me, "has it struck you there might be a danger of pressing down the ends of the blade, and making a convex cut?"

"That's obviated in the first place by these rollers under the blade."

"True; that goes for something. And in the second place?"

"In the second place, it would be impossible to make a convex cut with this apparatus even if you wanted to. The blade, you see, has a T-shaped back; that makes it practically impossible to bend it."

I fancy the Captain put forward some of his objections against his own conviction. Knowing all he did, he could have answered them himself better than I. On the other hand, there were points he did not notice, but which caused me some anxiety. A machine that was to be carried about in the woods must not be made with delicate mechanism. I was afraid, for instance, that the two steel guides might be easily injured, and either broken away, or so bent that the wheels would jam. No; the guides would have to be dispensed with, and the wheels set under the back of the saw. Altogether, my machine was far from complete....

The Captain went over to Falkenberg and said:

"I want you to drive the ladies tomorrow; they're going some way, and Petter's not well enough, it seems. Do you think you could?"

"Surely," said Falkenberg; "and welcome."

"Frøkenen's going back to the vicarage," said the Captain, as he turned to go. "You'll have to be out by six o'clock."

Falkenberg was in high spirits at this mark of confidence, and jestingly hinted that I envied him the same. Truth to tell, I did not envy him there in the least. I was perhaps a little hurt to find my comrade so preferred before myself, but I would most certainly stay here by myself in the quiet of the woods than sit on a box and drive in the cold.

Falkenberg was thoroughly pleased with himself.

"You're looking simply green with envy now," he said. "You'd better take something for it. Try a little castor-oil, now, do."

He was busy all the forenoon getting ready for the journey, washing down the carriage, greasing the wheels, and cleaning the harness after. I helped him with the work.

"I don't believe you can drive a pair at all, really," I said, just to annoy him. "But I'll give you a bit of a lesson, if you like, before you start."

"You've got it badly," he answered. "It's a pity to see a man looking like that, when a dose of castor-oil would put him right."

It was like that all the time—jesting and merriment from one to the other.

That evening the Captain came out to me.

"I didn't want to send you down with the ladies," he said, "because of your work. But now Frøken Elisabeth says she wants you to drive, and not the other man."

"Me?"

"Yes. Because she knows you."

"Why, as for that, 'twould have been safe enough as it was."

"Do you mind going at all?"

"No."

"Good! Then that's settled."

This thought came to my mind at once: "Aha, it's me the ladies fancy, after all, because I'm an inventor and proprietor of a patent saw, and not bad looking when I'm properly got up—not bad looking by any means."

But the Captain explained things to Falkenberg in an altogether different way, that upset my vanity completely: Frøken Elisabeth wanted me to go down to the vicarage once more, so that her father might have another try at getting me to take work there. She'd promised him to do so.

I thought and thought over this explanation.

"But if you get taken on at the vicarage, then it's all off with our railway work," said Falkenberg.

"I shan't," said I.

XXIII

I started early in the morning with the two ladies in a closed carriage. It was more than a trifle cold at first, and my woollen rug came in very handy; I used it alternately to put over my knees and wrap round my shoulders.

We drove the way I had walked up with Falkenberg, and I recognized place after place as we passed. There and there he had tuned the pianos; there we had heard the grey goose passing.... The sun came up, and it grew warmer; the hours went by; then, coming to cross-roads, the ladies knocked at the window and said it was dinner-time.

I could see by the sun it was too early for the ladies' dinner-time, though well enough for me, seeing I took my dinner with Falkenberg at noon. So I drove on.

"Can't you stop?" they cried.

"I thought ... you don't generally have dinner till three...."

"But we're hungry."

I turned off aside from the road, took out the horses, and fed and watered them. Had these strange beings set their dinner-time by mine? "Værsaagod!"

But I felt I could not well sit down to eat with them, so I remained standing by the horses.

"Well?" said Fruen.

"Thank you kindly," said I, and waited to be served. They helped me, both of them, as if they could never give me enough. I drew the corks of the beer bottles, and was given a liberal share here as well; it was a picnic by the roadside—a little wayfaring adventure in my life. And Fruen I dared look at least, for fear she should be hurt.

49

And they talked and jested with each other, and now and again with me, out of their kindliness, that I might feel at ease. Said Frøken Elisabeth:

"Oh, I think it's just lovely to have meals out of doors. Don't you?"

And here she said De, instead of Du, as she had said before.

"It's not so new to him, you know," said Fruen; "he has his dinner out in the woods every day."

Eh, but that voice of hers, and her eyes, and the womanly, tender look of the hand that held the glass towards me.... I might have said something in turn—have told them this or that of strange things from out in the wide world, for their amusement; I could have set those ladies right when they chattered on, all ignorant of the way of riding camels or of harvest in the vineyards....

I made haste to finish my meal, and moved away. I took the buckets and went down for more water for the horses, though there was no need. I sat down by the stream and stayed there.

After a little while Fruen called:

"You must come and stand by the horses; we are going off to see if we can find some wild hops or something nice."

But when I came up they decided that the wild hops were over, and there were no rowan berries left now, nor any richly coloured leaves.

"There's nothing in the woods now," said Frøkenen. And she spoke to me directly once again: "Well, there's no churchyard here for you to roam about in."

"No."

"You must miss it, I should think." And then she went on to explain to Fruen that I was a curious person who wandered about in graveyards by night and held meetings with the dead. And it was there I invented my machines and things.

By way of saying something, I asked about young Erik. He had been thrown by a runaway horse and badly hurt....

"He's better now," said Frøkenen shortly.—"Are you ready to go on again, Lovise?"

"Yes, indeed. Can we start?"

"Whenever you please," I answered.

And we drove on again.

The hours pass, the sun draws lower down the sky, and it is cooler—a chill in the air; then later wind and wet, half rain, half snow. We passed the annexe church, a couple of wayside stores, and farm after farm.

Then came a knocking on the window of the carriage.

"Wasn't it here you went riding one night on borrowed

50

horses?" said Frøkenen laughingly. "Oh, we know all about it, never fear!"

And both the ladies were highly amused.

I answered on a sudden thought:

"And yet your father would have me to take service with him— or wasn't it so?"

"Yes."

"While I think of it, Frøken, how did your father know I was working for Captain Falkenberg? You were surprised yourself to find me there."

She thought quickly, and glanced at Fruen and said:

"I wrote home and told them."

Fruen cast down her eyes.

Now it seemed to me that the young lady was inventing. But she put in excellent answers, and tied my tongue. It sounded all so natural; she writes an ordinary letter to her people at home, and puts in something like this: "And who do you think is here? The man who did those water-pipes for us; he's felling timber now for Captain Falkenberg...."

But when we reached the vicarage, the new hand was engaged already, and there at work—had been there three weeks past. He came out to take the horses.

After that, I thought and thought again—why had they chosen me to drive them down? Perhaps it was meant as a little treat for me, as against Falkenberg's being asked into the parlour to sing. But surely—didn't they understand, these people, that I was a man who had nearly finished a new machine, and would soon have no need of any such trifles!

I went about sharp and sullen and ill-pleased with myself, had my meal in the kitchen, where Oline gave me her blessing for the water-pipes, and went out to tend my horses. I took my rug and went over to the barn in the dark....

I woke to find some one touching me.

"You mustn't lie here, you know; it's simply freezing," said Præstefruen. "Come with me, and I'll show you...."

We talked of that a little; I was not inclined to move, and at last she sat down herself instead. A flame she was—nay, a daughter of Nature. Within her the music of a rapturous dance was playing yet.

XXIV

Next morning I was more content with things. I had cooled down and turned sensible—I was resigned. If only I had seen before what was best for me, I might have taken service here at the vicarage, and been the first of all equals. Ay, and settle down and taken root in a quiet countryish life.

Fru Falkenberg stood out in the courtyard. Her bright figure stood like a pillar, stood there free and erect in the open courtyard, and her head was bare.

I greeted her Godmorgen.

"Godmorgen!" she answered again, and came striding towards me. Then very quietly she asked: "I wanted to see how they put you up last night, only I couldn't get away. That is, of course, I got away, but ... you weren't in the barn, were you?"

The last words came to me as if in a dream, and I did not answer.

"Well, why don't you answer?"

"Yes ... in the barn? Yes."

"Were you? And was it quite all right?"

"Yes."

"Oh, well, then ... yes—yes. We shall be going back sometime to-day."

She turned and walked away, her face all in one great flush....

Harald came and asked me to make a kite.

"A kite?" I answered all confusedly. "Ay, I'll make you a kite, a huge one, that'll go right up to the clouds. That I will."

We worked at it for a couple of hours, Harald and I. He was good and quick, and so innocent in his eagerness; I, for my part, was thinking of anything but kites. We made a tail several metres long, and busied ourselves with paste and lashing and binding; twice Frøken Elisabeth came out to look on. She may have been every bit as sweet and bright as before, but I cared nothing for what she was, and gave no thought, to her.

Then came the order to harness ready to start. I should have obeyed the order at once, for we had a long drive before us, but, instead, I sent Harald in to ask if we might wait just half an hour more. And we worked on till the kite was finished. Next day, when the paste was dry, Harald could send up his kite and watch it rise, and feel unknown emotion within him, as I did now.

Ready to start.

Fruen comes out; all the family are there to see her off. The priest and his wife both know me again, return my greeting, and say a few words—but I heard nothing said of my taking service with them now. The priest knew me again—yes; and his blue-eyed wife looked at me with that sidelong glance of hers as she knew me again, for all she had known me the night before as well.

Frøken Elisabeth brings out some food for the journey, and wraps her friend up well.

"Sure you'll be warm enough, now?" she asks for the last time.

"Quite sure, thanks; it's more than warm enough with all these. Farvel, Farvel."

"See you drive as nicely as you did yesterday," says Frøken, with a nod to me as well.

And we drove off.

The day was raw and chilly, and I saw at once that Fruen was not warm enough with her rug.

We drive on for hour after hour; the horses know they are on the way home, and trot without asking. My bare hands stiffen about the reins. As we neared a cottage a little way from the road, Fruen knocked on the carriage window to say it was dinner-time. She gets out, and her face was pale with the cold.

"We'll go up there and have dinner," she says. "Come up as soon as you're ready, and bring the basket."

And she walked up the hill.

It must be because of the cold she chose to eat in a stranger's house, I thought to myself; she could hardly be afraid of me.... I tied up the horses and gave them their fodder. It looked like rain, so I put the oilskins over them, patted them, and went up to the cottage with the basket.

There is only an old woman at home. "Værsaagod!" she says, and "Come in." And she goes on tending her coffee-pot. Fruen unpacks the basket, and says, without looking at me:

"I suppose I am to help you again to-day?"

"Thank you, if you will."

We ate in silence, I sitting on a little bench by the door, with my plate on the seat beside me, Fruen at the table, looking out of the window all the time, and hardly eating anything at all. Now and again she exchanges a word with the old woman, or glances at my plate to see if it is empty. The little place is cramped enough, with but two steps from the window to where I sit; so we are all sitting together, after all.

When the coffee is ready, I have no room for my cup on the end of the bench, but sit holding it in my hand. Then Fruen turns full-face towards me calmly, and says with down-cast eyes:

"There is room here."

I can hear my own heart beating and I murmur something:

"Thanks; it's quite all right. I'd rather...."

No doubt but that she is uneasy; she is afraid lest I should say something. She sits once more looking away, but I can see she is breathing heavily. Ah, she need have no fear; I would not trouble her with so much as a word.

Now I had to take the empty plate and cup and set them back on the table, but I feared to startle her in my approach, for she was still sitting with averted head. I made a little noise with the things to draw her attention, set them down, and thanked her.

She tried to put on a housewifely tone:

"Won't you have some more? I'm sure you can't have...."

"No, thank you very much.... Shall I pack up the things now? But I doubt if I can."

I happened to glance at my hands; they had swelled up terribly in the warm room, and were all shapeless and heavy now. I could hardly pack up things with hands like that. She guessed my thought, looked first at my hands, then out across the room, and said, with a little smile:

"Have you no gloves?"

"No; I never wear them."

I went back to my place, waited till she should have packed up the things so I could carry the basket down. Suddenly she turned her head towards me, still without looking up, and asked again:

"Where do you come from?"

"From Nordland."

Pause.

I ventured to ask in my turn if Fruen had ever been there.

"Yes; when I was a child."

Then she looked at her watch, as if to check me from any more questions, and at the same time to hint it was getting late.

I rose at once and went out to the horses.

It was already growing dusk; the sky was darker, and a loose, wet sleet was beginning to fall. I took my rug down covertly from the box, and hid it under the front seat inside the carriage; when that was done, I watered the horses and harnessed up. A little after, Fruen came down the hill. I went up for the basket, and met her on the way.

"Where are you going?"

"To fetch the basket."

"You needn't trouble, thanks; there's nothing to take back."

We went down to the carriage; she got in, and I made to help her to rights with the rug she had. Then I pulled out my own from under the front seat, taking care to keep the border out of sight lest she should recognize it.

"Oh, what a blessing!" cried Fruen. "Why, where was it?"

"Under the seat here."

"Well.... Of course, I might have borrowed some more rugs from the vicarage, but the poor souls would never have got them back again.... Thanks; I can manage ... no, thank you; I can manage by myself. You can drive on now."

I closed the carriage door and climbed to my seat.

"Now, if she knocks at the window again, it's that rug," I thought to myself. "Well, I won't stop...."

Hour after hour passed; it was pitch dark now, raining and snowing harder than ever, and the road growing worse all the time. Now and again I would jump down from the box and run along beside the horses to keep warm; the water was pouring from my clothes.

We were nearing home now.

I was hoping there would not be too much light when we drove up, so that she recognized the rug. Unfortunately, there were lights in all the windows, waiting her arrival.

In desperation I checked the horses a little before we got to the steps, and got down to open the carriage door.

"But why ... what on earth have you pulled up here for?"

"I only thought if perhaps Fruen wouldn't mind getting out here. It's all mud on ahead ... the wheels...."

She must have thought I was trying to entice her into something, Heaven knows!...

"Drive on, man, do!" she said.

The horses moved on, and the carriage stopped just where the light was at its full.

Emma came out to receive her mistress. Fruen handed her the rugs all in a bundle, as she had rolled them up before getting out of the carriage.

"Thanks," she said to me, glancing round as she went in. "Heavens, how dreadfully wet you are!"

XXV

A curious piece of news awaited me: Falkenberg had taken service with the Captain as a farm-hand.

This upset the plan we had agreed on, and left me alone once more. I could not understand a word of it all. Anyhow, I could think it over tomorrow.... By two in the morning I was still lying awake, shivering and thinking. All those hours I could not get warm; then at last it turned hot, and I lay there in full fever.... How frightened she had been yesterday—dared not sit down to eat with me by the roadside, and never opened her eyes to me once through all the journey....

Coming to my senses for a moment, it occurs to me I might wake Falkenberg with my tossing about, and perhaps say things in my delirium. That would never do. I clench my teeth and jump up, get into my clothes again, scramble down the stairs, and set out over the fields at a run. After a little my clothes begin to warm me; I make towards the woods, towards the spot where we had been working; sweat and rain pour down my face. If only I can find the saw and work the fever out of my body—'tis an old and tried cure of mine, that. The saw is nowhere to be seen, but I come upon the ax I had left there Saturday evening, and set to work with that. It is almost too dark to see at all, but I feel at the cut now and then with my hands, and bring down several trees. The sweat pours off me now.

Then, feeling exhausted enough, I hide the ax in its old place; it is getting light now, and I set off at a run for home.

"Where have you been?" asks Falkenberg.

Now, I do not want him to know about my having taken cold the day before, and perhaps go making talk of it in the kitchen; I simply mutter something about not knowing quite where I have been.

"You've been up to see Rønnaug, I bet," he said.

I answered: yes, I had been with Rønnaug, since he'd guessed it.

"'Twas none so hard to guess," he said. "Anyhow, you won't see me running after any of them now."

"Going to have Emma, then?"

"Why, it looks that way. It's a pity you can't get taken on here, too. Then you might get one of the others, perhaps."

And he went on talking of how I might perhaps have got my pick of the other girls, but the Captain had no use for me. I wasn't even to go out tomorrow to the wood.... The words sound far away, reaching me across a sea of sleep that is rolling towards me.

Next morning the fever is gone; I am still a little weak, but make ready to go out to the wood all the same.

"You won't need to put on your woodcutting things again," says Falkenberg. "I told you that before."

True! Nevertheless, I put on those things, seeing the others are wet. Falkenberg is a little awkward with me now, because of breaking our plan; by way of excuse, he says he thought I was taking work at the vicarage.

"So you're not coming up to the hills, then?" I asked.

"H'm! No, I don't think so—no. And you know yourself, I'm sick of tramping around. I'll not get a better chance than this."

I make as if it was no great matter to me, and take up a sudden interest in Petter; worst of all for him, poor fellow, to be turned out and nowhere to go.

"Nowhere to go?" echoes Falkenberg. "When he's lain here the three weeks he's allowed to stay sick by law, he'll go back home again. His father's a farmer."

Then Falkenberg declares it's like losing part of himself to have me go. If it wasn't for Emma, he'd break his word to the Captain after all.

"Here," he says, "I'll give you these."

"What's that?"

"It's the certificates. I shan't want them now, but they may be the saving of you at a pinch. If you ever wanted to tune a piano, say."

And he hands me the papers and the key.

But, seeing I haven't his ear for music, the things are no use to me; and I tell him so. I could better handle a grindstone than a piano.

Whereat Falkenberg burst out laughing, relieved to find me ready with a jest to the last....

Falkenberg goes out. I have time to laze a little, and lie down all dressed on the bed, resting and thinking. Well, our work was at an end; we should have had to go anyhow. I could not reckon on staying here for all eternity. The only thing outside all calculation was that Falkenberg should stay. If only it had been me they'd offered his work, I'd have worked enough for two! Now, was there any chance of buying him off, I wondered? To tell the truth, I fancied I had noticed something before; as if the Captain were not altogether pleased to have this labourer about the place bearing his own name. Well, perhaps I had been wrong.

I thought and thought. After all, I had been a good workman, as far as I knew, and I had never stolen a moment of the Captain's time for work on my own invention....

I fell asleep again, and wakened at the sound of footsteps on the stairs. Before I had time to get properly to my feet, there was the Captain himself in the doorway.

"Don't get up," he said kindly, and turned as if to go again. "Still, seeing you're awake, we might settle up. What do you say?"

I said it was as he pleased, and many thanks.

"I ought to tell you, though, both your friend and I thought you were going to take service at the vicarage, and so.... And now the weather's broken up, there's no doing more among the timber—

and, besides, we've got down all there was to come. Well, now; I've settled with the other man. I don't know if you'd...."

I said I would be quite content with the same.

"H'm! Your friend and I agreed you ought to have more per day."

Falkenberg had said no word of this to me; it sounded like the Captain's own idea.

"I agreed with him we should share alike," said I.

"But you were sort of foreman; of course, you ought to have fifty øre per day extra."

I saw my hesitation displeased him, and let him reckon it out as he pleased. When he gave me the money, I said it was more than I had reckoned with. The Captain answered:

"Very pleased to hear it. And I've written a few lines here that might be useful, saying you've worked well the time you were here."

He handed me the paper.

A just and kindly man, the Captain. He said nothing now about the idea of laying on water to the house next spring; I took it he'd his reasons for that, and did not like to trouble him.

Then he asked:

"So you're going off now to work on the railway?"

I said I was not quite sure as to that.

"Well, well... anyhow, thanks for the time you've been with us."

He moved towards the door. And I, miserable weakling that I was, could not hold myself in check, but asked:

"You won't be having any work for me later on, perhaps, in the spring?"

"I don't know; we shall see. I ... well, it all depends. If you should happen to be anywhere near, why.... What about that machine of yours?"

I ventured to ask if I might leave it on the place.

"Certainly," said the Captain.

When he had gone I sat down on the bed. Well, it was all over now. Ay, so it was—and Lord have mercy on us all! Nine o'clock; she is up—she is there in the house I can see from this very window. Well, let me get away and have done with it.

I get out my sack and stow away my things, put on my wet jacket over my blouse, and am ready to start. But I sit down again.

Emma comes in: "Værsaagod; there's something ready for you in the kitchen."

To my horror she had my rug over one arm.

"And Fruen told me to ask if this wasn't your rug."

"Mine? No; I've got mine here with my things."

Emma goes off again with the rug.

Well, how could I say it was mine? Devil take the rug!... Should I go down to the kitchen or not? I might be able to say good-bye and thanks at the same time—nothing strange in that.

Emma came in again with the rug and laid it down neatly folded on a stool.

"If you don't hurry up, the coffee'll be cold," she says.

"What did you put that rug there for?"

"Fruen told me to."

"Oh, well, perhaps it's Falkenberg's," I muttered.

Emma asks:

"Are you going away now for good?"

"Yes, seeing you won't have anything to do with me."

"You!" says Emma, with a toss of her head.

I went down with Emma to the kitchen; sitting at table, I saw the Captain going out to the woods. Good he was gone—now, perhaps, Fruen might come out.

I finished my meal and got up. Should I go off now, and leave it at that? Of course; what else? I took leave of the maids, with a jesting word to each in turn.

"I'd have liked to say good-bye to Fruen, too, but...."

"Fruen's indoors. I'll...."

Emma goes in, and comes back a moment later.

"Fruen's lying down with a headache. She sent her very good wishes."

"Come again!" said all the girls as I set off.

I walked away out of the place, with my sack under my arm. Then suddenly I remembered the ax; Falkenberg might not find it where I'd put it. I went back, knocked at the kitchen door, and left a message for him where it was.

Going down the road, I turned once or twice and looked back towards the windows of the house. Then all was out of sight.

XXVI

I circled round all that day, keeping near to Øvrebø; looked in at one or two farms to ask for work, and wandered on again like an outcast, aimlessly. It was a chill, unkindly day, and I had need of all my walking to keep warm.

Towards evening I made over to my old working place among the Captain's timber. I heard no sound of the ax; Falkenberg had gone home. I found the trees I had felled the night before, and

59

laughed outright at the ghastly looking stumps I had left. Falkenberg would surely have seen the havoc, and wondered who could have done it. Possibly he might have set it down to witchcraft, and fled home accordingly before it got dark. Falkenberg!... Hahaha!

But it was no healthy merriment, I doubt—a thing born of the fever and the weakness that followed it. And I soon turned sorrowful once more. Here, on this spot, she had stood one day with that girl friend of hers; they had come out and talked to us in the woods....

When it was dark enough I started down towards the house. Perhaps I might sleep in the loft again to-night; then to-morrow, when her headache was gone, she might come out. I went down near enough to see the lights of the house, then I turned back. No, perhaps it was too early yet.

Then for a time—I should reckon about two hours—I wandered round and sat down a bit, wandered again and sat down a bit; then I moved up towards the house again. Now I could perfectly well go up in the loft and lie down there. As for Falkenberg—miserable worm!—let him dare to say a word! Now I know what I will do. I will hide my sack in the woods before I go up, so as to look as if I had only come back for some little thing I had forgotten.

And I go back to the woods.

No sooner have I hidden the sack than I realize I am not concerned at all with Falkenberg and sleeping in the loft. I am a fool and a madman, for the thing I want is not shelter for the night, but a sight of just one creature there before I leave the place. And I say to myself: "My good sir, was it not you that set out to live a quiet life among healthy folk, to win back your peace of mind?"

I pull out my sack from its hiding-place, fling it over my shoulder, and move towards the house for the third time, keeping well away from the servants' quarters, and coming round on the south side of the main building. There is a light in the parlour.

And now, although it is dark, I let down the sack from over my shoulder, not to look like a beggar, and thrust it under my arm as if it were a parcel. So I steal up cautiously towards the house. When I have got near enough, I stop, stand there upright and strong before the windows, take off my cap and stand there still. There is no one to be seen within, not a shadow. The dining-room is all dark; they have finished their evening meal. It must be late, I tell myself.

Suddenly the lamp in the parlour goes out, and the whole house seems dead and deserted. I wait a little, then a solitary light shines out upstairs. That must be her room. The light burns for half an hour, perhaps, and then goes out again. She had gone to rest. Good-night!

Good-night for ever!

And, of course, I shall not come back to this place in the spring. A ridiculous idea!

When I got down on to the high road, I shouldered my sack once more and set out on my travels....

In the morning I go on again, having slept in a barn where it was terribly cold, having nothing to wrap round me; moreover, I had to start out again just at the coldest hour, about daybreak, lest I should be found there.

I walk on and on. The woods change from pine to birch and back again. Coming upon a patch of fine, straight-stemmed juniper, I cut myself a staff, and sit down at the edge of the wood to trim it. Here and there among the trees a yellow leaf or so still hangs, but the birches are full of catkins set with pearly drops. Now and again half, a dozen small birds swoop down on one of these birches, to peck at the catkins, and then look about for a stone or a rough tree trunk to rub the gum from their beaks. Each is jealous of the rest; they watch and chase and drive one another away, though there are millions of catkins for them to take all they will. And the one that is chased never does anything but take to flight. If a little bird comes bearing down towards a bigger one, the bigger one will move away; even a full-grown thrush offers no resistance to a sparrow, but simply takes itself off. I fancy it must be the speed of the attack that does it.

The cold and discomfort of the morning gradually disappear; it amuses me to watch the various things I meet with on my way, and think a little, idly enough, of every one. The birds were most diverting; also, it was cheering to reflect that I had my pocket full of money.

Falkenberg had chanced to mention that morning where Petter's home was, and I now made for that. There would hardly be work for me on so small a place; but now that I was rich, it was not work I sought for first of all. Petter would be coming home soon, no doubt, and perhaps have some news to tell.

I managed so as to reach the farm in the evening. I said I brought news of their son, that he was much better now, and would soon be home again. And could they put me up for the night?

61

XXVII

I have been staying here a couple of days; Petter has come home, but had nothing to tell.

"Is all well at Øvrebø?"

"Ay, there's nothing wrong that I know of."

"Did you see them all before you left? The Captain, Fruen?"

"Yes."

"Nobody ill?"

"No. Why, who should there be?"

"Well, Falkenberg said something about he'd hurt his hand. But I suppose it's all right now, then."

There was little comfort in this home, though they seemed to be quite well off. Petter's father was deputy to the Storting, and had taken to sitting reading the papers of an evening. Eh, reading and reading—the whole house suffered under it, and the daughters were bored to death. When Petter came home the entire family set to work reckoning out whether he had gotten his full pay, and if he had lain sick at Øvrebø for the full time allowed him by law, or "provided by statute," as his father, the deputy, put it. Yesterday, when I happened to break a window—a little pane that cost next to nothing—there was no end of whispering about it, and unfriendly glances at me from all sides; so today I went up to the store and bought a new pane, and fixed it in properly with putty. Then said the deputy: "You needn't have taken all that trouble over a pane of glass."

To tell the truth, it was not only for that I had been up to the store; I also bought a couple of bottles of wine, to show I did not care so much for the price of a pane of glass or so. Also, I bought a sewing-machine, to give the girls when I went away. We could drink the wine this evening; tomorrow would be Sunday, and we should all have time to lie abed. But on Monday morning I would start off again.

Things turned out otherwise, however. The two girls had been up in the loft, sniffing at my sack; both the wine and the sewing-machine had put fancies into their heads; they imagined all sorts of things, and began throwing out hints. Wait a bit, thought I to myself; my time will come!

In the evening I sit with the family in the parlour, talking. We have just finished supper, and the master of the house had put on his spectacles to read the papers. Then some one coughs outside. "There's some one coming in," I say. The girls exchange glances and go out. A little after they open the door and show in two young men. "Come in and sit down," says the wife.

It struck me just then that these two peasant lads had been invited on the strength of my wine, and that they were sweethearts with the girls. Smart young creatures—eighteen, nineteen years old, and already up to anything. Well, if they reckoned on that wine now, they'd be mistaken! Not a drop....

There was some talking of the weather; how it was no better than could be looked for that time of year, but a pity the wet had stopped the ploughing. There was no sort of life in this talk, and one of the girls turned to me and said I was very quiet this evening. How could it be?

"Maybe because I'm going away," I answered. "I've a good long way to go between now and Monday morning."

"Then perhaps we ought to have a parting glass tonight?"

There was some giggling at this, as a well-deserved thrust at me for keeping back the wine that miserly fashion. But I did not know these girls, and cared nothing for them, otherwise I had acted differently.

"What do you mean?" I asked. "I've bought three bottles of wine that I've to take with me to a certain place."

"And you're going to carry it all that way?" asked the girl, amid much laughter. "As if there were never a store on the road."

"Frøkenen forgets that it's Sunday tomorrow, and the stores on the road will be shut," said I.

The laugh died away, but I could see the company was no more kindly disposed towards me now for speaking straight out. I turned to the wife, and asked coldly how much I owed her for the time I had stayed.

But surely there was no hurry—wouldn't it do tomorrow?

I was in a hurry—thank you. I had been there two days—what did that come to?

She thought over it quite a while; at last she went out, and got her husband to go with her and work it out together.

Seeing they stayed so long away, I went up to the loft, packed my sack all ready, and carried it down into the passage. I proposed to be even more offended, and start off now—that very night. It would be a good way of taking leave, as things were.

When I came into the room again, Petter said:

"You don't mean to say you're starting out tonight?"

"Yes, I do."

"You've no call to heed the girls' nonsense, anyway."

"Herregud, let the old fellow go if he wants to," said his sister.

At last the deputy and his wife came in again, stiffly and stubbornly silent.

Well! And how much did I owe them?

63

H'm! They would leave it to me.

They were all alike—a mean and crafty lot; I felt myself stifling, and picking out the first note that came to hand I flung it at the woman.

Was that enough?

H'm! A tidy bit, for sure, but still.... And some might say 'twas enough, but....

How much was it I had given her?

A five-Kroner note.

Well, perhaps it was barely enough; I felt in my pocket for some more.

"No, mother, it was a ten-Kroner," said Petter. "And that's too much; you'll have to give him something back."

The old woman opens her hand, looks at the note, and turns so very surprised all at once.

"Why, so it is, ten Kroner, yes.... I didn't properly look. Why, then, 'tis right enough, and many thanks...."

Her husband, in embarrassment, starts talking to the two lads of what he'd been reading in the paper; nasty accident; hand crushed in a threshing-machine. The girls pretended not to notice me, but sat like two cats all the time, with necks drawn in and eyes as thin as knife blades. Nothing to stay for here—good-bye to them all.

The old woman comes out in the passage and tries making up to me.

"If only you'd lend us just one of those bottles now," she says, "'twould be a real kindness, that it would. With the two lads sitting there and all."

"Farvel," said I shortly, and would hear no more.

I had my sack over my shoulder, and the sewing-machine in one hand; it was a heavy load, and the muddy road made things no easier. But for all that I walked with a light heart. It was a miserable business altogether, and I might as well admit I had acted a trifle meanly. Meanly? Not a bit! I formed myself into a little committee, and pointed out that those infernal girls had planned to entertain their sweethearts with my wine. Well and good; but was not my ill-will towards that idea male selfishness on my part? If two strange girls had been invited, instead of two young men, should I not have uncorked the wine without a murmur? Certainly! And then as to their calling me an old fellow; after all, it was perfectly right. Old indeed I must be, since I took offence at being set aside in favour of stray plough-boys....

But my sense of injury cooled down in the course of that hard walking. The committee meeting was adjourned, and I toiled along hour after hour with my ridiculous burden—three bottles of wine and a sewing-machine. It was mild and slightly foggy; I could not see the lights of a farm till quite close up, and then mostly the dogs would come dashing out on me and hinder me from stealing into a barn. Later and later it grew; I was tired and discouraged, and plagued myself too with anxiety about the future. Had I not already wasted a heap of money on the most useless trash? I must sell that sewing-machine again now, and get some of it back.

At long last I came to a place where there was no dog. There was still a light in the window, and, without more ado, I walked up and asked shelter for the night.

XXVIII

A young girl sat at a table sewing; there was no one else in the room. When I asked for shelter, she answered brightly and trustingly that she would see, and went into a little room at the side. I called after her as she went that I would be glad only to sit here by the stove till daylight.

A little after the girl came in again with her mother, who was still buttoning her clothes about her. Godkvæld! Shelter for the night? Well, well, there wasn't that room in the place they could make me properly comfortable, but I'd be welcome to the bedroom, such as it was.

And where would they sleep themselves?

Why, it was near day now, and the girl'd be sitting up anyhow for a bit with her sewing.

What was she sewing to sit up for all night? A new dress?

No, only the skirt. She was to wear it to church in the morning, but wouldn't hear of her mother helping.

I brought up my sewing-machine, and said jestingly that a skirt more or less was a mere trifle for a thing like this. Wait, and I'd show them.

Was I a tailor, then?

No. But I sold sewing-machines.

I took out the printed directions and studied them to see how it worked. The girl listened attentively; she was a mere child; her thin fingers were all blue with the dye from the stuff. There was something so poor-looking about those blue fingers; I brought out some wine and poured out for all of us. Then we go on sewing again—I with the printed paper, and the girl working the machine. She is delighted to see how easily it goes, and her eyes are all aglow.

65

How old was she?

Sixteen. Confirmed last year.

And what was her name?

Olga.

Her mother stands watching us, and would dearly like to try the machine herself, but every time she comes near, Olga says: "Be careful, mother, you'll despise it." And when the spool needs filling, and her mother takes the shuttle in her hand a moment, the child is once more afraid it may be "despised."[4]

The old woman puts on the coffee-pot, and tends the fire; the room is soon warm and cosy. The lonely folk are as trusting and kindly as could be. Olga laughs when I make a little jest about the machine. I noted that neither of them asked how much the thing cost, though I had told them it was for sale. They looked on it as hopelessly beyond their reach. But they could still take a delight in seeing it work.

I hinted that Olga really ought to have a machine like that, seeing she'd got the way of it so neatly all at once.

Her mother answered it would have to wait till she'd been out in service for a bit.

Was she going out in service?

Why, yes, she hoped so, anyway. Both her other daughters were in service, and doing well—thank God. Olga would be meeting them at church in the morning.

There was a little cracked mirror hanging on one of the walls, on the other a few cheap prints had been tacked up—pictures of soldiers on horseback and royalties with a great deal of finery. One of these pictures is old and frayed. It is a portrait of the Empress Eugenie, and evidently not a recent purchase. I asked where it had come from.

The good woman did not know. Must be something her husband had bought in his time.

"Did he buy it here?"

More likely 'twould have been at Hersæt, where he had been in service as a young man. Might be thirty years gone now.

I have a little plan in my head already, and say:

"That picture is worth a deal of money."

---

4 Foragte, literally "despise." The word is evidently to be understood as used in error by the girl herself, in place of some equivalent of "spoil (destroy)," the author's purpose being to convey an impression of something touchingly "poor," as with the dye-stained fingers earlier and her awkward gait and figure later mentioned. Precisely similar characteristics are used to the same end in Pan, and elsewhere.

The woman thinks I am making game of her, so I make a close inspection of the picture, and declare emphatically that it is no cheap print—no.

But the woman is quite stupid, and simply says: well, did I think so, now? The thing had hung there ever since the house was built. It was Olga's, by the way, she had called it hers from the time she was a little one.

I put on a knowing, mysterious air, and ask for further details of the case—where Hersæt might be.

Hersæt was in the neighbouring parish, some eight miles away. The Lensmand lived there....

The coffee is ready, and Olga and I call a halt. There are only the fastenings to be done now. I ask to see the blouse she is to wear with the skirt, and it appears that this is not a real blouse at all, but a knitted kerchief. But she has a left-off jacket that one of her sisters gave her, and that will go outside and hide all the rest.

Olga is growing so fast, I am told, that there's no sense in buying a blouse for her this twelvemonth to come.

Olga sits sewing on hooks and eyes, and that is soon done. Then she turns so sleepy, it's a sight to see; wherefore I put on an air of authority and order her to bed. Her mother feels constrained to sit up and keep me company, though I tell her myself to go back to bed again.

"You ought to be properly thankful, I'm sure," says the mother, "to the strange man for all the way he's helped you."

And Olga comes up to me and gives her hand to thank me, and I turn her round and shuffle her across to the bedroom door.

"You'd better go too," I say to her mother. "I won't sit talking any more, for I'm tired myself."

And, seeing I settle down by the stove with my sack under my head, she shakes her head with a smile and goes off too.

XXIX

I am happy and comfortable here; it is morning; the sun coming in through the window, and both Olga and her mother with their hair so smooth and plastered down, a wonder to see.

After breakfast, which I share with the two of them, getting quantities of coffee with it, Olga gets herself up in her new skirt and her knitted kerchief and the jacket. Eh, that wonderful jacket; lasting at the edge all round, and two rows of buttons of the same, and the neck and sleeves trimmed with braid. But little Olga could not fill it out. Nothing near it! The child is all odd corners and angles, like a young calf.

"Couldn't we just take it in a bit at the sides?" I ask. "There's plenty of time."

But mother and daughter exchange glances, plainly saying, 'tis Sunday, and no using needle or knife that day. I understand them well enough, for I would have thought exactly the same myself in my childhood. So I try to find a way out by a little free-thinking: 'tis another matter when it's a machine that does the work; no more than when an innocent cart comes rumbling down the road, as it may any Sunday.

But no; this is beyond them. And anyhow, the jacket must give her room to grow; in a couple of years it would fit her nicely.

I thought about for something I could slip into Olga's hand as she went; but I've nothing, so I gave her a silver Krone. And straightway she gives her hand in thanks, and shows the coin to her mother, and whispers she will give it to her sister at church. Her eyes are simply glowing with joy at the thought. And her mother, hardly less moved herself, answers yes, perhaps she ought....

Olga goes off to church in her long jacket; goes shambling down the hill with her feet turning in and out any odd way. A sweet and heartening thing to see....

Hersæt now; was that a big place?

Yes, a fine big place.

I sit for a while blinking sleepy eyes and making excursions in etymology. Hersæt might mean Herresæte.[5] Or possibly some herse[6] might have held sway there. And the herse's daughter was the proudest maiden for far around, and the Jarl himself comes to ask her hand. And the year after she bears him a son, who becomes king....

In a word, I would go to Hersæt. Seeing it was all the same where I went, I would go there. Possibly I might get work at the Lensmand's, or there was always the chance of something turning up; at any rate, I should see new people. And having thus decided upon Hersæt, I felt I had a purpose before me.

The good woman gives me leave to lie down on her bed, for I am drowsy and stupid for lack of sleep. A fine blue spider clambers slowly up the wall, and I lie watching it till I fall asleep.

After a couple of hours I wake suddenly, feeling rested and fresh. The woman was cooking the dinner. I pack up my sack, pay

---

[5] Manor.
[6] Local chieftain in ancient times.

her for my stay, and end up by saying I'd like to make an exchange; my sewing-machine for Olga's picture there.

The woman incredulous as ever.

Never mind, say I; if she was content, why, so was I. The picture was of value; I knew what I was doing.

I took down the picture from the wall, blew the dust from it, and rolled it up carefully; the wall showed lighter in a square patch where it had been. Then I took my leave.

The woman followed me out: wouldn't I wait now, till Olga came back, so she could thank me? Oh, now if I only would!

I couldn't. Hadn't time. Tell her from me, if there was anything she couldn't make out, to look in the directions....

The woman stood looking after me as I went. I swaggered down the road, whistling with satisfaction at what I had done. Only the sack to carry now; I was rested, the sun was shining, and the road had dried up a little. I fell to singing with satisfaction at what I had done.

Neurasthenia....

I reached Hersæt the following day. At first I felt like passing by, it looked so big and fine a place; but after I had talked a bit with one of the farm-hands, I decided to try the Lensmand after all. I had worked for rich people before—let me see, there was Captain Falkenberg of Øvrebø....

The Lensmand was a little, broad-shouldered man, with a long white beard and dark eyebrows. He talked gruffly, but had kindly eyes; afterwards, I found he was a merry soul, who could laugh and jest heartily enough at times. Now and again, too, he would show a touch of pride in his position, and his wealth, and like to have it recognized.

"No, I've no work for you. Where do you come from?"

I named some places I had lately passed.

"No money, I suppose, and go about begging?"

No, I did not beg; I had money enough.

"Well, you'll have to go on farther. I've nothing for you to do here; the ploughing's done. Can you cut staves for a fence?

"Yes."

"H'm. Well, I don't use wooden fences any more. I've put up wire. Do bricklayer's work?"

"Yes."

"That's a pity. I've had bricklayers at work here for weeks; you might have got a job. But it's all done now."

He stood poking his stick in the ground.

"What made you come to me?"

"Every one said go to the Lensmand if I wanted work."

"Oh, did they? Well, I've always got a crowd here working at something or other—those bricklayers, now. Can you put up a fence that's proof against fowls?—For that's more than any soul on earth ever could, haha!—

"Worked for Captain Falkenberg, you said, at Øvrebø?"

"Yes."

"What were you doing there?"

"Felling timber."

"I don't know him—he lives a long way off. But I've heard of him. Any papers from him?"

I showed him what the Captain had written.

"Come along with me," said the Lensmand abruptly. He led me round the house and into the kitchen.

"Give this man a thorough good meal—he's come a long way, and...."

I sat down in the big, well-lighted kitchen to the best meal I had had for a long time. I had just finished when the Lensmand came out again.

"Look here, you...." he began.

I got up at once and stood straight as an arrow—a piece of politeness which I fancy was not lost on him.

"No, no, finish your meal, go on. Finished? Sure? Well, I've been thinking.... Come along with me."

He took me out to the woodshed.

"You might do a bit of work getting in firewood; what do you say to that? I've two men on the place, but one of them I shall want for summoners' work, so you'll have to go woodcutting with the other. You can see there's plenty of wood here as it is, but it'll take no harm lying here, can't have too much of that sort of thing. You said you had money; let me see."

I showed him the notes I had.

"Good. I'm an official, you see, and have to know my folk. Though I don't suppose you've anything on your conscience, seeing you come to the Lensmand, haha! Well, as I said, you can give yourself a rest today, and start cutting wood tomorrow."

I set to work getting ready for the next day, looked to my clothes, filed the saw, and ground my ax. I had no gloves, but it was hardly weather for gloves as yet, and there was nothing else I was short of.

The Lensmand came out to me several times, and talked in a casual way; it amused him, perhaps, to talk to a strange wanderer. "Here, Margrethe!" he called to his wife, as she went across the courtyard; "here's the new man; I'm going to send him out cutting wood."

70

XXX

We had no special orders, but set to work as we thought best, felling dry-topped trees, and in the evening the Lensmand said it was right enough. But he would show us himself the next day.

I soon realized that the work here would not last till Christmas. With the weather we were having, and the ground as it was, frost at night and no snow, we felled a deal each day, and nothing to hinder the work; the Lensmand himself though we were devilish smart at felling trees, haha! The old man was easy to work with; he often came out to us in the woods and chatted and made jokes, and as I never joked in return, he took me, no doubt, for a dull dog, but a steady fellow. He began sending me on errands now, with letters to and from the post.

There were no children on the place, no young folk at all save the maids and one of the farm-hands, so the evenings fell rather long. By way of passing the time, I got hold of some tin and acids and re-tinned some old pots and kettles in the kitchen. But that was soon done. And then one evening I came to write the following letter:

"If only I were where you are, I would work for two."

Next day I had to go to the post for the Lensmand; I took my letter with me and posted it. I was very uneasy. Moreover, the letter looked clumsy as I sent it, for I had got the paper from the Lensmand, and had to paste a whole strip of stamps along the envelope to cover where his name was printed on. I wondered what she would say when she got it. There was no name, nor any place given in the letter.

And so we work in the woods, the other man and I, talk of our little affairs, working with heart and soul, and getting on well together. The days passed; already, worse luck, I could see the end of our work ahead, but I had a little hope the Lensmand might find something else for me to do when the woodcutting was finished. Something would surely turn up. I had no wish to set out wandering anew before Christmas.

Then one day I go to the post again, and there is a letter for me. I cannot understand that it is for me, and I stand turning and twisting it confusedly; but the man knows me now; he reads from the envelope again and says yes, it is my name right enough, and care of the Lensmand.

Suddenly a thought strikes me, and I grasp the letter. Yes, it is for me; I forgot ... yes, of course....

And I hurry out into the road, with something ringing in my ears all the time, and open the letter, and read:

71

"Skriv ikke til mig—"[7]

No name, no place, but so clear and lovely. The first word was underlined.

I do not know how I got home. I remember I sat on a stone by the roadside and read the letter and put it in my pocket, and walked on till I came to another stone and did the same again. Skriv ikke. But—did that mean I might come and perhaps speak with her? That little, dainty piece of paper, and the swift, delicate characters. Her hands had held it, her eyes had looked on it, her breath had touched it. And then at the end a dash. Which might have a world of meaning.

I came home, handed in the Lensmand's post, and went out into the wood. I was dreaming all the time. My comrade, no doubt, must have found me an incomprehensible man, seeing me read a letter again and again, and put it back with my money.

How splendid of her to have found me! She must have held the envelope up to the light, no doubt, and read the Lensmand's name under the stamps; then laid her beautiful head on one side and half closed her eyes and thought for a moment: he is working for the Lensmand at Hersæt now....

That evening, when we were back home, the Lensmand came out and talked to us of this and that, and asked:

"Didn't you say you'd been working for Captain Falkenberg at Øvrebø?"

"Yes."

"I see he's invented a machine."

"A machine?"

"A patent saw for timber work. It's in the papers."

I started at this. Surely he hadn't invented my patent saw?

"There must be some mistake," I said. "It wasn't the Captain who invented it."

"Oh, wasn't it?"

"No it wasn't. But the saw was left with him."

And I told the Lensmand all about it. He went in to fetch the paper, and we both read what it said: "New Invention.... Our Correspondent on the spot.... Of great importance to owners of timber lands.... Principle of the mechanism is as follows:..."

"You don't mean to say it's your invention?"

"Yes, it is."

"And the Captain is trying to steal it? Why, this'll be a pretty case, a mighty pretty case. Leave it to me. Did any one see you working on the thing?"

"Yes, all his people on the place did."

---

[7] "Do not write (skrive) to me."

"Lord save me if it's not the stiffest bit of business I've heard for a long time. Walk off with another man's invention! And the money, too ... why, it might bring you in a million!"

I was obliged to confess I could not understand the Captain.

"Don't you? Haha, but I do! I've not been Lensmand all this time far nothing. No; I've had my suspicions that he wasn't so rich as he pretended. Well, I'll send him a bit of a letter from me, just a line or so—what do you say to that? Hahaha! You leave it to me."

But at this I began to feel uneasy. The Lensmand was too violent all at once; it might well be that the Captain was not to blame in the matter at all, and that the newspaper man had made the mistake himself. I begged the Lensmand to let me write myself.

"And agree to divide the proceeds with that rascal? Never! You leave the whole thing in my hands. And, anyhow, if you were to write yourself, you couldn't set it out properly the way I can."

But I worked on him until at last he agreed that I should write the first letter, and then he should take it up after. I got some of the Lensmand's paper again.

I got no writing done that evening; it had been an exciting day, and my mind was all in a turmoil still. I thought and reckoned it out; for Fruen's sake I would not write directly to the Captain, and risk causing her unpleasantness as well; no, I would send a line to my comrade, Lars Falkenberg, to keep an eye on the machine.

That night I had another visit from the corpse—that miserable old woman in her night-shift, that would not leave me in peace on account of her thumbnail. I had had a long spell of emotion the day before, so this night she took care to come. Frozen with horror, I saw her come gliding in, stop in the middle of the room, and stretch out her hand. Over against the other wall lay my fellow-woodcutter in his bed, and it was a strange relief to me to hear that he too lay groaning and moving restlessly; at any rate there were two of us to share the danger. I shook my head, to say I had buried the nail in a peaceful spot, and could do no more. But the corpse stood there still. I begged her pardon; but then, suddenly, I was seized with a feeling of annoyance; I grew angry, and told her straight out I'd have no more of her nonsense. I'd borrowed that nail of hers at a pinch, but I'd done all I could do months ago, and buried it again.... At that she came gliding sideways over to my pillow, trying to get behind me. I flung myself up in bed and gave a shriek.

"What is it?" asked the lad from the other bed.

I rub my eyes and answer I'd been dreaming, that was all.

"Who was it came in just now?" asks the boy.

"I don't know. Was there any one in here?"

"I saw some one going..."

XXXI

After a couple of days, I set myself down calmly and loftily to write to Falkenberg. I had a bit of a saw thing I'd left there at Øvrebø, I wrote; it might be a useful thing for owners of timber lands some day, and I proposed to come along and fetch it away shortly. Please keep an eye on it and see it doesn't get damaged.

Yes, I wrote in that gentle style. That was the most dignified way. And since Falkenberg, of course, would mention it in the kitchen, and perhaps show the letter round, it had to be delicacy itself. But it was not all delicacy and nothing else; I fixed a definite date, to make it serious: I will come for the machine on Monday, 11th December.

I thought to myself: there, that's clear and sound; if the machine's not there that Monday, why, then, something will happen.

I took the letter to the post myself, and stuck a strip of stamps across the envelope as before....

My beautiful ecstasy was still on me. I had received the loveliest letter in the world; here it was in my breast pocket; it was to me. Skriv ikke. No, indeed, but I could come. And then a dash at the end.

There wasn't anything wrong, by any chance, about that underlining the word: as, for instance, meaning to emphasize the whole thing as an order? Ladies were always so fond of underlining all sorts of words, and putting in dashes here, there, and everywhere. But not she; no, not she!

A few days more, and the work at the Lensmand's would be at an end; it fitted in very well, everything worked out nicely; on the 11th I was to be at Øvrebø. And that perhaps not a minute too soon. If the Captain really had any idea of his own about my machine, it would be necessary to act at once. Was a stranger to come stealing my hard-earned million? Hadn't I toiled for it? I almost began to regret the gentleness of my letter to Falkenberg; I might have made it a good deal sharper; now, perhaps, he would imagine I was too soft to stand up for myself. Why, he might even take it into his head to bear witness against me, and say I hadn't invented the machine at all! Hoho, Master Falkenberg, just try it on! In the first place, 'twill cost you your eternal salvation; and if that's not enough, I'll have you up for perjury before my friend and patron, the Lensmand. And you know what that'll mean.

"Of course you must go," said the Lensmand when I spoke to him about it. "And just come back here to me with your machine.

You must look after your interests, of course; it may be a question of something considerable."

The following day's post brought a piece of news that changed the situation in a moment; there was a letter from Captain Falkenberg himself in the paper, saying it was due to a misunderstanding that the new timber saw had been stated as being of his invention. The apparatus had been designed by a man who had worked on his estate some time back. As to its value, he would not express any opinion.—Captain Falkenberg.

The Lensmand and I looked at each other.

"Well, what do you say now?" he asked.

"That the Captain, at any rate, is innocent."

"Ho! D'you know what I think?"

Pause. The Lensmand playing Lensmand from top to toe, unravelling schemes and plots.

"He is not innocent," said he.

"Really?"

"Ah, I've seen that sort of thing before. Drawing in his horns, that's all. Your letter put him on his guard. Haha!"

At this I had to confess to the Lensmand that I had not written to the Captain at all but had merely sent a bit of a note to one of the hands at Øvrebø; and even that letter could not have reached there yet, seeing it was only posted the night before.

This left the Lensmand dumb, and he gave up unravelling things. On the other hand, he seemed from now onward to be greatly in doubt as to whether the whole thing had any value at all.

"Quite likely the machine's no good at all," he said. But then he added kindly: "I mean, it may need touching up a bit, and improving. You've seen yourself how they're always altering things like warships and flying-machines. Are you still determined to go?"

No more was said about my coming back here and bringing the machine with me. But the Lensmand wrote me a very nice recommendation. He would gladly have kept me on longer, it said, but the work was interrupted by private affairs of my own elsewhere....

In the morning, when I was ready to start, a little girl stood in the courtyard waiting for me to come out. It was Olga. Was there ever such a child? She must have been afoot since midnight to get here so early. And there she stood in her blue skirt and her jacket.

"That you, Olga? Where are you going?"

She had come to see me.

How did she know I was here?

She had asked about me and found out where I was. And

75

please was it true she was to keep the sewing-machine? But of course it couldn't....

Yes, the machine was hers all right; hadn't I taken her picture in exchange? Did it work all right?

Yes, it worked all right.

We did not talk much together; I wanted to get her away before the Lensmand came out and began asking questions.

"Well, run along home now, child; you've a long way to go."

Olga gives me her hand—it is swallowed up completely in mine, and she lets it lie there as long as I will. Then she thanks me, and shambles gaily off again. And her toes turning in and out all odd ways.

XXXII

I am nearly at my goal.

Sunday evening I lay in a watchman's hut not far from Øvrebø, so as to be on the place early Monday morning. By nine o'clock every one would be up, then surely I must be lucky enough to meet the one I sought.

I had grown dreadfully nervous, and kept imagining ugly things. I had written a nice letter to Falkenberg, using no sharp words, but the Captain might after all have been offended at my fixing the date like that; giving him so and so much time.... If only I had never written at all!

Coming up towards the house I stoop more and more, and make myself small, though indeed I had done no wrong. I turn off from the road up, and go round so as to reach the outbuildings first—and there I come upon Falkenberg. He is washing down the carriage. We gave each other greeting, and were the same good comrades as before.

Was he going out with the carriage?

No, just come back the night before. Been to the railway station.

Who had gone away, then?

Fruen.

Fruen?

Fruen, yes.

Pause.

Really? And where was Fruen gone to?

Gone to stay in town for a bit.

Pause.

"Stranger man's been here writing in the papers about that machine of yours," says Falkenberg.

"Is the Captain gone away too?"

"No, Captain's at home. You should have seen his face when your letter came."

I got Falkenberg to come up to the old loft. I had still two bottles of wine in my sack, and I took them out and we started on them together; eh, those bottles that I had carried backward and forward, mile after mile, and had to be so careful with, they served me well just now. Save for them Falkenberg would never have said so much.

"What was that about the Captain and my letter? Did he see it?"

"Well, it began like this," said Falkenberg. "Fruen was in the kitchen when I came in with the post. 'What letter's that with all those stamps on?' she says. I opened it, and said it was from you, to say you were coming on the 11th."

"And what did she say?"

"She didn't say any more. Yes, she asked once again, 'Coming on the 11th, is he?' And I said yes, he was."

"And then, a couple of days after, you got orders to drive her to the station?"

"Why, yes, it must have been about a couple of days. Well, then, I thought, if Fruen knows about the letter, then Captain surely knows too. D'you know what he said when I brought it in?"

I made no answer to this, but thought and thought. There must be something behind all this. Was she running away from me? Madman! the Captain's Lady at Øvrebø would not run away from one of her labourers. But the whole thing seemed so strange. I had hoped all along she would give me leave to speak with her, since I was forbidden to write.

Falkenberg went on, a little awkwardly:

"Well, I showed the Captain your letter, though you didn't say I was to. Was there any harm in that?"

"It doesn't matter. What did he say?"

"'Yes, look after the machine, do,' he said, and made a face. 'In case any one comes to steal it,' he said."

"Then the Captain's angry with me now?"

"Nay, I shouldn't think so. I've heard no more about it since that day."

It mattered little after all about the Captain. When Falkenberg had taken a deal of wine, I asked him if he knew where Fruen was staying in town. No, but Emma might, perhaps. We get hold of

77

Emma, treat her to wine, talk a lot of nonsense, and work gradually round to the point; at last asking in a delicate way. No, Emma didn't know the address. But Fruen had gone to buy things for Christmas, and she was going with Frøken Elisabeth from the vicarage, so they'd know the address there. What did I want it for, by the way?

Well, it was only about a filigree brooch I had got hold of, and wanted to ask if she'd care to buy it.

"Let's look."

Luckily I was able to show her the brooch; it was a beautiful piece of old work; I had bought it of one of the maids at Hersæt.

"Fruen wouldn't have it," said Emma. "I wouldn't have it myself."

"Not if you got me into the bargain, Emma, what?" And I forced myself to jest again.

Emma goes off. I try drawing out Falkenberg again. Falkenberg was sharp enough at times to understand people.

Did he still sing for Fruen?

Lord, no; that was all over. Falkenberg wished he hadn't taken service here at all; 'twas nothing but trouble and misery about the place.

Trouble and misery? Weren't they friends, then, the Captain and his Lady?

Oh yes, they were friends. In the same old way. Last Saturday she had been crying all day.

"Funny thing it should be like that," say I, "when they're so upright and considerate towards each other." And I watch to see what Falkenberg says to that.

"Eh, but they're ever weary," says Falkenberg in his Valdres dialect. "And she's losing her looks too. Only in the time you've been gone, she's got all pale and thin."

I sat up in the loft for a couple of hours, keeping an eye on the main building from my window, but the Captain did not appear. Why didn't he go out? It was hopeless to wait any longer; I should have to go without making my excuses to the Captain. I could have found good grounds enough; I might have put the blame on to the first article in the paper, and said it had rather turned my head for the moment—and there was some truth in that. Well, all I had to do now was to tie up the machine in a bundle, cover it up as far as possible with my sack, and start off on my wanderings again.

Emma stole some food for me before I went.

It was another long journey this time; first to the vicarage—though that was but a little out of the way—and then on to the railway station. A little snow was falling, which made it rather heavy walking; and what was more, I could not take it easy now, but must get on as fast as I could. The ladies were only staying in town for their Christmas shopping, and they had a good start already.

On the following afternoon I came to the vicarage. I had reckoned out it would be best to speak with Fruen.

"I'm on my way into town," I told her. "And I've this machine thing with me; if I might leave the heaviest of the woodwork here meanwhile?"

"Are you going into town?" says Fruen. "But you'll stay here till tomorrow, surely?"

"No, thanks all the same. I've got to be in town tomorrow."

Fruen thinks for a bit and then says:

"Elisabeth's in town. You might take a parcel in for her—something she's forgotten."

That gives me the address! I thought to myself.

"But I've got to get it ready first."

"Then Frøken Elisabeth might be gone again before I got there?"

"Oh no, she's with Fru Falkenberg, and they're staying in town for the week."

This was grand news, joyous news. Now I had both the address and the time.

Fruen stands watching me sideways, and says:

"Well, then, you'll stay the night, won't you? You see, it's something I've got to get ready first...."

I was given a room in the main building, because it was too cold to sleep in the barn. And when all the household had gone to rest that night, and everything was quiet, came Fruen to my room with the parcel, and said:

"Excuse my coming so late. But I thought you might be going early to-morrow morning before I was up."

XXXIII

So here I am once more in the crush and noise of a city, with its newspapers and people. I have been away from all this for many months now, and find it not unpleasant. I spend a morning taking it all in; get hold of some other clothes, and set off to find Frøken Elisabeth at her address. She was staying with some relatives.

And now—should I be lucky enough to meet the other one? I am restless as a boy. My hands are vulgarly unused to gloves, and I pull them off; then going up the step I notice that my hands do not go at all well with the clothes I am wearing, and I put on my gloves again. Then I ring the bell.

"Frøken Elisabeth? Yes, would you wait a moment?"

Frøken Elisabeth comes out. "Goddag. You wished to speak to.... Oh, is it you?"

I had brought a parcel from her mother. Værsaagod.

She tears open the parcel and looks inside. "Oh, fancy Mama thinking of that. The opera-glasses! We've been to the theatre already.... I didn't recognize you at first."

"Really! It's not so very long since...."

"No, but.... Tell me, isn't there any one else you'd like to inquire about? Haha!"

"Yes," said I.

"Well, she's not here. I'm only staying here with my relations. No, she's at the Victoria."

"Well, the parcel was for you," said I, trying to master my disappointment.

"Wait a minute. I was just going out again; we can go together."

Frøken Elisabeth puts on some over-things, calls out through a door to say she won't be very long, and goes out with me. We take a cab and drive to a quiet café. Frøken Elisabeth says yes, she loves going to cafés. But there's nothing very amusing about this one.

Would she rather go somewhere else?

"Yes. To the Grand."

I hesitated; it might be hardly safe. I had been away for a long time now, and if we met any one I knew I might have to talk to them. But Frøkenen insisted on Grand. She had had but a few days' practice in the capital, and had already gained a deal of self-assurance. But I liked her so much before.

We drove off again to Grand. It was getting towards evening. Frøkenen picks out a seat right in the brightest spot, beaming all over herself at the fun of it. I ordered some wine.

"What fine clothes you're wearing now," she says, with a laugh.

"I couldn't very well come in here in a workman's blouse."

"No, of course not. But, honestly, that blouse ... shall I tell you what I think?"

"Yes, do."

"The blouse suited you better."

There! Devil take these town clothes! I sat there with my head full of other things, and did not care for this sort of talk.

"Are you staying long in town?" I asked.

"As long as Lovise does. We've finished our shopping. No, I'm

80

sorry; it's all too short." Then she turns gay once more, and asks laughingly: "Did you like being with us out in the country?"

"Yes. That was a pleasant time."

"And will you come again soon? Haha!"

She seemed to be making fun of me. Trying, of course, to show she saw through me: that I hadn't played—my part well enough as a country labourer. Child that she was! I could teach many a labourer his business, and had more than one trade at my finger-ends. Though in my true calling I manage to achieve just the next best of all I dream....

"Shall I ask Papa to put up a notice on the post next spring, to say you're willing to lay down water-pipes and so on?"

She closed her eyes and laughed—so heartily she laughed.

I am torn with excitement, and her merriment pains me, though it is all good-humoured enough. I glance round the place, trying to pull myself together; here and there an acquaintance nods to me, and I return it; it all seems so far away to me. I was sitting with a charming girl, and that made people notice us.

"You know these people, it seems?"

"Yes, one or two of them. Have you enjoyed yourself in town?"

"Oh yes, immensely. I've two boy cousins here, and then there were their friends as well."

"Poor young Erik, out in the country," said I jestingly.

"Oh, you with your young Erik. No, there's one here in town; his name's Bewer. But I'm not friends with him just now."

"Oh, that won't last long."

"Do you think so? Really, though, I'm rather serious about it. I've an idea he might be coming in here this evening."

"You must point him out to me if he does."

"I thought, as we drove out here, that you and I could sit here together, you know, and make him jealous."

"Right, then, we will."

"Yes, but.... No, you'd have to be a bit younger. I mean...."

I forced myself to laugh. Oh, we would manage all right. Don't despise us old ones, us ancient ones, we can be quite surprisingly useful at times. "Only you'd better let me sit on the sofa beside you there, so he can't see I'm bald at the back."

Eh, but it is hard to take that perilous transition to old age in any quiet and beautiful way. There comes a forcedness, a play of jerky effort and grimaces, the fight against those younger than ourselves, and envy.

"Frøken...." I ask this of her now with all my heart. "Frøken, couldn't you ring up Fru Falkenberg and get her to come round here now?"

81

She thinks for a moment.

"Yes, we will," she says generously.

We go out to the telephone, ring up the Victoria: Fruen is there.

"Is that you, Lovise? You'd never guess who I'm with now? Won't you come along? Oh, good! We're at the Grand. No, I can't tell you now. Yes, of course it's a man—only he's a gentleman now—I won't say who it is. Are you coming? Why, you said just now you would! Some people? Oh, well, do as you like, of course, but I do think.... Yes, he's standing here. You are in a hurry...."

Frøken Elisabeth rang off, and said shortly:

"She had to go and see some friends."

We went back to our seat, and had some more wine; I tried to be cheerful, and suggested champagne. Yes, thanks. And then, as we're sitting there, Frøkenen says suddenly:

"Oh, there's Bewer! I'm so glad we're drinking champagne."

But I have only one idea in my mind, and being now called upon to show what I can do, and charm this young lady to the ultimate advantage of some one else, I find myself saying one thing and thinking another. Which, of course, leads to disaster. I cannot get that telephone conversation out of my head; she must have had an idea—have realized that it was I who was waiting for her here. But what on earth had I done? Why had I been dismissed so suddenly from Øvrebø, and Falkenberg taken on in my place. Quite possibly the Captain and his wife were not always the best of friends, but the Captain had scented danger in my being there, and wished to save his wife at least from such an ignominious fall. And now, here she was, feeling ashamed that I had worked on her place, that she had used me to drive her carriage, and twice shared food with me by the way. And she was ashamed, too, of my being no longer young....

"This will never do," says Frøken Elisabeth.

So I pull myself together again, and start saying all manner of foolish things, to make her laugh. I drink a good deal and that helps; at last, she really seems to fancy I am making myself agreeable to her on her own account. She looks at me curiously.

"No, really, though, do you think I'm nice?"

"Oh, please—don't you understand?—I was speaking of Fru Falkenberg."

"Sh!" says Frøken Elisabeth. "Of course it is Fru Falkenberg; I know that perfectly well, but you need not say so.... I really think we're beginning to make an impression on him over there. Let's go on like we are doing, and look interested."

So she hadn't imagined I was trying on my own account, after

82

all. I was too old for that sort of thing, anyway. Devil take it, yes, of course.

"But you can't get Fru Falkenberg," she says, beginning again. "It's simply hopeless."

"No, I can't get her. Nor you either."

"Are you speaking to Fru Falkenberg now again?"

"No, it was to you this time."

Pause.

"Do you know I was in love with you? Yes, when I was at home."

"This is getting quite amusing," said I, shifting up on the sofa. "Oh, we'll manage Bewer, never fear."

"Yes, only fancy, I used to go up to the churchyard to meet you in the evenings. But you, foolish person, you didn't see it a bit."

"Now you're talking to Bewer, of course," said I.

"No, it's perfectly true. And I came over one day when you were working in the potato fields. It wasn't your young Erik I came to see, not a bit."

"Only think, that it should have been me," I say, putting on a melancholy air.

"Yes, of course you think it was strange. But really, you know, people who live in the country must have some one to be fond of too."

"Does Fru Falkenberg say the same?"

"Fru Falkenberg? No, she says she doesn't want to be fond of anybody, only play her piano and that sort of thing. But I was speaking of myself. Do you know what I did once? No, really, I can't tell you that. Do you want to know?"

"Yes, tell me."

"Well, then ... for, after all, I'm only a child compared to you, so it doesn't matter. It was when you were sleeping in the barn; I went over there one day and laid your rugs together properly, and made a proper bed."

"Was it you did that?" I burst out quite sincerely, forgetting to play my part.

"You ought to have seen me stealing in. Hahaha!"

But this young girl was—not artful enough, she changed colour at her little confession, and laughed forcedly to cover her confusion.

I try to help her out, and say:

"You're really good-hearted, you know. Fru Falkenberg would never have done a thing like that."

"No; but then she's older. Did you think we were the same age?"

"Does Fru Falkenberg say she doesn't want to be fond of anybody?"

"Yes. Oh no ... bother, I don't know. Fru Falkenberg's married, of course; she doesn't say anything. Now talk to me again a little.... Yes, and do you remember the time we went up to the store to buy things, you know? And I kept walking slower and slower for you to catch up...."

"Yes ... that was nice of you. And now I'll do something for you in return."

I rose from my seat, and walked across to where young Bewer sat, and asked if he would not care to join us at our table. I brought him along; Frøken Elisabeth flushed hotly as he came up. Then I talked those two young people well together, which done, I suddenly remembered I had some business to do, and must go off at once. "I'm ever so sorry to leave just now. Frøken Elisabeth, I'm afraid you've turned my head, bewitched me completely; but I realize it's hopeless to think of it. It's a marvel to me, by the way...."

XXXIV

I shambled over to Raadhusgaten, and stood awhile by the cab stand, watching the entrance to the Victoria. But, of course, she had gone to see some friends. I drifted into the hotel, and got talking to the porter.

Yes, Fruen was in. Room No. 12, first floor.

Then she was not out visiting friends?

No.

Was she leaving shortly?

Fruen had not said so.

I went out into the street again, and the cabmen flung up their aprons, inviting my patronage. I picked out a cab and got in.

"Where to?"

"Just stay where you are. I'm hiring you by the hour."

The cabmen walk about whispering, one suggesting this, another that: he's watching the place; out to catch his wife meeting some commercial traveller.

Yes, I am watching the place. There is a light in one or two of the rooms, and suddenly it strikes me that she might stand at a window and see me. "Wait," I say to the cabman, and go into the hotel again.

"Whereabouts is No. 12?"

"First floor."

84

"Looking out on to Raadhusgaten?"

"Yes."

"Then it must have been my sister," I say, inventing something in order to slip past the porter.

I go up the stairs, and, to give myself no chance of turning back, I knock at the door the moment I have seen the number. No answer. I knock again.

"Is it the maid?" comes a voice from within.

I could not answer yes; my voice would have betrayed me. I tried the handle—the door was locked. Perhaps she had been afraid I might come; possibly she had seen me outside.

"No, it's not the maid," I say, and I can hear how the words quiver strangely.

I stand listening a long while after that; I can hear someone moving inside, but the door remains closed. Then come two short rings from one of the rooms down to the hall. It must be she, I say to myself; she is feeling uneasy, and has rung for the maid. I move away from her door, to avoid any awkwardness for her, and, when the maid comes, I walk past as if going downstairs. Then the maid says, "Yes, the maid," and the door is opened.

"No, no." says the maid; "only a gentleman going downstairs."

I thought of taking a room at the hotel, but the idea was distasteful to me; she was not a runaway wife meeting commercial travellers. When I came down, I remarked to the porter as I passed that Fruen seemed to be lying down.

Then I went out and got into my cab again. The time passes, a whole hour; the cabman wants to know if I do not feel cold? Well, yes, a little. Was I waiting for some one? Yes.... He hands me down his rug from the box, and I tip him the price of a drink for his thoughtfulness.

Time goes on; hour after hour. The cabmen talk unrestrainedly now, saying openly one to another that I'm letting the horse freeze to death.

No, it was no good. I paid for the cab, went home, and wrote the following letter:

"You would not let me write to you; will you not let me see you once again? I will ask for you at the hotel at five to-morrow afternoon."

Should I have fixed an earlier hour? But the light in the forenoon was so white; if I felt moved and my mouth twitched, I should look a dreadful sight.

I took the letter round myself to the hotel, and went home again.

A long night—oh, how long were those hours! Now, when I

85

ought to sleep and stretch myself and feel refreshed, I could not. Day dawned, and I got up. After a long ramble through the streets I came back home again, and slept.

Hours pass. When I awake and come to my senses, I hurry anxiously to the telephone to ask if Fruen had left.

No, Fruen had not left.

Thank Heaven then, it seemed she did not wish to run away from me; she must have had my letter long since. No; I had called at an awkward hour the evening before, that was all.

I had something to eat, lay down, and slept again. When I woke it was past noon. I stumble in to the telephone again and ring up as before.

No, Fruen had not left yet. But her things were packed. She was out just now.

I got ready at once, and hurried round to Raadhusgaten to stand on watch. In the course of half an hour I saw a number of people pass in and out, not the one I sought. It was five o'clock now, and I went in and spoke to the porter.

Fruen was gone.

Gone?

"Was it you that rang up? She came just at that moment and took her things. But I've a letter here."

I took the letter, and, without opening it, asked about the train.

"Train left at 4.45," says the porter, looking at his watch. "It's five now."

I had thrown away half an hour keeping watch outside.

I sit down on one of the steps, staring at the floor.

The porter keeps on talking. He must be well aware it was not my sister.

"I said to Fruen there was a gentleman had just rung up. But she only said she hadn't time, and would I give him this letter."

"Was there another lady with her when she left?"

"No."

I got up and went out. In the street I opened the letter and read:

"You must not follow me about any more—"

Impassively I put the thing away. It had not surprised me, had made no new impression. Thoroughly womanly, hasty words, written on impulse, with underlining and a dash....

Then it occurred to me to go round to Frøken Elisabeth's address; there was still a glimmer of hope. I heard the door bell ring inside the house as I pressed, and stood listening as in a whirling desert.

86

Frøken Elisabeth had left an hour before.

Then wine, and then whisky. And then endless whisky. And altogether a twenty-one days' debauch, in the course of which a curtain falls and hides my earthly consciousness. In this state, it enters my head one day to send something to a little cottage in the country. It is a mirror, in a gay gilt frame. And it was for a little maid, by name Olga, a creature touching and sweet to watch as a young calf.

Ay, for I've not got over my neurasthenia yet.

The timber saw is in my room. But I cannot put it together, for the bulk of the wooden parts I left behind at a vicarage in the country. It matters little now, my love for the thing is dulled. My neurasthenic friends, believe me, folk of our sort are useless as human beings, and we should not even do for any kind of beast.

One day I suppose I shall grow tired of this unconsciousness, and go out and live on an island once again.

A WANDERER PLAYS ON MUTED STRINGS

INTRODUCTION

It looks to be a fine year for berries, yes; whortleberries, crowberries, and fintocks. A man can't live on berries; true enough. But it is good to have them growing all about, and a kindly thing to see. And many a thirsty and hungry man's been glad to find them.

I was thinking of this only yesterday evening.

There's two or three months yet till the late autumn berries are ripe; yes, I know. But there are other joys than berries in the wilds. Spring and summer they are still only in bloom, but there are harebells and ladyslippers, deep, windless woods, and the scent of trees, and stillness. There is a sound as of distant waters from the heavens; never so long-drawn a sound in all eternity. And a thrush may be singing as high as ever its voice can go, and then, just at its highest pitch, the note breaks suddenly at a right angle; clear and clean as if cut with a diamond; then softly and sweetly down the scale once more. Along the shore, too, there is life; guillemot, oyster-catcher, tern are busy there; the wagtail is out in search of food, advancing in little spurts, trim and pert with its pointed beak and swift little flick of a tail; after a while it flies up to perch on a fence and sing with the rest. But when the sun has set, may come the cry of a loon from some hill-tarn; a melancholy hurrah. That is the last; now there is only the grasshopper left. And there's nothing to say of a grasshopper, you never see it; it doesn't count, only he's there gritting his resiny teeth, as you might say.

I sit and think of all these things; of how summer has its joys for a wanderer, so there's no sort of need to wait till autumn comes.

And here I am writing cool words of these quiet things—for all the world as if there were no violent and perilous happenings ahead. 'Tis a trick, and I learned it of a man in the southern hemisphere—of a Mexican called Rough. The brim of his huge hat was hung with tinkling sequins: that in itself was a thing to remember. And most of all, I remember how calmly he told the story of his first murder: "I'd a sweetheart once named Maria," said Rough, with that patient look of his; "well, she was no more than sixteen, and I was nineteen then. She'd such little hands when you touched them; fingers thin and slight, you know the sort. One evening the master called her in from the fields to do some sewing for him. No help for it then; and it wasn't more than a day again before he calls her in same as before. Well, it went on like that a few weeks, and then stopped. Seven months after Maria died, and they buried her, little hands and all. I went to her brother Inez and said: 'At six tomorrow morning the master rides to town, and he'll be alone.' 'I know,' said he. 'You might lend me that little rifle of yours to shoot him with.' 'I shall be using it myself,' said he. Then we talked for a bit about other things: the crops, and a big new well we'd dug. And when I left, I reached down his rifle from the wall and took it with me. In the timber I heard Inez at my heels, calling to me to stop. We sat down and talked a bit more this way and that; then Inez snatched the rifle away from me and went home. Next morning I was up early, and out at the gate ready to open it for the master; Inez was there too, hiding in the bushes. I told him he'd better go on ahead; we didn't want to be two to one. 'He's pistols in his belt.' said Inez; 'but what about you?' 'I know,' said I; 'but I've a lump of lead here, and that makes no noise.' I showed him the lump of lead, and he thought for a bit; then he went home. Then the master came riding up; grey and old he was, sixty at least. 'Open the gate!' he called out. But I didn't. He thought I must be mad, no doubt, and lashed out at me with his whip, but I paid no heed. At last he had to get down himself to open the gate. Then I gave him the first blow: it got him just by one eye and cut a hole. He said, 'Augh!' and dropped. I said a few words to him, but he didn't understand; after a few more blows he was dead. He'd a deal of money on him; I took a little to help me on my way, then I mounted and rode off. Inez was standing in the doorway as I rode past his place. 'It's only three and a half days to the frontier,' he said."

So Rough told his story, and sat staring coolly in front of him when it was ended.

I have no murders to tell of, but joys and sufferings and love. And love is no less violent and perilous than murder.

Green in all the woods now, I thought to myself this morning as I dressed. The snow is melting on the hills, and everywhere the cattle in their sheds are eager and anxious to be out; in houses and cottages the windows are opened wide. I open my shirt and let the wind blow in upon me, and I mark how I grow starstruck and uncontrollable within; ah, for a moment it is all as years ago, when I was young, and a wilder spirit than now. And I think to myself: maybe there's a tract of woodland somewhere east or west of this, where an old man can find himself as well bested as a young. I will go and look for it.

Rain and sun and wind by turns; I have been many days on the road already. Too cold yet to lie out in the open at night, but there is always shelter to be had at farmsteads by the way. One man thinks it strange that I should go tramping about like this for nothing; he takes me, no doubt, for somebody in disguise, just trying to be original like Wergeland.[8] The man knows nothing of my plans, how I am on my way to a place I know, where live some people I have a fancy to see again. But he is a sensible fellow enough, and involuntarily I nod as if to agree there is something in what he says. There's a theatrical touch in most of us that makes us feel flattered at being taken for more than we are. Then up come his wife and daughter, good, ordinary souls, and carry all away with their kindly gossip; he's no beggar, they say; be paid for his supper and all. And at last I turn crafty and cowardly and say never a word, and let the man lay more to my charge and still never a word. And we three hearty souls outwin his reasoning sense, and he has to explain he was only jesting all the time; surely we could see that. I stayed a night and a day there, and greased my shoes with extra care, and mended my clothes.

But then the man begins to suspect once more. "There'll be a handsome present for that girl of mine when you leave, I know," says he. I made as if his words had no effect, and answered with a laugh: "You think so?" "Yes," says he; "and then when you're gone we'll sit thinking you must have been somebody grand, after all."

A detestable fellow this! I did the only thing I could: ignored his sarcasm and asked for work. I liked the place, I said, and he'd need of help; I could turn my hand to anything now in the busy time.

"You're a fool," said he, "and the sooner you're off the place the better I'll be pleased."

Clearly he had taken a dislike to me, and there was none of the womenfolk at hand to take my part. I looked at the man, at a loss to understand what was in his mind.

His glance was steady; it struck me suddenly that I had never seen such wisdom in the eyes of man or woman. But he carried his ill-will too far, and made a false step. He asked: "What shall we say your name was?" "No need to say anything at all," I answered. "A wandering Eilert Sundt?" he suggested. And I entered into the jest and answered: "Yes, why not?" But at that he fired up and snapped out sharply: "Then I'm sorry for Fru Sundt, that's all." I shrugged my shoulders in return, and said: "You're wrong there, my good man; I am not married." And I turned to go. But with an unnatural readiness he called after me: "'Tis you that's wrong: I meant for the mother that bore you."

---

[8] A Norwegian poet.

A little way down the road I turned, and saw how his wife and daughter took him up. And I thought to myself: no, 'tis not all roses when one goes a-wandering.

At the next place I came to I learned that he had been with the army, as quartermaster-sergeant; then he went mad over a lawsuit he lost, and was shut up in an asylum for some time. Now in the spring his trouble broke out again; perhaps it was my coming that had given the final touch. But the lightning insight in his eyes at the moment when the madness came upon him! I think of him now and again; he was a lesson to me. 'Tis none so easy to judge of men, who are wise or mad. And God preserve us all from being known for what we are!

That day I passed by a house where a lad sat on the doorstep playing a mouth-organ. He was no musician to speak of, but a cheerful soul he must surely be, to sit there playing to himself like that. I would not disturb him, but simply raised one hand to my cap, and stood a little distance off. He took no notice of me, only wiped his mouth-organ and went on playing. This went on for some time; then at last, waiting till he stopped to wipe his instrument again, I coughed.

"That you, Ingeborg?" he called out. I thought he must be speaking to someone in the house behind him, and made no answer. "You there, I mean," he said again.

I was confused at this. "Can't you see me?" I said.

He did not answer, but fumbled with his hands to either side, as if trying to get up, and I realized that he was blind, "Sit still; don't be afraid of me," I said, and set myself down beside him.

We fell into talk: been blind since he was fourteen, it seemed; he would be eighteen now, and a big, strong fellow he was, with a thick growth of down on his chin. And, thank Heaven, he said, his health was good. But his eyesight, I asked; could he remember what the world looked like? Yes, indeed; there were many pleasant things he could remember from the time when he could see. He was happy and content enough. He was going in to Christiania this spring, to have an operation; then perhaps he might at least be able to see well enough to walk; ay, all would be well in time, no doubt. He was dull-witted, looked as if he ate a lot; was stout and strong as a beast. But there was something unhealthy-looking, something of the idiot about him; his acceptance of his fate was too unreasonable. To be hopeful in that way implies a certain foolishness, I thought to myself; a man must be lacking in sense to some degree if he can go ahead feeling always content with life, and even reckoning to get something new, some good out of it into the bargain.

But I was in the mood to learn something from all I chanced

on in my wandering; even this poor creature on his doorstep made me the wiser by one little thing. How was it he could mistake me for a woman; the woman Ingeborg he had called by name? I must have walked up too quietly. I had forgotten the plodding cart-horse gait; my shoes were too light. I had lived too luxuriously these years past; I must work my way back to the peasant again.

Three more days now to the goal my curious fancy had set before me: to Øvrebø, to Captain Falkenberg's. It was an opportune time to walk up there just now and ask for work; there would be plenty to do on a big place like that in the spring. Six years since I was there last; time had passed, and for the last few weeks I had been letting my beard grow, so that none should recognize me now.

It was in the middle of the week; I must arrange to get there on the Saturday evening. Then the Captain would let me stay over the Sunday while he thought about taking me on. On Monday he would come and say yes or no.

Strangely enough, I felt no excitement at the thought of what was to come; nothing of unrest, no; calmly and comfortably I took my way by farmstead, wood, and meadow. I thought to myself how I had once, years ago, spent some adventurous weeks at that same Øvrebø, even to being in love with Fruen herself, with Fru Lovise. Ay, that I was. She had fair hair and grey, dark eyes; like a young girl she was. Six years gone, ay, so long it is ago; would she be greatly changed? Time has had its wear on me; I am grown dull and faded and indifferent; I look upon a woman now as literature, no more. It has come to the end. Well, and what then? Everything comes to an end. When first I entered on this stage I had a feeling as if I had lost something; as if I had been favoured by the caresses of a pickpocket. Then I set to and felt myself about, to see if I could bear myself after this; if I could endure myself as I was now. Oh well, yes, why not? Not the same as before, of course, but it all passed off so noiselessly, but peacefully, but surely. Everything comes to an end.

In old age one takes no real part in life, but keeps oneself on memories. We are like letters that have been delivered; we are no longer on the way, we have arrived. It is only a question whether we have whirled up joys and sorrows out of what was in us, or have made no impression at all. Thanks be for life; it was good to live!

But Woman, she was, as the wise aforetime knew, infinitely poor in mind, but rich in irresponsibility, in vanity, in wantonness. Like a child in many ways, but with nothing of its innocence.

I stand by the guide-post where the road turns off to Øvrebø. There is no emotion in me. The day lies broad and bright over meadow and woods; here and there is ploughing and harrowing in the fields, but all moves slowly, hardly seems to move at all, for it is full noon and a blazing sun. I walk a little way on beyond the post, dragging out the time before going up to the house. After an hour, I go into the woods and wander about there for a while; there are berries in flower and a scent of little green leaves. A crowd of thrushes go chasing a crow across the sky, making a great to-do, like a clattering confusion of faulty castanets. I lie down on my back, with my sack under my head, and drop off to sleep.

A little after I wake again, and walk over to the nearest ploughman. I want to find out something about the Falkenbergs, if they are still there and all well. The man answers cautiously; he stands blinking, with his little, crafty eyes, and says: "All depends if Captain's at home."

"Is he often away, then?"

"Nay, he'll be at home."

"Has he got the field work done?"

The man smiled: "Nay, I doubt it's not finished yet."

"Are there hands enough to the place?"

"That's more than I can say; yes, I doubt there's hands enough. And the field work's done; leastways, the manure's all carted out."

The man clicks to his horses and goes on ploughing; I walked on beside him. There was not much to be got out of him; next time the horses stopped for a breathing space I worried out of him a few more contradictions as to the family at Øvrebø. The Captain, it seemed was away on manoeuvres all through the summer, and Fruen was at home alone. Yes, they had always a heap of visitors, of course; but the Captain was away. That is to say, not because he wanted to; he liked best to stay at home, by all accounts, but, of course, he'd his duty as well. No, they'd no children as yet; didn't look as if Fruen was like to have any. What was I talking about? They might have children yet, of course; any amount of them for that. On again.

We plough on to the next stop. I am anxious not to arrive at an awkward time, and ask the man, therefore, if he thinks there would be visitors or anything of that sort up at the house today. No, he thought not. They'd parties and visitors now and again, but.... Ay, and music and playing and fine goings-on as often as could be, but.... And well they might, for that matter, seeing they were fine folks, and rich and well-to-do as they were.

He was a torment, was that ploughman. I tried to find out something about another Falkenberg, who could tune pianos at a pinch. On this the ploughman's information was more definite. Lars? Ay, he was here. Know him? Why, of course he knew Lars well enough. He'd finished with service at Øvrebø, but the Captain had

93

given him a clearing of land to live on; he married Emma, that was maid at the house, and they'd a couple of children. Decent, hardworking folk, with feed for two cows already out of their clearing.

Here the furrow ended, and the man turned his team about. I thanked him, and went on my way.

When I came to the house, I recognized all the buildings; they wanted painting. The flagstaff I had helped to raise six years before, it stood there still; but there was no cord to it, and the knob at the top was gone.

Well, here I was, and that was four o'clock in the afternoon of the 26th day of April.

Old folk have a memory for dates.

I

It turned out otherwise than I had thought. Captain Falkenberg came out, heard what I had to say, and answered no on the spot. He had all the hands he wanted, and the field work was all but done.

Good! Might I go over to the men's room and sit down and rest a while?

Certainly.

No invitation to stay over Sunday. The Captain turned on his heel and went indoors again. He looked as if he had only just got out of bed, for he was wearing a night-shirt tucked into his trousers, and had no waistcoat on; only a jacket flung on loosely and left unbuttoned. He was going grey about the ears, and his beard as well.

I sat down in the men's quarters and waited till the farmhands came in for their afternoon meal. There were only two of them—the foreman and another. I got into talk with them, and it appeared the Captain had made a mistake in saying the field work was all but done. Well, 'twas his own affair. I made no secret of the fact that I was looking for a place, and, as for being used to the work, I showed them the fine recommendation I had got from the Lensmand at Hersæt years ago. When the men went out again, I took my sack and walked out with them, ready to go on my way. I peeped in at the stables and saw a surprising number of horses, looked at the cowshed, at the fowls, and the pigs. I noticed that there was dung in the pit from the year before that had not been carted out yet.

I asked how that could be.

"Well, what are we to do?" answered the foreman. "I looked to it from the end of the winter up till now, and nobody but myself on the place. Now there's two of us at least, in a sort of way, but now there's all the ploughing and harrowing to be done."

'Twas his affair.

I bade him farewell, and went on my way. I was going to my good friend, Lars Falkenberg, but I did not tell them so. There are some new little buildings far up in the wood I can see, and that I take to be the clearing.

But the man I had just left must have been inwardly stirred by the thought of getting an extra hand to help with the work. I saw him tramp across the courtyard and up to the house as I went off.

I had gone but a couple of hundred yards when he comes hurrying after me to say I am taken on after all. He had spoken to the Captain, and got leave to take me on himself. "There'll be nothing to do now till Monday, but come in and have something to eat."

He is a good fellow, this; goes with me up to the kitchen and tells them there: "Here's a new man come to work on the place; see he gets something to eat."

A strange cook and strange maids. I get my food and go out again. No sign of master or mistress anywhere.

But I cannot sit idle in the men's room all the evening; I walk up to the field and talk to my two fellow-workers. Nils, the foreman, is from a farm a little north of here, but, not being the eldest son, and having no farm of his own to run, he has been sensible enough to take service here at Øvrebø for the time being. And, indeed, he might have done worse. The Captain himself was not paying more and more attention to his land, rather, perhaps, less and less, and he was away so much that the man had to use his own judgment many a time. This last autumn, for instance, he has turned up a big stretch of waste land that he is going to sow. He points out over the ground, showing where he's ploughed and what's to lie over: "See that bit there how well it's coming on."

It is good to hear how well this young man knows his work; I find a pleasure in his sensible talk. He has been to one of the State schools, too, and learned how to keep accounts of stock, entering loads of hay in one column and the birth dates of the calves in another. His affair. In the old days a peasant kept such matters in his head, and the womenfolk knew to a day when each of their twenty or fifty cow was due to calve.

But he is a smart young fellow, nevertheless, and not afraid of work, only a little soured and spoiled of late by having more on his hands than a man could do. It was plain to see how he brightened up now he had got a man to help with the work. And he settles there and then that I am to start on Monday with the harrow horse, carting out manure, the lad to take one of the Captain's carriage horses for the harrow; he himself would stick to the ploughing. Ay, we would get our sowing done this year.

Sunday.

I must be careful not to show any former knowledge of things about the place here; as, for instance, how far the Captain's timber runs, or where the various out-houses and buildings are, or the well, or the roads. I took some time getting things ready for tomorrow—greased the wheels of the cart, and did up the harness, and gave the horse an extra turn. In the afternoon I went for a four or five hours' ramble through the woods, passed by Lars Falkenberg's place without going in, and came right out to where the Captain's land joined that of the neighbouring village before I turned back. I was surprised to see the mass of timber that had been cut.

When I got back, Nils asked: "Did you hear them singing and carrying on last night?"

"Yes; what was it?"

"Visitors," said he, with a laugh.

Visitors! yes, there were always visitors at Øvrebø just now.

There was an extremely fat but sprightly man among them; he wore his moustache turned up at the ends, and was a captain in the same arm of the service as the master. I saw him and the other guests come lounging out of the house in the course of the evening. There was a man they called Ingeniør,[9] he was young, a little over twenty, fairly tall, brown-skinned and clean shaven. And there was Elisabet from the vicarage. I remember Elisabet very well, and recognized her now at once, for all she was six years older and more mature. Little Elisabet of the old days was no longer a girl—her breast stood out so, and gave an impression of exaggerated health. I learned she is married; she took Erik after all, a farmer's son she had been fond of as a child. She was still friendly with Fru Falkenberg, and often came to stay. But her husband never came with her.

Elisabet is standing by the flagstaff, and Captain Falkenberg comes out. They talk a little, and are occupied with their own affairs. The Captain glances round every time he speaks; possibly he is not talking of trifles, but of something he must needs be careful with.

Then comes the other Captain, the fat and jovial one; we can hear his laugh right over in the servants' quarters. He calls out to Captain Falkenberg to come along, but gets back only a curt answer. A few stone steps lead down to the lilac shrubbery; the Captain goes down there now, a maid following after with wine and glasses. Last of all comes the engineer.

Nils bursts out laughing: "Oh, that Captain! look at him!"

"What's his name?"

"They all call him Bror;[10] it was the same last year as well. I don't know his proper name."

"And the Engineer?"

"His name's Lassen, so I've heard. He's only been here once before in my time."

Then came Fru Falkenberg out on the steps; she stopped for a moment and glanced over at the two by the flagstaff. Her figure is

---

[9] Engineer. Men are frequently addressed and referred to by the title of their occupation, with or without adding the name.

[10] Brother. Not so much a nickname as a general term of jovial familiarity.

slight and pretty as ever; but her face seems looser, as if she had been stouter once and since grown thin. She goes down to the shrubbery after the others, and I recognize her walk again—light and firm as of old. But little wonder if time has taken something of her looks in all those years.

More people come out from the house—an elderly lady wearing a shawl, and two gentlemen with her.

Nils tells me it is not always there are so many guests in the house at once; but it was the Captain's birthday two days ago, and two carriage loads of people had come dashing up; the four strange horses were in the stables now.

Now voices are calling again for the couple by the flagstaff; the Captain throws out an impatient "Yes!" but does not move. Now he brushes a speck of dust from Elisabet's shoulder; now, looking round carefully, he lays one hand on her arm and tells her something earnestly.

Says Nils:

"They've always such a lot to talk about, those two. She never comes here but they go off for long walks together."

"And what does Fru Falkenberg say to that?"

"I've never heard she troubled about it any way."

"And Elisabet, hasn't she any children either?"

"Ay, she's many."

"But how can she get away so often with that big place and the children to look after?"

"It's all right as long as Erik's mother's alive. She can get away all she wants."

He went out as he spoke, leaving me alone. In this room I had sat once working out the construction of an improved timber saw. How earnest I was about it all! Petter, the farm-hand, lay sick in the room next door, and I would hurry out eagerly whenever I'd any hammering to do, and get it done outside. Now that patent saw's just literature to me, no more. So the years deal with us all.

Nils comes in again.

"If the visitors aren't gone tomorrow, I'll take a couple of their horses for the ploughing," says he, thinking only of his own affairs.

I glanced out of the window; the couple by the flagstaff have moved away at last.

In the evening things grew more and more lively down in the shrubbery. The maids went backwards and forwards with trays of food and drink; the party were having supper among the lilacs. "Bror! Bror!" cried one and another, but Bror himself was loudest of all. A chair had broken under his enormous weight, and a message comes out to the servants' quarters to find a good, solid, wooden

98

chair that would bear him. Oh, but they were merry down in the shrubbery! Captain Falkenberg walked up now and again in front of the house to show he was still steady on his legs, and was keeping a watchful eye on things in general. "You mark my words," said Nils, "he'll not be the first to give over. I drove for him last year, and he was drinking all the way, but never a sign was there to see."

The sun went down. It was growing chilly, perhaps, in the garden; anyway, the party went indoors. But the big windows were thrown wide, and waves of melody from Fru Falkenberg's piano poured out. After a while it changed to dance tunes; jovial Captain Bror, no doubt, was playing now.

"Nice lot, aren't they?" said Nils. "Sit up playing and dancing all night, and stay in bed all day. I'm going to turn in."

I stayed behind, looking out of the window, and saw my mate Lars Falkenberg come walking across the courtyard and go up into the house. He had been sent for to sing to the company. When he has sung for a while, Captain Bror and some of the others begin to chime in and help, making a fine merry noise between them. After about an hour in comes Lars Falkenberg to the servants' quarters with a half-bottle of spirit in his pocket for his trouble. Seeing no one but me, a stranger, in the room, he goes in to Nils in the bedroom next door, and they take a dram together; after a little they call to me to come in. I am careful not to say too much, hoping not to be recognized; but when Lars gets up to go home, he asks me to go part of the way with him. And then it appears that I am discovered already; Lars knows that I am his former mate of the woodcutting days.

The Captain had told him.

Well and good, I think to myself. Then I've no need to bother about being careful any more. To tell the truth, I was well pleased at the way things had turned out; it meant that the Captain was completely indifferent as to having me about the place; I could do as I pleased.

I walked all the way home with Lars, talking over old times, and of his new place, and of the people at Øvrebø. It seemed that the Captain was not looked up to with the same respect as before; he was no longer the spokesman of the district, and neighbours had ceased to come and ask his help and advice. The last thing of any account he did was to have the carriage drive altered down to the high road, but that was five years ago. The buildings needed painting, but he had put it off and never had it done; the road across the estate was in disrepair, and he had felled too much timber by far. Drink? Oh, so folk said, no doubt, but it couldn't be fairly said he drank—not that way. Devil take the gossiping fools. He drank a little, and now and again he would drive off somewhere and stay away for a bit; but when he did come home again things never seemed to go well with him, and that was the pity of it! An evil spirit seemed to have got hold of him, said Lars.

And Fruen?

Fruen! She went about the house as before, and played on her piano, and was as pretty and neat as ever any one could wish. And they keep open house, with folk for ever coming and going; but taxes and charges on this and that mount up, and it costs a deal to keep up the place, with all the big buildings to be seen to. But it is a sin and a shame for the Captain, and Fruen as well, to be so dead-weary of each other, you'd never think. If they do say a word to each other, it's looking to the other side all the time, and hardly opening their lips. They barely speak at all, except to other people month after month the same. And all summer the Captain's out on manoeuvres, and never comes home to see how his wife and the place are getting on. "No, they've no children; that's the trouble," says Lars.

Emma comes out and joins us. She looks well and handsome still, and I tell her so.

"Emma?" says Lars. "Ay, well, she's none so bad. But she's for ever having children, the wretch!" and, pouring out a drink from his half-bottle, he forces her to drink it off. Now Emma presses us to come in; we might just as well be sitting down indoors as standing about out here.

"Oh, it's summer now!" says Lars, evidently none so anxious to have me in. Then, when I set off for home, he walks down again with me a bit of the way, showing me where he's dug and drained and fenced about his bit of land. Small as it is, he has made good and sensible use of it. I find a strange sense of pleasure coming over me as I look at this cosy homestead in the woods. There is a faint soughing of the wind in the forest behind; close up to the house are foliage trees, and the aspens rustle like silk.

I walk back home. Night is deepening; all the birds are silent; the air calm and warm, in a soft bluish gloom.

"Let us be young to-night!" It is a man's voice, loud and bright, from behind the lilacs. "Let's go and dance, or do something wild."

"Have you forgotten what you were like last year?" answers Fru Falkenberg. "You were nice and young then, and never said such things."

"No, I never said such things. To think you should remember that! But you scolded me one evening last year too. I said how beautiful you were that evening, and you said no, you weren't beautiful any more; and you called me a child, and told me not to drink so much."

"Yes, so I did," says Fru Falkenberg, with a laugh.

"So you did, yes. But as to your being beautiful or not, surely I ought to know when I was sitting looking at you all the time?"

"Oh, you child!"

"And this evening you're lovelier still."

"There's some one coming!"

Two figures rise up suddenly behind the lilacs. Fruen and the young engineer. Seeing it is only me, they breathe more easily again, and go on talking as if I did not exist. And mark how strange is human feeling; I had been wishing all along to be ignored and left in peace, yet now it hurt me to see these two making so little account of me. My hair and beard are turning grey, I thought to myself; should they not respect me at least for that?

"Yes, you're lovelier still tonight," says the man again. I come up alongside them, touching my cap carelessly, and pass on.

"I'll tell you this much: you'll gain nothing by it," says Fruen. And then: "Here, you've dropped something," she calls to me.

Dropped something? My handkerchief lay on the path; I had dropped it on purpose. I turned round now and picked it up, said thank you, and walked on.

"You're very quick to notice things of no account," says the engineer. "A lout's red-spotted rag.... Come, let's go and sit in the summer-house."

"It's shut up at night," says Fruen. "I dare say there's somebody in there."

After that I heard no more.

My bedroom is up in the loft in the servants' quarters, and the one open window looks out to the shrubbery. When I come up I can still hear voices down there among the bushes, but cannot make out what is said. I thought to myself: why should the summer-house be shut up at night, and whose idea could it be? Possibly some very crafty soul, reckoning that, if the door were always kept locked, it would be less risky to slip inside one evening in good company, take out the key, and stay there.

Some way down along the way I had just come were two people walking up—Captain Bror and the old lady with the shawl. They had been sitting somewhere among the trees, no doubt, when I passed by, and I fell to wondering now if, by any chance, I could have been talking to myself as I walked, and been overheard.

Suddenly I see the engineer get up from behind the bushes and walk swiftly over to the summer-house. Finding it locked, he sets his shoulder against the door and breaks it open with a crash.

101

"Come along, there's nobody here!" he cries.

Fru Falkenberg gets up and says: "Madman! Whatever are you doing?"

But she goes towards him all the same.

"Doing?" says he. "What else should I do? Love isn't glycerine—it's nitro-glycerine."

And he takes her by the arm and leads her in.

Well, 'tis their affair....

But the stout Captain and his lady are coming up; the pair in the summer-house will hardly be aware of their approach, and Fru Falkenberg would perhaps find it far from agreeable to be discovered sitting there with a man just now. I look about for some means of warning them; here is an empty bottle; I go to the window and fling it as hard as I can over towards the summer-house. There is a crash, bottle and tiles are broken, and the pieces go clattering down over the roof; a cry of dismay from within, and Fru Falkenberg rushes out, her companion behind her still grasping her dress. They stop for a moment and look about them. "Bror!" cries Fru Falkenberg, and sets off at a run down the shrubbery. "No, don't come," she calls back over her shoulder. "You mustn't, I tell you."

But the engineer ran after her, all the same. Wonderfully young he was, and all inflexible.

Now the stout Captain and his lady come up, and their talk is a marvel to hear. Love: there is nothing like it, so it seems. The stout cavalier must be sixty at the least, and the lady with him, say forty; their infatuation was a sight to see.

The Captain speaks:

"And up to this evening I've managed to hide it somehow, but now—well, it's more than any man can. You've bewitched me Frue, completely."

"I didn't think you cared so much, really," she answers gently, trying to help him along.

"Well, I do," he says. "And I can't stand it any longer, and that's the truth. When we were up in the woods just now, I still thought I could get through one more night, and didn't say anything much at the time. But now; come back with me, say you will!"

She shook her head.

"No; oh, I'd love to give you ... do what you...."

"Ah!" he exclaims, and, throwing his arms about her, stands pressing his round paunch against hers. There they stood, looking like two recalcitrants that would not. Oh, that Captain!

"Let me go," she implored him.

He loosened his hold a trifle and pressed her to him again. Once more it looked as if both were resisting.

102

"Come back up into the wood," he urged again and again.

"Oh, it's impossible!" she answered. "And then it's all wet with the dew."

But the Captain was full of passionate words—full and frothing over.

"Oh, I used to think I didn't care much about eyes! Blue eyes—huh! Grey eyes—huh! Eyes any sort of colour—huh! But then you came with those brown eyes of yours...."

"They are brown, yes...."

"You burn me with them; you—you roast me up!"

"To tell the truth, you're not the first that's said nice things about my eyes. My husband now...."

"Ah, but what about me!" cries the Captain. "I tell you, Frue, if I'd only met you twenty years ago, I wouldn't have answered for my reason. Come; there's no dew to speak of up in the wood."

"We'd better go indoors, I think," she suggests.

"Go in? There's not a corner anywhere indoors where we can be alone."

"Oh, we'll find somewhere!" she says.

"Well, anyhow, we must have an end of it to-night," says the Captain decisively.

And they go.

I asked myself: was it to warn anybody I had thrown that empty bottle?

At three in the morning I heard Nils go out to feed the horses. At four he knocked to rouse me out of bed. I did not grudge him the honour of being first up, though I could have called him earlier myself, any hour of that night indeed, for I had not slept. 'Tis easy enough to go without sleep a night or two in this light, fine air; it does not make for drowsiness.

Nils sets out for the fields, driving a new team. He has looked over the visitors' horses, and chosen Elisabet's. Good country-breds, heavy in the leg.

II

More visitors arrive, and the house-party goes on. We farm-hands are busy measuring, ploughing, and sowing; some of the fields are sprouting green already after our work—a joy to see.

But we've difficulties here and there, and that with Captain Falkenberg himself. "He's lost all thought and care for his own good," says Nils. And indeed an evil spirit must have got hold of him; he was half-drunk most of the time, and seemed to think of little else beyond playing the genial host. For nearly a week past, he and his guests had played upside down with day and night. But what with the noise and rioting after dark the beasts in stable and shed could get no rest; the maids, too, were kept up at all hours, and, what was more, the young gentlemen would come over to their quarters at night and sit on their beds talking, just to see them undressed.

We working hands had no part in this, of course, but many a time we felt shamed instead of proud to work on Captain Falkenberg's estate. Nils got hold of a temperance badge and wore it in the front of his blouse.

One day the Captain came out to me in the fields and ordered me to get out the carriage and fetch two new visitors from the station. It was in the middle of the afternoon; apparently he had just got up. But he put me in an awkward position here—why had he not gone to Nils? It struck me that he was perhaps, after all, a little shy of Nils with his temperance badge.

The Captain must have guessed my difficulty, for he smiled and said:

"Thinking what Nils might say? Well, perhaps I'd better talk to him first."

But I wouldn't for worlds have sent the Captain over to Nils just then, for Nils was still ploughing with visitors' horses, and had asked me to give him warning if I saw danger ahead. I took out my handkerchief to wipe my face, and waved a little; Nils saw it, and slipped his team at once. What would he do now, I wondered? But Nils was not easily dismayed; he came straight in with his horses, though it was in the middle of a working spell.

If only I could hold the Captain here a bit while he got in! Nils realizes there is no time to be lost—he is already unfastening the harness on the way.

Suddenly the Captain looks at me, and asks:

"Well, have you lost your tongue?"

"'Twas Nils," I answer then. "Something gone wrong, it looks like; he's taken the horses out."

"Well, and what then?"

"Nay, I was only thinking...."

But there I stopped. Devil take it, was I to stand there playing the hypocrite? Here was my chance to put in a word for Nils; the next round he would have to manage alone.

"It's the spring season now," I said, "and there's green showing already where we're done. But there's a deal more to do yet, and we...."

"Well, and what then—what then?"

"There's two and a half acres here, and Nils with hard on three acres of corn land; perhaps Captain might give it another thought."

At that the Captain swung on his heel and left me without a word.

"That's my dismissal," I thought to myself. But I walked up after him with my cart and team, ready to do as he had said.

I was in no fear now about Nils; he was close up to the stables by now. The Captain beckoned to him, but without avail. Then "Halt!" he cried, military fashion; but Nils was deaf.

When we reached the stables the horses were back in their places already. The Captain was stiff and stern as ever, but I fancied he had been thinking matters over a little on the way.

"What have you brought the horses in for now?" he asked.

"Plough was working loose," answered Nils. "I brought them in just while I'm setting it to rights again; it won't take very long."

The Captain raps out his order:

"I want a man to drive to the station."

Nils glances at me, and says half to himself:

"H'm! So that's it? A nice time for that sort of thing."

"What's that you're muttering about?"

"There's two of us and a lad," says Nils, "for the season's work this spring. 'Tis none so much as leaves any to spare."

But the Captain must have had some inkling as to the two brown horses Nils had been in such a hurry to get in; he goes round patting the animals in turn, to see which of them are warm. Then he comes back to us, wiping his fingers with his handkerchief.

"Do you go ploughing with other people's horses, Nils?"

Pause.

"I'll not have it here; you understand?"

"H'm! No," says Nils submissively. Then suddenly he flares up: "We've more need of horses this spring than any season ever at Øvrebø: we're taking up more ground than ever before. And here were these strange cattle standing here day after day eating and eating, and doing never so much as the worth of the water they drank. So I took them out for a bit of a spell now and then, just enough to keep them in trim."

"I'll have no more of it. You hear what I say?" repeated the Captain shortly.

Pause.

"Didn't you say one of the Captain's plough horses was ailing yesterday?" I put in.

Nils was quick to seize his chance.

"Ay. So it was. Standing all a-tremble in its box. I couldn't have taken it out anyway."

The Captain looked me coldly up and down.

"What are you standing here for?" he asked sharply.

"Captain said I was to drive to the station."

"Well, then, be off and get ready."

But Nils took him up on the instant.

"That can't be done."

"Bravo, Nils!" said I to myself. The lad was thoroughly in the right, and he looked it, sturdily holding his own. And as for the horses, our own had been sorely overdone with the long season's work, and the strange cattle stood there eating their heads off and spoiling for want of exercise.

"Can't be done?" said the Captain, astounded. "What do you mean?"

"If Captain takes away the help I've got, then I've finished here, that's all," says Nils.

The Captain walked to the stable door and looked out, biting his moustache and thinking hard. Then he asked over his shoulder:

"And you can't spare the lad, either?"

"No," said Nils; "he's the harrowing to do."

This was our first real encounter with the Captain, and we had our way. There were some little troubles again later on, but he soon gave in.

"I want a case fetched from the station," he said one day. "Can the boy go in for it?"

"The boy's as ill to spare as a man for us now," said Nils. "If he's to drive in to the station now, he won't be back till late tomorrow; that's a day and a half lost."

"Bravo!" I said to myself again. Nils had spoken to me before about that case at the station; it was a new consignment of liquor; the maids had heard about it.

There was some more talk this way and that. The Captain frowned; he had never known a busy season last so long before. Nils lost his temper, and said at last: "If you take the boy off his field work, then I go." And then he did as he and I had agreed beforehand, and asked me straight out:

"Will you go, too?"

"Yes," said I.

At that the Captain gave way, and said with a smile: "Conspiracy, I see. But I don't mind saying you're right in a way. And you're good fellows to work."

But the Captain saw but little of our work, and little pleasure it gave him. He looked out now and again, no doubt, over his fields, and saw how much was ploughed and sown, but that was all. But we farm-hands worked our hardest, and all for the good of our master; that was our way.

Ay, that was our way, no doubt.

But maybe now and again we might have just a thought of question as to that zeal of ours, whether it was so noble after all. Nils was a man from the village who was anxious to get his field work done at least as quickly as any of his neighbours; his honour was at stake. And I followed him. Ay, even when he put on that temperance badge, it was, perhaps, as much as anything to get the Captain sober enough to see the fine work we had done. And here again I was with him. Moreover, I had perhaps a hope that Fruen, that Fru Falkenberg at least, might understand what good souls we were. I doubt I was no better than to reckon so.

The first time I saw Fru Falkenberg close to was one afternoon as I was going out of the kitchen. She came walking across the courtyard, a slender, bareheaded figure. I raised my cap and looked at her; her face was strangely young and innocent to see. And with perfect indifference she answered my "Goddag," and passed on.

It could not be all over for good between the Captain and his wife. I based this view upon the following grounds:

Ragnhild, the parlour-maid, was her mistress's friend and trusted spy. She noted things on Fruen's behalf, went last to bed, listened on the stairs, made a few swift, noiseless steps when she was outside and somebody called. She was a handsome girl, with very bright eyes, and fine and warm-blooded into the bargain. One evening I came on her just by the summer-house, where she stood sniffing at the lilacs; she started as I came up, pointed warningly towards the summer-house, and ran off with her tongue between her teeth.

The Captain was aware of Ragnhild's doings, and once said to his wife so all might hear—he was drunk, no doubt, and annoyed at something or other:

"That Ragnhild's an underhanded creature; I'd be glad to be rid of her."

Fruen answered:

"It's not the first time you've wanted to get Ragnhild out of the way; Heaven knows what for! She's the best maid we've ever had."

"For that particular purpose, I dare say," he retorted.

This set me thinking. Fruen was perhaps crafty enough to keep this girl spying, simply to make it seem as if she cared at all what her husband did. Then people could imagine that Fruen, poor thing, went about secretly longing for him, and being constantly disappointed and wronged. And then, of course, who could blame

107

her if she did the like in return, and went her own way? Heaven knows if that was the way of it!

One day later on the Captain changed his tactics. He had not managed to free himself from Ragnhild's watchfulness; she was still there, to be close at hand when he was talking to Elisabet in some corner, or making towards the summer-house late in the evening to sit there with some one undisturbed. So he tried another way, and began making himself agreeable to that same Ragnhild. Oho! 'twas a woman's wit—no doubt, 'twas Elisabet—had put him up to that!

We were sitting at the long dining-table in the kitchen, Nils and I and the lad; Fruen was there, and the maids were busy with their own work. Then in comes the Captain from the house with a brush in his hand.

"Give my coat a bit of a brush, d'you mind?" says he to Ragnhild.

She obeyed. When she had finished, he thanked her, saying: "Thank you, my child."

Fruen looked a little surprised, and, a moment after, sent her maid upstairs for something. The Captain looked after her as she went, and said:

"Wonderfully bright eyes that girl has, to be sure."

I glanced across at Fruen. Her eyes were blazing, her cheeks flushed, as she moved to leave the room. But in the doorway she turned, and now her face was pale. She seemed to have formed her resolution already. Speaking over her shoulder, she said to her husband:

"I shouldn't be surprised if Ragnhild's eyes were a little too bright."

"Eh?" says the Captain, in surprise.

"Yes," says Fruen, with a slight laugh, nodding over towards the table where we sat. "She's getting a little too friendly with the men out here."

Silence.

"So perhaps she'd better go," Fruen went on.

It was incomparable audacity on Fruen's part, of course, to say such a thing to our face, but we could not protest; we saw she was only using us to serve her need.

When we got outside, Nils said angrily:

"I'm not sure but I'd better go back and say a word or two myself about that."

But I dissuaded him, saying it was not worth troubling about.

A few days passed. Again the Captain found an opportunity of paying barefaced compliments to Ragnhild: "... with a figure like yours," he said.

And the tone of everything about the house now—badly changed from of old. Gone down, grown poorer year by year, no doubt, drunken guests doing their share to help, and idleness and indifference and childlessness for the rest.

In the evening, Ragnhild came to me and told me she was given notice; Fruen had made some reference to me, and that was all.

Once more a piece of underhand work. Fruen knew well I should not be long on the place; why not make me the scapegoat? She was determined to upset her husband's calculations, that was the matter.

Ragnhild, by the way, took it to heart a good deal, and sobbed and dabbed her eyes. But after a while she comforted herself with the thought that, as soon as I was gone, Fruen would take back her dismissal and let her stay. I, for my part, was inwardly sure that Fruen would do nothing of the kind.

Yes, the Captain and Elisabet might be content: the troublesome parlour-maid was to be sent packing, surely enough.

But who was to know? I might be out in my reckoning after all. New happenings set me questioning anew; ay, forced me to alter my judgment once again. 'Tis a sorely difficult thing to judge the truth of humankind.

I learned now, beyond doubt, that Fru Falkenberg was truly and honestly jealous of her husband; not merely pretending to be, as so by way of covering her own devious ways. Far, indeed, from any pretence here. True, she did not really believe for a moment that he was interested in her maid. But it suited her purpose to pretend she did; in her extremity, she would use any means that came to hand. She had blushed during that scene in the kitchen; yes, indeed, but that was a sudden and natural indignation at her husband's ill-chosen words, nothing more.

But she had no objections to her husband's imagining she was jealous of the girl. This was just what she wanted. Her meaning was clear enough. I'm jealous again, yes; you can see it's all the same as before with me: here I am! Fru Falkenberg was better than I had thought. For many years now the pair had slipped farther and farther from each other through indifference, partly perhaps towards the last, in defiance; now she would take the first step and show that she cared for him still. That was it, yes. But, in face of the one she feared most of all, she would not show her jealousy for worlds—and that was Elisabet, this dangerous friend of hers who was so many years younger than herself.

Yes, that was the way of it.

And the Captain? Was he moved at all to see his wife flush at his words to her maid? Maybe a shadow of memory from the old days, a tingle of wonder, a gladness. But he said no word. Maybe he was grown prouder and more obstinate with the years that had passed. It might well seem so from his looks.

Then it was there came the happenings I spoke of.

III

Fru Falkenberg had been playing with her husband now for some little time. She affected indifference to his indifference, and consoled herself with the casual attentions of men staying in the house. Now one and now another of them left, but stout Captain Bror and the lady with the shawl stayed on, and Lassen, the young engineer, stayed too. Captain Falkenberg looked on as if to say: "Well and good, stay on by all means, my dear fellow, as long as you please." And it made no impression on him when his wife said "Du" to Lassen and called him Hugo. "Hugo!" she would call, standing on the steps, looking out. And the Captain would volunteer carelessly: "Hugo's just gone down the road."

One day I heard him answer her with a bitter smile and a wave of his hand towards the lilacs: "Little King Hugo is waiting for you in his kingdom." I saw her start; then she laughed awkwardly to cover her confusion, and went down in search of Lassen.

At last she had managed to wring some expression of feeling out of him. She would try it again.

This was on a Sunday.

Later in the day Fruen was strangely restless; she said a few kindly words to me, and mentioned that both Nils and I had managed our work very well.

"Lars has been to the post office today," she said, "to fetch a letter for me. It's one I particularly want. Would you mind going up to his place and bringing it down for me?"

I said I would with pleasure.

"Lars won't be home again till about eleven. So you need not start for a long time yet."

Very good.

"And when you get back, just give the letter to Ragnhild."

It was the first time Fru Falkenberg had spoken to me during my present stay at Øvrebø; it was something so new, I went up afterwards to my bedroom and sat there by myself, feeling as if something had really happened. I thought over one or two things a little as well. It was simply foolishness, I told myself to go on playing the stranger here and pretending nobody knew. And a full beard was a nuisance in the hot weather; moreover, it was grey, and made me look ever so old. So I set to and shaved it off.

About ten o'clock I started out towards the clearing. Lars was not back. I stayed there a while with Emma, and presently he came in. I took the letter and went straight home. It was close on midnight.

Ragnhild was nowhere to be seen, and the other maids had gone to bed. I glanced in at the shrubbery. There sat Captain Falkenberg and Elisabet, talking together at the round stone table; they took no notice of me. There was a light in Fruen's bedroom upstairs. And suddenly it occurred to me that to-night I looked as I had done six years before, clean-shaven as then. I took the letter out of my pocket and went in the main entrance to give it to Fruen myself.

At the top of the stairs Ragnhild comes slipping noiselessly towards me and takes the letter. She is evidently excited. I can feel the heat of her breath as she points along the passage. There is a sound of voices from the far end.

It looked as if she had taken up her post here on guard, or had been set there by some one to watch; however, it was no business of mine. And when she whispered: "Don't say a word; go down again quietly!" I obeyed, and went to my room.

My window was open. I could hear the couple down among the bushes: they were drinking wine. And there was still light upstairs in Fruen's room.

Ten minutes passed; then the light went out.

A moment later I heard some one hurrying up the stairs in the house, and looked down involuntarily to see if it was the Captain. But the Captain was sitting as before.

Now came the same steps down the stairs again, and, a little after, others. I kept watch on the main entrance. First comes Ragnhild, flying as if for her life over towards the servants' quarters; then comes Fru Falkenberg with her hair down, and the letter in her hand showing white in the gloom. After her comes the engineer. The pair of them move down towards the high road.

Ragnhild comes rushing in to me and flings herself on a chair, all out of breath and bursting with news. Such things had happened this evening, she whispered. Shut the window! Fruen and that engineer fellow—never a thought of being careful—'twas as near as ever could be but they'd have done it. He was holding on to her when Ragnhild went in with the letter. Ugh! Up in Fruen's room, with the lamp blown out.

"You're mad," said I to Ragnhild.

111

But the girl had both heard and seen well enough, it seemed. She was grown so used to playing the spy that she could not help spying on her mistress as well. An uncommon sort, was Ragnhild.

I put on a lofty air at first and would have none of her tale-bearing, thank you, listening at keyholes. Fie!

But how could she help it, she replied. Her orders were to bring up the letter as soon as her mistress put out the light, and not before. But Fruen's windows looked out to the shrubbery, where the Captain was sitting with Elisabet from the vicarage. No place for Ragnhild there. Better to wait upstairs in the passage, and just take a look at the keyhole now and again, to see if the light was out.

This sounded a little more reasonable.

"But only think of it," said Ragnhild suddenly, shaking her head in admiration. "What a fellow he must be, that engineer, to get as near as that with Fruen."

As near as what! Jealousy seized me; I gave up my lofty pose, and questioned Ragnhild searchingly about it all. What did she say they were doing? How did it all come about?

Ragnhild could not say how it began. Fruen had given her orders about a letter that was to be fetched from Lars Falkenberg's, and when it arrived, she was to wait till the light went out in Fruen's room, and then bring it up. "Very good," said Ragnhild. "But not till I put out the light, you understand," said Fruen again. And Ragnhild had set herself to wait for the letter. But the time seemed endless, and she fell to thinking and wondering about it all; there was something strange about it. She went up into the passage and listened. She could hear Fruen and the engineer talking easily and without restraint; stooping down to the keyhole, she saw her mistress loosening her hair, with the engineer looking on and saying how lovely she was. And then—ah, that engineer—he kissed her.

"On the lips, was it?..."

Ragnhild saw I was greatly excited, and tried to reassure me.

"Well, perhaps not quite. I won't be sure; but still ... and he's not a pretty mouth, anyway, to my mind.... I say, though, you've shaved all clean this evening. How nice! Let me see...."

"But what did Fruen say to that? Did she slip away?"

"Yes, I think so; yes, of course she did—and screamed."

"Did she, though?"

"Yes; out loud. And he said 'Sh!' And every time she raised her voice he said 'Sh!' again. But Fruen said let them hear, it didn't matter; they were sitting down there making love in the shrubbery themselves. That's what she said, and it was the Captain and Elisabet from the vicarage she meant. 'There, you can see them,' she said, and went to the window. 'I know, I know,' says the engineer;

112

'but, for Heaven's sake, don't stand there with your hair down!' and he went over and got her away from the window. Then they said a whole heap of things, and every time he tried to whisper Fruen talked out loud again. 'If only you wouldn't shout,' he said. 'We could be ever so quiet up here.' Then she was quiet for a bit, and just sat there smiling at him without a word. She was ever so fond of him."

"Was she?"

"Yes, indeed, I could see that much. Only fancy, a fellow like that! He leaned over towards her, and put his hand so—there."

"And Fruen sat still and let him?"

"Well, yes, a little. But then she went over to the window again, and came back, and put out her tongue like that—and went straight up to him and kissed him. I can't think how she could. For his mouth's not a bit nice, really. Then he said, 'Now we're all alone, and we can hear if anybody comes.' 'What about Bror and his partner?' said she. 'Oh; they are out somewhere, at the other end of the earth,' said he. 'We're all alone; don't let me have to keep on asking you now!' And then he took hold of her and picked her up— oh, he was so strong, so strong! 'No, no; leave go!' she cried."

"Go on!" I said breathlessly. "What next?"

"Why, it was just then you came up with the letter, and I didn't see what happened next. And when I went back, they'd turned the key in the lock, so I could hardly see at all. But I heard Fruen saying: 'Oh, what are you doing? No, no, we mustn't!' She must have been in his arms then. And then at last she said: 'Wait, then; let me get down a minute.' And he let her go. 'Blow out the lamp,' she said. And then it was all dark ... oh!...."

"But now I was at my wits' end what to do," Ragnhild went on. "I stood a minute all in a flurry, and was just going to knock at the door all at once—"

"Yes, yes; why didn't you? What on earth made you wait at all?"

"Why, if I had, then Fruen'd have known in a moment I'd been listening outside," answered the girl. "No, I slipped away from the door and down the stairs, then turned back and went up again, treading hard so Fruen could hear the way I came. The door was still fastened, but I knocked, and Fruen came and opened it. But the engineer was just behind; he'd got hold of her clothes, and was simply wild after her. 'Don't go! don't go!' he kept on saying, and never taking the slightest notice of me. But then, when I turned to go, Fruen came out with me. Oh, but only think. It was as near as could be!...."

A long, restless night.

At noon, when we men came home from the fields next day, the maids were whispering something about a scene between the Captain and his wife. Ragnhild knew all about it. The Captain had noticed his wife with her hair down the night before, and the lamp out upstairs, and laughed at her hair and said wasn't it pretty! And Fruen said nothing much at first, but waited her chance, and then she said: "Yes, I know. I like to let my hair down now and again, and why not? It isn't yours!" She was none so clever, poor thing, at answering back in a quarrel.

Then Elisabet had come up and put in her word. And she was smarter—prrr! Fruen did manage to say: "Well, anyhow we were in the house, but you two were sitting out among the bushes!" And Elisabet turned sharp at that, and snapped out: "We didn't put out the light!" "And if we did," said Fruen, "it made no difference; we came down directly after."

Heavens! I thought to myself, why ever didn't she say they put the light out because they were going down?

That was the end of it for a while. But then, later on, the Captain said something about Fruen being so much older than Elisabet. "You ought always to wear your hair down," he said. "On my word, it made you look quite a girl!" "Oh yes, I dare say I need it now," answered Fruen. But seeing Elisabet turn away laughing, she flared up all of a sudden and told her to take herself off. And Elisabet put her hands on her hips, and asked the Captain to order her carriage. "Right!" says the Captain at that; "and I'll drive you myself!"

All this Ragnhild had heard for herself standing close by.

I thought to myself they were jealous, the pair of them—she, of this sitting out in the shrubbery, and he, of her letting her hair down and putting out the light.

As we came out of the kitchen, and were going across for a rest, there was the Captain busy with Elisabet's carriage. He called me up and said:

"I ought not to ask you now, when you're having your rest, but I wish you'd go down and mend the door of the summer-house for me."

"Right!" I said.

Now that door had been wrong ever since the engineer burst it open several nights before. What made the Captain so anxious to have it put right just at this moment? He'd have no use for the summerhouse while he was driving Elisabet home. Was it because he wanted to shut the place up so no one else should use it while he was away? It was a significant move, if so.

I took some tools and things and went down to the shrubbery.

And now I had my first look at the summer-house from inside. It was comparatively new; it had not been there six years before. A roomy place, with pictures on the walls, and even an alarm clock—now run down—chairs with cushions, a table, and an upholstered settee covered with red plush. The blinds were down.

I set a couple of pieces in the roof first, where I'd smashed it with my empty bottle; then I took off the lock to see what was wrong there. While I was busy with this the Captain came up. He had evidently been drinking already that day, or was suffering from a heavy bout the night before.

"That's no burglary," he said. "Either the door must have been left open, and slammed itself to bits, or some one must have stumbled up against it in the dark. One of the visitors, perhaps, that left the other day."

But the door had been roughly handled, one could see: the lock was burst open, and the woodwork on the inside of the frame torn away.

"Let me see! Put a new bolt in here, and force the spring back in place," said the Captain, examining the lock. He sat down in a chair.

Fru Falkenberg came down the stone steps to the shrubbery, and called:

"Is the Captain there?"

"Yes," said I.

Then she came up. Her face was twitching with emotion.

"I'd like a word with you," she said. "I won't keep you long."

The Captain answered, without rising:

"Certainly. Will you sit down, or would you rather stand? No, don't run away, you! I've none too much time as it is," he said sharply to me.

This I took to mean that he wanted the lock mended so he could take the key with him when he went.

"I dare say it wasn't—I oughtn't to have said what I did," Fruen began.

The Captain made no answer.

But his silence, after she had come down on purpose to try and make it up, was more than she could bear. She ended by saying: "Oh, well, it's all the same; I don't care."

And she turned to go.

"Did you want to speak to me?" asked the Captain.

"Oh no, it doesn't matter. Thanks, I shan't trouble."

"Very well," said the Captain. He smiled as he spoke. He was drunk, no doubt, and angry about something.

But Fruen turned as she passed by me in the doorway, and said:

"You ought not to drive down there today. There's gossip enough already."

"You need not listen to it," he answered.

"It can't go on like this, you know," she said again. "And you don't seem to think of the disgrace...."

"We're both a little thoughtless in that respect," he answered carelessly, looking round at the walls.

I took the lock and stepped outside.

"Here, don't go running away now!" cried the Captain. "I'm in a hurry!"

"Yes, you're in a hurry, of course," repeated Fruen. "Going away again. But you'd do well to think it over just for once. I've been thinking things over myself lately; only you wouldn't see...."

"What do you mean?" he asked, haughty and stiff as ever. "Was it your fooling about at night with your hair down and lights out you thought I wouldn't see? Oh yes, no doubt!"

"I'll have to finish this on the anvil," said I, and hurried off.

I stayed away longer than was needed, but when I came back Fruen was still there. They were talking louder than before.

"And do you know what I have done?" said Fruen "I've lowered myself so far as to show I was jealous. Yes, I've done that. Oh, only about the maid ... I mean...."

"Well, and what then?" said the Captain.

"Oh, won't you understand? Well, have it your own way, then. You'll have to take the consequences later; make no mistake about that!"

These were her last words, and they sounded like an arrow striking a shield. She stepped out and strode away.

"Manage it all right?" said the Captain as I came up. But I could see his thoughts were busy with other things; he was trying to appear unconcerned. A little after, he managed to yawn, and said lazily: "Ugh, it's a long drive. But if Nils can't spare a hand I must go myself."

I had only to fix the lock in its place, and set a new strip down the inside of the door-frame; it was soon done. The Captain tried the door, put the key in his pocket, thanked me for the work, and went off.

A little later he drove away with Elisabet.

"See you again soon," he called to Captain Bror and Engineer Lassen, waving his hand to them both. "Mind that you have a good time while I'm away!"

IV

Evening came. And what would happen now? A great deal, as it turned out.

It started early; we men were at supper while they were having dinner up at the house, and we could hear them carrying on as gaily as could be. Ragnhild was taking in trays of food and bottles, and waiting at table; once when she came out, she laughed to herself and said to the other girls: "I believe Fruen's drunk herself tonight."

I had not slept the night before, nor had my midday rest; I was troubled and nervous after all that had happened the last two days. So, as soon as I had finished my supper, I went out and up to the woods to be alone. I stayed there a long while.

I looked down towards the house. The Captain away, the servants gone to rest, the beasts in stable and shed fast asleep. Stout Captain Bror and his lady, too, had doubtless found a quiet corner all to themselves after dinner; he was simply wild about the woman, for all he was old and fat and she herself no longer young. That left only Fru Falkenberg and the young engineer. And where would they be now?

'Twas their affair.

I sauntered home again, yawning and shivering a little in the cool night, and went up to my room. After a while Ragnhild came up, and begged me to keep awake and be ready to help in case of need. It was horrible, she said; they were carrying on like mad things up at the house, walking about from one room to another, half undressed and drunk as well. Was Fruen drunk, too? Yes, she was. And was she walking about half undressed? No, but Captain Bror was, and Fruen clapped her hands and cried "Bravo!" And the engineer as well. It was one as bad as the other. And Ragnhild had just taken in two more bottles of wine, though they were drunk already.

"Come over with me and you can hear them yourself," said Ragnhild. "They're up in Fruen's room now."

"No," I said. "I'm going to bed. And you'd better go, too."

"But they'll ring in a minute and be wanting something if I do."

"Let them ring!"

And then it was Ragnhild confessed that the Captain himself had asked her to stay up that night in case Fruen should want her.

This altered the whole aspect of affairs in a moment. Evidently the Captain had feared something might happen, and set

117

Ragnhild on guard in case. I put on my blouse again and went across with her to the house.

We went upstairs and stood in the passage; we could hear them laughing and making a noise in Fruen's room. But Fruen herself spoke as clearly as ever, and was not drunk at all. "Yes, she is," said Ragnhild, "anyhow, she's not like herself tonight."

I wished I could have seen her for a moment.

We went back to the kitchen and sat down. But I was restless all the time; after a little I took down the lamp from the wall and told Ragnhild to follow me. We went upstairs again.

"No; go in and ask Fruen to come out here to me," I said.

"Why, whatever for?"

"I've a message for her."

And Ragnhild knocked at the door and went in.

It was only at the last moment I hit on any message to give. I could simply look her straight in the face and say: "The Captain sent his kind regards."[11] Would that be enough? I might say more: "The Captain was obliged to drive himself, because Nils couldn't spare any one to go."

But a moment can be long at times, and thought a lightning flash. I found time to reject both these plans and hatch out another before Fruen came. Though I doubt if my last plan was any better.

Fruen asked in surprise:

"Well, what do you want?"

Ragnhild came up, too, and looked at me wonderingly.

I turned the lamp towards Fruen's face and said:

"I beg pardon for coming up so late. I'll be going to the post first thing tomorrow; I thought if perhaps Fruen had any letters to go?"

"Letters? No," she answered, shaking her head.

There was an absent look in her eyes, but she did not look in the least as if she had been drinking.

"No, I've no letters," she said, and moved to go.

"Beg pardon, then," I said.

"Was it the Captain told you to go to the post?" she asked.

"No, I was just going for myself."

She turned and went back to her room. Before she was well through the door I heard her say to the others:

"A nice pretext, indeed."

---

[11] Kapteinen bad mig hilse Dem: literally, "The Captain bade me greet you." Such a message would not seem quite so uncalled for in Norway, such greetings (Hilsen) being given and sent more frequently, and on slighter occasions, than with us.

Ragnhild and I went down again. I had seen her.

Oh, but I was humbled now indeed! And it did not ease my mind at all when Ragnhild incautiously let out a further piece of news. It seemed she had been romancing before; it was not true about the Captain's having asked her to keep a look out. I grew more and more convinced in my own mind: Ragnhild was playing the spy on her own account, for sheer love of the game.

I left her, and, went up to my room. What had my clumsy intrusion gained for me, after all? A pretext, she had said; clearly she had seen through it all. Disgusted with myself, I vowed that for the future I would leave things and people to themselves.

I threw myself down fully dressed on the bed.

After a while I heard Fru Falkenberg's voice outside in front of the house; my window was open, and she spoke loudly enough. The engineer was with her, putting in a word now and again. Fruen was in raptures over the weather, so fine it was, and such a warm night. Oh, it was lovely out now—ever so much nicer than indoors!

But her voice seemed a trifle less clear now than before.

I ran to the window, and saw the pair of them standing by the steps that led down to the shrubbery. The engineer seemed to have something on his mind that he had not been able to get said before. "Do listen to me now," he said. Then followed a brief and earnest pleading, which was answered—ay, and rewarded. He spoke as if to one hard of hearing, because she had been deaf to his words so long; they stood there by the stone steps, neither of them caring for any one else in the world. Let any listen or watch who pleased; the night was theirs, the world was theirs, and the spring-time was about them, drawing them together. He watched her like a cat; every movement of her body set his blood tingling; he was ready to spring upon her in a moment. And when it came near to action there was a power of will in his manner towards her. Ay, the young spark!

"I've begged and prayed you long enough," he said breathlessly. "Yesterday you all but would; today you're deaf again. You think you and Bror and Tante[12] and the rest are to have a good time and no harm done, while I look on and play the nice young man? But, by Heaven, you're wrong! Here's you yourself, a garden of all good things right in front of me, and a fence ... do you know what I'm going to do now with that silly fence?"

"What are you going to do? No, Hugo, you've had too much to drink this evening. You're so young. We've both drunk more than we ought," she said.

"And then you play me false into the bargain, with your tricks.

---

[12] "Auntie." Evidently Captain Bror's lady is meant.

You send a special messenger for a letter that simply can't wait, and at the same time you're cruel enough to let me think ... to promise me...."

"I'll never do it again, Hugo."

"Never do it again? What do you mean by that? When you can go up to a man—yes, to me, and kiss me like you did.... What's the good of saying you'll never do it any more; it's done, and a kiss like that's not a thing to forget. I can feel it still, and it's a mad delight, and I thank you for it You've got that letter in your dress; let me see it."

"You're so excited, Hugo. No, it's getting late now. We'd better say good-night."

"Will you show me that letter?"

"Show you the letter? Certainly not!"

At that he made a half-spring, as if to take it by force, but checked himself, and snapped out:

"What? You won't? Well, on my word you are.... Mean's not the word for it. You're something worse...."

"Hugo!"

"Yes, you are!"

"If you will see the letter, here it is!" She thrust her hand into her blouse, took out the letter, opened it, and waved it at him, flourishing her innocence. "Here's the letter—from my mother; there's her signature—look. From mother—and now what have you to say?"

He quailed as if at a blow, and only said:

"From your mother. Why, then, it didn't matter at all?"

"No; there you are. Oh, but of course it did matter in a way, but still...."

He leaned up against the fence, and began to work it out:

"From your mother.... I see. A letter from your mother came and interrupted us. Do you know what I think? You've been cheating. You've been fooling me all along. I can see it all now."

She tried again.

"It was an important letter. Mama is coming—she's coming here to stay very soon. And I was waiting to hear."

"You were cheating all the time, weren't you?" he said again. "Let them bring in the letter just at the right moment, when we'd put out the light. Yes, that's it. You were just leading me on, to see how far I'd go, and kept your maid close at hand to protect you."

"Oh, do be sensible! It's ever so late; we must go in."

"Ugh! I had too much to drink up there, I think. Can't talk straight now."

He could think of nothing but the letter, and went on about it again:

"For there was no need to have all that mystery about a letter from home. No; I see it all now. Want to go in, you say? Well then, go in, Fru, by all means. Godnat, Frue. My dutiful respects, as from a son."

He bowed, and stood watching her with a sneering smile.

"A son? Oh yes," she replied, with sudden emotion. "I am old, yes. And you are so young, Hugo, that's true. And that's why I kissed you. But I couldn't be your mother—no, it's only that I'm older, ever so much older than you. But I'm not quite an old woman yet, and that you should see if only . . . But I'm older than Elisabet and every one else. Oh, what am I talking about? Not a bit of it. I don't know what else the years may have done to me, but they haven't made me an old woman yet. Have they? What do you think yourself? Oh, but what do you know about it? . . ."

"No, no," he said softly. "But is there any sense in going on like this? Here are you, young as you are, with nothing on earth to do all the time but keep guard over yourself and get others to do the same. And the Lord in heaven knows you promised me a thing, but it means so little to you; you take a pleasure in putting me off and beating me down with your great white wings."

"Great white wings," she murmured to herself.

"Yes, you might have great red wings. Look at yourself now, standing there all lovely as you are, and all for nothing."

"Oh, I think the wine has gone to my head! All for nothing, indeed!"

Then suddenly she takes his hand and leads him down the steps. I can hear her voice: "Why should I care? Does he imagine Elisabet's so much better?"

They pass along the path to the summer-house. Here she hesitates, and stops.

"Oh, where are we going?" she asks. "Haha, we must be mad! You wouldn't have thought I was mad, would you? I'm not, either—that is to say, yes, I am, now and again. There, the door's locked; very well, we'll go away again. But what a mean trick to lock the door, when we want to go in."

Full of bitterness and suspicion, he answered:

"Now, you're cheating again. You knew well enough the door was locked."

"Oh, must you always think the worst of me? But why should he lock the door so carefully and have the place all to himself? Yes, I did know it was locked, and that's why I came with you. I dare not. No, Hugo, I won't, I mean it. Oh, are you mad? Come back!"

121

She took his hand again and tried to turn back; they stood struggling a little, for he would not follow. Then in his passion and strength he threw both arms round her and kissed her again and again. And she weakened ever more and more, speaking brokenly between the kisses:

"I've never kissed any other man before—never! It's true—I swear it. I've never kissed...."

"No, no, no," he answers impatiently, drawing her step by step the way he will.

Outside the summer-house he looses his hold of her a moment, flings himself, one shoulder forward, heavily against the door, and breaks it open for the second time. Then in one stride he is beside her once more. Neither speaks.

But even at the door, she checks again—stands clinging to the door-post, and will not move.

"No, no, I've never been unfaithful to him yet. I won't; I've never—never...."

He draws her to him suddenly, kisses her a full minute, two minutes, a deep, unbroken kiss; she leans back from the waist, her hand slips where it holds, and she gives way....

A white mist gathers before my eyes. So ... they have come to it now. Now he takes her, has his will and joy of her....

A melancholy weariness and rest comes over me. I feel miserable and alone. It is late; my heart has had its day....

Through the white mist comes a leaping figure; it is Ragnhild coming up from among the bushes, running with her tongue thrust out.

The engineer came up to me, nodded Godmorgen, and asked me to mend the summer-house door.

"Is it broken again?"

"Yes, it got broken last night."

It was early for him to be about—no more than halfpast four; we farm-hands had not yet started for the fields. His eyes showed small and glittering, as if they burned; likely enough he had not slept all night. But he said nothing as to how the door had got broken.

Not for any thought of him, but for Captain Falkenberg's sake, I went down at once to the summer-house and mended the door once again. No need for such haste, maybe; the Captain had a long drive there and back, but it was close on twenty-four hours now since he started.

The engineer came down with me. Without in the least perceiving how it came about, I found myself thinking well of him; he had broken open that door last night—quite so, but he was not

122

the man to sneak out of it after. He and no one other it was who had it mended. Eh, well, perhaps after all 'twas only my vanity was pleased. I felt flattered at his trusting to my silence. That was it. That was how I came to think well of him.

"I'm in charge of some timber-rafting on the rivers," he said. "How long are you staying here?"

"Not for long. Till the field-work's over for the season."

"I could give you work if you'd care about it."

Now this was work I knew nothing of, and, what was more, I liked to be among field and forest, not with lumbermen and proletariat. However, I thanked him for the offer.

"Very good of you to come and put this right. As a matter of fact, I broke it open looking for a gun. I wanted to shoot something, and I thought there might be a gun in there."

I made no answer; it would have pleased me better if he had said nothing.

"So I thought I'd ask you before you started out to work," he said, to finish off.

I put the lock right and set it in its place again, and began nailing up the woodwork, which was shattered as before. While I was busy with this, we heard Captain Falkenberg's voice; through the bushes we could see him unharnessing the horses and leading them in.

The engineer gave a start; he fumbled for his watch, and got it out, but his eyes had grown all big and empty—they could see nothing. Suddenly he said:

"Oh, I forgot, I must . . ."

And he hurried off far down the garden.

"So he's going to sneak out of it, after all," I thought to myself.

A moment later the Captain himself came down. He was pale, and covered with dust, and plainly had not slept, but perfectly sober. He called to me from a distance:

"Hei! how did you get in there?"

I touched my cap, but said nothing.

"Somebody been breaking in again?"

"It was only . . . I just remembered I'd left out a couple of nails here yesterday. It's all right now. If Captain will lock up again . . ."

Fool that I was! If that was the best excuse I could find, he would see through it all at once.

He stood for a few seconds looking at the door with half-closed eyes; he had his suspicions, no doubt. Then he took out the key, locked up the place, and walked off. What else could he do?

V

All the guests are gone—stout Captain Bror, the lady with the shawl, Engineer Lassen as well. And Captain Falkenberg is getting ready to start for manoeuvres at last. It struck me that he must have applied for leave on very special grounds, or he would have been away on duty long before this.

We farm-hands have been hard at work in the fields the last few days—a heavy strain on man and beast. But Nils knew what he was doing; he wanted to gain time for something else.

One day he set me to work cleaning up all round outside the house and buildings. It took all the time gained and more, but it made the whole place look different altogether. And that was what Nils wanted—to cheer the Captain up a little before he left home. And I turned to of my own accord and fixed up a loose pale or so in the garden fence, straightened the door of a shed that was wry on its hinges, and such-like. And the barn bridge, too, needed mending. I thought of putting in new beams.

"Where will you be going when you leave here?" asked the Captain.

"I don't know. I'll be on the road for a bit."

"I could do with you here for a while; there's a lot of things that want doing."

"Captain was thinking of paintwork, maybe?"

"Painting, too—yes. I'm not sure about that, though; it would be a costly business, with the outbuildings and all. No, I was thinking of something else. Do you know anything about timber, now? Could you mark down for yourself?"

It pleased him, then, to pretend he did not recognize me from the time I had worked in his timber before. But was there anything left now to fell? I answered him:

"Ay, I'm used to timber. Where would it be this year?"

"Anywhere. Wherever you like. There must be something left, surely."

"Ay, well."

I laid the new beams in the barn bridge, and when that was done, I took down the flagstaff and put on a new knob and line. Øvrebø was looking quite nice already, and Nils said it made him feel better only to look at it. I got him to talk to the Captain and put in a word about the paintwork, but the Captain had looked at him with a troubled air and said: "Yes, yes, I know. But paint's not the only thing we've got to think about. Wait till the autumn and see how the crops turn out. We've sowed a lot this year."

But when the flagstaff stood there with the old paint all

124

scraped off, and a new knob and halliards, the Captain could not help noticing it, and ordered some paint by telegraph. Though, to be sure there was no such hurry as all that; a letter by the post had been enough.

Two days passed. The paint arrived, but was put aside for the time being; we had not done with the field-work yet by a long way, though we were using both the carriage horses for sowing and harrowing, and when it came to planting potatoes, Nils had to ask up at the house for the maids to come and help. The Captain gave him leave, said yes to all that was asked, and went off to manoeuvres. So we were left to ourselves.

But there was a big scene between husband and wife before he went.

Every one of us on the place knew there was trouble between them, and Ragnhild and the dairymaid were always talking about it. The fields were coming on nicely now, and you could see the change in the grassland from day to day; it was fine spring weather, and all things doing well that grew, but there was trouble and strife at Øvrebø. Fruen could be seen at times with a face that showed she had been crying; or other times with an air of exaggerated haughtiness, as if she cared nothing for any one. Her mother came—a pale, quiet lady with spectacles and a face like a mouse. She did not stay long—only a few days; then she went back to Kristianssand—that was where she lived. The air here did not agree with her, she said.

Ah, that great scene! A bitter final reckoning that lasted over an hour—Ragnhild told us all about it afterwards. Neither the Captain nor Fruen raised their voices, but the words came slow and strong. And in their bitterness the pair of them agreed to go each their own way from now on.

"Oh, you don't say so!" cried all in the kitchen, clasping their hands.

Ragnhild drew herself up and began mimicking:

"'You've been breaking into the summer-house again with some one?' said the Captain. 'Yes,' said Fruen. 'And what more?' he asked. 'Everything,' said she. The Captain smiled at that and said: 'There's something frank and open about an answer like that; you can see what is meant almost at once.' Fruen said nothing to that. 'What you can see in that young puppy, I don't know—though he did help me once out of a fix.' Fruen looked at him then, and said: 'Helped you?' 'Yes,' said the Captain; 'backed a bill for me once.' And Fruen asked: 'I didn't know that.' Then the Captain: 'Didn't he tell you that?' Fruen shook her head. 'Well, what then?' he said again. 'Would it have made any difference if he had?' 'Yes,' said

125

Fruen at first, and then, 'No.' 'Are you fond of him?' he asked. And she turned on him at once. 'Are you fond of Elisabet?' 'Yes,' answered the Captain; but he sat smiling after that. 'Well and good,' said Fruen sharply. Then there was a long silence. The Captain was the first to speak, 'You were right when you said that about thinking over things. I've been doing so. I'm not a vicious man, really; queerly enough, I've never really cared about drinking and playing the fool. And yet I suppose I did, in a way. But there's an end of it now.' 'So much the better for you,' she answered sullenly. 'Quite so,' says he again. 'Though it would have been better if you'd been a bit glad to hear it.' 'You can get Elisabet to do that,' says she. 'Elisabet,' says he—just that one word—and shakes his head. Then they said nothing for quite a while. 'What are you going to do now?' asks the Captain. 'Oh, don't trouble yourself about me,' said Fruen very slowly. 'I can be a nurse, if you like, or cut my hair short and be a school teacher, if you like.' 'If I like,' says he; 'no, decide for yourself.' 'I want to know what you are going to do first,' she says, 'I'm going to stay here where I am,' he answered, 'but you've turned yourself out of doors.' And Fruen nodded and said: 'Very well.'"

"Oh," from all in the kitchen. "Oh but, Herregud! it will come right again surely," said Nils, looking round at the rest of us to see what we thought.

For a couple of days after the Captain had gone, Fruen sat playing the piano all the time. On the third day Nils drove her to the station; she was going to stay with her mother at Kristianssand. That left us more alone than ever. Fruen had not taken any of her things with her; perhaps she felt they were not really hers; perhaps they had all come from him originally, and she did not care to have them now. Oh, but it was all a misery.

Ragnhild was not to go away, her mistress had said. But it was cook that was left in charge of everything, and kept the keys, which was best for all concerned.

On Saturday the Captain came back home on leave. Nils said he never used to do that before. Fine and upright in his bearing he was, for all that his wife was gone away, and he was sober as could be. He gave me orders, very short and clear, about the timber; came out with me and showed me here and there. "Battens, down to smallest battens, a thousand dozen. I shall be away three weeks this time," he said. On the Sunday afternoon he went off again. He was more determined in his manner now—more like himself.

We were through with the field-work at last, and the potato-planting was done; after that, Nils and the lad could manage the daily work by themselves, and I went up to my new work among the timber.

126

Good days these were for me, all through. Warm and rainy at first, making the woods all wet, but I went out all the same, and never stayed in on that account. Then a spell of hot weather set in, and in the light evenings, after I got home from work, it was a pleasure to go round mending and seeing to little things here and there—a gutter-pipe, a window, and the like. At last I got the escape ladder up and set to scraping the old paint from the north wall of the barn—it was flaking away there of itself. It would be a neat piece of work if I could get the barn done this summer after all, and the paint was there all ready.

But there was another thing that made me weary at times of the work and the whole place. It was not the same working there now as when the Captain and Fruen were home; I found here confirmation of the well-known truth that it is well for a man to have some one over him at his work, that is, if he is not himself in charge as leading man. Here were the maids now, going about the place with none to look after them. Ragnhild and the dairymaid were always laughing and joking noisily at meal-times and quarreling now and again between themselves; the cook's authority was not always enough to keep the peace, and this often made things uncomfortable. Also, it seemed that some one must have been talking to Lars Falkenberg, my good old comrade that had been, and made him suspicious of me now.

Lars came in one evening and took me aside; he had come to say he forbade me to show myself on his place again. His manner was comically threatening.

Now, I had not been there more than a few times with washing—maybe half a dozen times in all; he had been out, but Emma and I had talked a bit of old things and new. The last time I was there Lars came home suddenly and made a scene the moment he got inside the door, because Emma was sitting on a stool in her petticoat. "It's too hot for a skirt," she said. "Ho, yes, and your hair all down your back—too hot to put it up, I suppose?" he retorted. Altogether he was in a rage with her. I said good-night to him as I left, but he did not answer.

I had not been there since. Then what made him come over like this all of a sudden? I set it down as more of Ragnhild's mischievous work.

When he had told me in so many words he forbade me to enter his house, Lars nodded and looked at me; to his mind, I ought now to be as one dead.

"And I've heard Emma's been down here," he went on. "But she'll come no more, I fancy, after this."

"She may have been here once or twice for the washing."

127

"Ho, yes, the washing, of course. And you coming up yourself Heaven knows how many times a week—more washing! Bring up a shirt one day and a pair of drawers the next, that's what you do. But you can get Ragnhild to do your washing now."

"Well and good."

"Aha, my friend, I know you and your little ways. Going and visiting and making yourself sweet to folk when you find them all alone. But not for me, thank you!"

Nils comes up to us now, guessing, no doubt, what's the trouble, and ready to put in a word for me, like the good comrade he is. He catches the last words, and gives me a testimonial on the spot, to the effect that he's never seen anything wrong about me all the time I've been on the place.

But Lars Falkenberg bridles up at once and puts on airs, looking Nils up and down with contempt. He has a grudge against Nils already. For though Lars had managed well enough since he got his own little place up in the wood, he had never equalled Nils' work here on the Captain's land. And Lars Falkenberg feels himself aggrieved.

"What have you got to come cackling about?" he asks.

"I'm saying what is the truth, that's all," answers Nils.

"Ho, are you, you goat? If you want me to wipe the floor with you, I'll do it on the spot!"

Nils and I walked away, but Lars still shouted after us. And there was Ragnhild, of course, sniffing at the lilacs as we passed.

That evening I began to think about moving on again as soon as I had finished my work in the timber. When the three weeks were up, the Captain came back as he had said. He noticed I had scraped the northern wall of the barn, and was pleased with me for that. "End of it'll be you'll have to paint that again, too," he said. I told him how far I had got with the timber; there was not much left now. "Well, keep at it and do some more," was all he said. Then he went back to his duty again for another three weeks.

But I did not care to stay another three weeks at Øvrebø as things were now. I marked down a few score dozen battens, and reckoned it all out on my paper—that would have to do. But it was still too early for a man to live in the forests and hills; the flowers were come, but there were no berries yet. Song and twitter of birds at their mating, flies and midges and moths, but no cloudberries, no angelica.

In town.

I came in to Engineer Lassen, Inspector of rafting sections, and he took me on as he had promised, though it was late in the season now. To begin with, I am to make a tour of the water and see

128

where the logs have gathered thickest, noting down the places on a chart. He is quite a good fellow, the engineer, only still very young. He gives me over-careful instructions about things he fancies I don't know already. It makes him seem a trifle precocious.

And so this man has helped Captain Falkenberg out of a mess? The Captain was sorry for it now, no doubt, anxious to free himself from the debt—that was why he was cutting down his timber to the last lot of battens, I thought. And I wished him free of it myself. I was sorry now I had not stayed on marking down a few more days, that he might have enough and to spare. What if it should prove too little, after all?

Engineer Lassen was a wealthy man, apparently. He lived at an hotel, and had two rooms there. I never got farther than the office myself, but even there he had a lot of costly things, books and papers, silver things for the writing-table, gilt instruments and things; a light overcoat, silk-lined, hung on the wall. Evidently a rich man, and a person of importance in the place. The local photographer had a large-sized photograph of him in the show-case outside. I saw him, too, out walking in the afternoons with the young ladies of the town. Being in charge of all the timber traffic, he generally walked down to the long bridge—it was four hundred and sixty feet—across the foss, halted there, and stood looking up and down the river. Just by the bridge piers, and on the flat rocks below them, was where the logs were most inclined to jam, and he kept a gang of lumbermen regularly at hand for this work alone. Standing on the bridge there, watching the men at work among the logs, he looked like an admiral on board a ship, young and strong, with power to command. The ladies with him stopped willingly, and stood there on the bridge, though the rush of water was often enough to make one giddy. And the roar of it was such that they had to put their heads together when they spoke.

But just in this position, at his post on the bridge, standing there and turning this way and that, there was something smallish and unhandsome about his figure; his sports jacket, fitting tightly at the waist, seemed to pinch, and showed up over-heavy contours behind.

The very first evening, after he'd given me my orders to start off up the river next day, I met him out walking with two ladies. At sight of me he stopped, and kept his companions waiting there, too, while he gave me the same instructions all over again. "Just as well I happened to meet you," he said. "You'll start off early, then, tomorrow morning, take a hooking pole with you, and clear all the logs you can manage. If you come across a big jam, mark it down on the chart—you've got a copy of the chart, haven't you? And keep on up river till you meet another man coming down. But remember to mark in red, not blue. And let me see how well you can manage.—A man I've got to work under me," he explained to the ladies. "I really can't be bothered running up and down all the time."

So serious he was about it all; he even took out a notebook and wrote something down. He was very young, and could not help showing off a little with two fair ladies to look on.

Next morning I got away early. It was light at four, and by that time I was a good way up the river. I carried food with me, and my hooking pole—which is like a boat-hook really.

No young, growing timber here, as on Captain Falkenberg's land; the ground was stony and barren, covered with heather and pine needles for miles round. They had felled too freely here; the sawmills had taken over much, leaving next to no young wood. It was a melancholy country to be in.

By noon I had cleared a few small jams, and marked down a big one. Then I had my meal, with a drink of water from the river. A bit of a rest, and I went on again, on till the evening. Then I came upon a big jam, where a man was already at work among the logs. This was the man I had been told to look out for. I did not go straight up to him at first, but stopped to look at him. He worked very cautiously, as if in terror of his life; he was even afraid of getting his feet wet. It amused me to watch him for a little. The least chance of being carried out into the stream on a loosened log was enough to make him shift at once. At last I went up close and looked at him—why ... yes, it was my old friend, Grindhusen.

Grindhusen, that I had worked with as a young man at Skreia—my partner in the digging of a certain well six years before.

And now to meet him here.

We gave each other greeting, and sat down on the logs to talk, asking and answering questions for an hour or more. Then it was too late to get any more done that day. We got up and went back a little way up the river, where Grindhusen had a bit of a log hut. We crept in, lit a fire, made some coffee, and had a meal. Then, going outside again, we lit our pipes and lay down in the heather.

Grindhusen had aged, and was in no better case than I myself; he did not care to think of the gay times in our youth, when we had danced the whole night through. He it was that had once been as a red-haired wolf among the girls, but now he was thoroughly cowed by age and toil, and had not even a smile. If I had only had a drop of spirits with me it might have livened him up a little, but I had none.

In the old days he had been a stiff-necked fellow, obstinate as could be; now he was easy-going and stupid. "Ay, maybe so," was his answer to everything. "Ay, you're right," he would say. Not that he meant it; only that life had taught him to seek the easiest way. So life does with all of us, as the years go by—but it was an ill thing to see, meeting him so.

Ay, he got along somehow, he said, but he was not the man he used to be. He'd been troubled with gout of late, and pains in the chest as well. His pains in the chest were cardialgic. But it was none so bad as long as he'd the work here for Engineer Lassen. He knew the river right up, and worked here all spring and early summer in his hut. And as for clothes, he'd nothing to wear out save breeches and blouse all the year round. Had a bit of luck, though, last year, he said suddenly. Found a sheep with nobody to own it. Sheep in the forest? Up that way, he said, pointing. He'd had meat on Sundays half through the winter off that sheep. Then he'd his folks in America as good as any one else: children married there and well-to-do. They sent him a little to help the first year or so, but now they'd stopped; it was close on two years now since he'd heard from them at all. Eyah! well, that's how things were now with him and his wife. And getting old....

Grindhusen lapsed into thought.

A dull, rushing sound from the forest and the river, like millions of nothings flowing and flowing on. No birds here, no creatures hopping about, but if I turn up a stone, I may find some insect under it.

"Wonder what these tiny things live on?" I say.

"What tiny things?" says Grindhusen. "Those? That's only ants and things."

"It's a sort of beetle," I tell him. "Put one on the grass and roll a stone on top of it, and it'll live."

Grindhusen answers: "Ay, maybe so," but thinking never a word of what I've said, and I think the rest to myself; but put an ant there under the stone as well, and very soon there'll be no beetle left.

And the rush of the forest and river goes on: 'tis one eternity that speaks with another, and agrees. But in the storms and in thunder they are at war.

"Ay, so it is," says Grindhusen at last. "Two years come next fourteenth of August since the last letter came. There was a smart photograph in, from Olea, it was, that lives in Dakota, as they call it. A mighty fine photograph it was, but I never got it sold. Eyah, but we'll manage somehow, please the Lord," says Grindhusen, with a yawn. "What was I going to say now?... What is he paying for the work?"

"I don't know."

131

But Grindhusen looks at me suspiciously, thinking it is only that I will not say.

"Ay, well, 'tis all the same to me," he says. "I was only asking."

To please him, I try to guess a wage. "I dare say he'll give me a couple of Kroner a day, or perhaps three, d'you think?"

"Ay, dare say you may," he answers enviously. "Two Kroner's all I get, and I'm an old hand at the work."

Then fancying, perhaps, I may go telling of his grumbling, he starts off in praise of Engineer Lassen, saying what a splendid fellow he is in every way. "He'll do what's fair by me, that I know. Trust him for that! Why, he's been as good as a father to me, and that's the truth!"

It sounds quaint, indeed, to hear Grindhusen, half his teeth gone with age, talking of the young engineer as a father. I felt pretty sure I could find out a good deal about my new employer from this quarter, but I did not ask.

"He didn't say anything about me coming down into town?" asked Grindhusen.

"No."

"He sends up for me now and again, and when I get there, it's not for anything particular—only wants to have a bit of a chat with me, that's all. Ay, a fine fellow is the engineer!"

It is getting late. Grindhusen yawns again, creeps into the hut and lies down.

Next morning we cleared the jam. "Come up with me my way a bit," says Grindhusen. And I went. After an hour's walking, we sighted the fields and buildings of a hill farm up among the trees. And suddenly I recollect the sheep Grindhusen had found.

"Was it up this way you found that sheep?" I ask.

Grindhusen looks at me.

"Here? No, that was ever so far away—right over toward Trovatn."

"But Trovatn's only in the next parish, isn't it?"

"Yes, that's what I say. It's ever so far away from here."

But now Grindhusen does not care to have my company farther; he stops, and thanks me for coming up so far. I might just as well go up to the farm with him, and I say so; but Grindhusen, it seems, is not going up to the farm at all—he never did. And I'd just have an easy day back into town, starting now.

So I turned and went back the way I had come.

VI

It was no sort of work this for a man; I was not satisfied. Nothing but walk, walk up and down the river, clearing a few logs here and there, and then on again. And after each trip, back to my lodging-house in the town. All this time I had but one man to talk to—the boots or porter at the hotel where the engineer was staying. He was a burly fellow, with huge fists, and eyes like a child's. He had fallen down and hurt his head as a youngster, he said, and never got on in life beyond hauling things and carrying heavy loads. I had a talk with him now and again, but found no one else to talk to in the town.

That little town!

When the river is high, a mighty roar of sound goes rushing through the place, dividing it in two. Folk live in their little wooden houses north or south of the roar, and manage, no doubt, to make ends meet from day to day. Of all the many children crossing the bridge and running errands to the shops, there are none that go naked, probably few that suffer want, and all are decent looking enough. And here are big, tall, half-grown girls, the quaintest of all, with their awkward movements, and their laughter, and their earnest occupation with their own little affairs. Now and again they stop on the bridge to watch the lumbermen at work among the logs below, and join in the song of the men as they haul—"Hoi-aho!"—and then they giggle and nudge one another and go on.

But there are no birds here.

Strange, that there should be no birds! On quiet evenings, at sunset-time, the great enclosed pool lies there with its deep waters unmoved; moths and midges hover above it, the trees on the banks are reflected there, but there are no birds in the trees. Perhaps it is because of the roar of the water, that drowns all other sound; birds cannot thrive there, where none can hear another's song. And so it comes about that the only winged creatures here are flies and moths. But God alone knows why even the crows and common birds shun us and our town.

Every small town has its daily event that every one turns out for—and, as for that, the big towns too, with their promenades. Out Vestland way it is the postpacket. Living in Vestland, it's hard to keep away from the quay when the little vessel comes in. Here, in this inland town, with a dozen miles or more to the sea, and nothing but rocks and hills all about, here we have the river. Has the water risen or fallen in the night? Will they be clearing logs from the booms today? Oh, we are all so interested! True, we have a little railway as well, but that doesn't count for much. The line ends here;

it runs as far as it can go, and then stops, like a cork in a bottle. And there's something cosy and pleasant about the tiny carriages on the trains; but folk seem ashamed of them, they are so ridiculously old and worse for wear, and there's not even room to sit upright with a hat on!

Not but what we've other things besides—a market, and a church, and schools, and post office, and all. And then there's the sawmills and works by the riverside. But as for grocery shops and stores, there's more than you'd believe.

We've so many things altogether. I am a stranger here myself—as indeed I am everywhere—yet I could reckon up a host of things we have besides the river. Was the town a big place once upon a time? No, it has been a little town for two hundred and fifty years. But there was once a great man over all the smaller folk—one who rode lordly fashion with a servant behind him—a great landowner. Now we are all equal; saving, perhaps, with Engineer Lassen, this something-and-twenty-year-old Inspector of rafting sections, who can afford two rooms at his hotel.

I have nothing to do, and find myself pondering over the following matter:

Here is a big house, somewhere about a couple of hundred years old, the house of the wealthy Ole Olsen Ture. It is of enormous size, a house of two stories, the length of a whole block; it is used as a depot now. In the days when that house was built there was no lack of giant timber hereabouts; three beams together make the height of a man, and the wood is hard as iron; nothing can bite on it. And inside the building are halls and cells as in a castle. Here Ture the Great ruled like a prince in his day.

But times changed. Houses were made not only big, not only to live in for shelter from cold and rain, but also to look on with pleasure to the eye. On the opposite side of the river stands an old archaic building with carefully balanced verandah in the Empire style, pillars, fronton, and all. It is not faultless, but handsome all the same; it stands out like a white temple on the green hillside. One other house I have seen and stopped to look at; one near the market-place. Its double street door has old handles and carved rococo mirrors, but the frames cannelated in the style of Louis XVI. The cartouche above the doorway bears the date 1795 in Arabic numerals—that was our transition period here! So there were folk here at that time who kept in touch with the times, without the aid of steam and telegraph.

But later on, again, houses were built to keep off rain and snow and nothing else. They were neither big nor beautiful to look at. The idea was to put up some sort of a dwelling, Swiss fashion—a place to keep a wife and children in, and that was all. And we learned from a miserable little people up in the Alps, a people that throughout its history has never been or done anything worth speaking of—we learned to pay no heed to what a homestead really looked like, as long as it met with the approval of loafing tourist. Is there something of the calm and beauty of a temple about that white building on the hillside? And pray, what's the use of it if there is? And the great big house that dates from the time of Ole Olsen Ture, why hasn't it been pulled down long ago? There would be room for a score of cheap dwellings on the site.

Things have gone downhill, gone to the depths. And now the little cobbler-soul can rejoice—not because we're all grown equally great, but because we're all equally small. 'Tis our affair!

The long bridge is pleasant to walk on because it is paved with planks, and even as a floor; all the young ladies can walk gracefully here. And the bridge is light and open at the sides, making an excellent lookout place for us inquisitive folk.

Down on the raft of tangled logs the men are shouting, as they strain to free the timber that has caught and stuck fast among the rocks and boulders in the river-bed. Stick after stick comes floating down and joins the mass already gathered; the jam grows and grows; at times there may be a couple of hundred dozen balks hung up at one spot. But if all goes well, the gang can clear the jam in time. And if fate will have it ill, some unlucky lumberman may be carried down as well, down the rapids to his death.

There are ten men with boat-hooks on the jam, all more or less wet from falling in. The foreman points out the log next to be freed, but we, watching from the bridge, can see now and again that all the gang are not agreed. There is no hearing what is said, but we can see some of them are inclined to get another log out first; one of the old hands protests. Knowing his speech as I do, I fancy I can hear him say stubbornly and calmly: "I doubt we'd better see and get that one clear first." Ten pairs of eyes are turned towards the stick he has chosen, tracing the lie of it in among its tangled fellows; if the men agree, ten boat-hooks are thrust into it. Then for a moment the poles stand out from the log like the strings of a harp; a mighty "Ho!" from the gang, a short, tense haul, and it moves a trifle forward. A fresh grip, another shout, and forward again. It is like watching half a score of ants about a twig. And at last the freed log slides out and away down the foss.

But there are logs that are almost immovable, and often it is just one of the worst that has to be cleared before anything else can be done. Then the men spread out and surround it, fixing their hooks wherever they can get a sight of it in the tangle, some hauling,

135

others thrusting outward; if it is dry, they splash water over it to make it slippery. And here the poles are nowise regularly set like harp-strings, but lie crosswise at all angles like a cobweb.

Sometimes the shouting of the gang can be heard all day long from the river, silenced only for meals; ay, it may happen that it goes on for days together. Then suddenly a new sound falls on the ear: the stroke of the ax; some devil of a log has fixed itself so cunningly there is no hauling it free, and it has to be cut through. It does not take many strokes to do it, for the pressure on it already is enormous; soon it breaks, the great confused mass yields, and begins to move. All the men are on their guard now, holding back to see what is coming next; if the part they are standing on shows signs of breaking loose, they must leap with catlike swiftness to a safer spot. Their calling is one of daily and hourly peril; they carry their lives in their hands.

But the little town is a living death.

It is pitiful to see such a dead place, trying to pretend it is alive. It is the same with Bruges, the great city of the past, and with many cities in Holland, in South Germany, the north of France, the Orient. Standing in the marketplace of such a town one cannot but think: "Once, once upon a time this was a living place; there are still human beings walking in the streets!"

Strange, this town of ours is hidden away, shut in by the hills—and yet for all that it has no doubt its local feminine beauty and its local masculine ambition just as all other towns. Only it is such a queer, outlandish life that is lived here, with little crooked fingers, with eyes as of a mouse, and ears filled day and night with the eternal rushing of the waters. A beetle on its way in the heather, a stub of yellow grass sticks up here and there—huge trees they seem to the beetle's eye! Two local merchants walk across the bridge. Going to the post, no doubt. They have this very day decided to go halves in a whole sheet of stamps, buying them all at once for the sake of the rebate on a quantity!

Oh, those local tradesmen!

Each day they hang out their stocks of ready-made clothes, and dress their windows with their stuffs and goods, but rarely do I see a customer go in. I thought to myself at first: But there must surely be some one now and then—a peasant from somewhere up the valley, coming into town. And I was right; I saw that peasant today, and it was strange and pleasant to see him.

He was dressed like the pictures in our folk-tales—a little short jacket with silver buttons, and grey breeches with a black leather seat. He was driving a tiny little haycart with a tiny little horse, and up in the cart was a little red-flanked cow—on its way to the butcher's, I suppose. All three—man, horse, and cow—were undersized; palaeolithic figures; dwarf creatures from the underworld on a visit to the haunts of men. I almost looked to see them vanish before my eyes. All of a sudden the cow in its Lilliputian cart utters a throaty roar—and even that unromantic sound was like a voice from another world.

A couple of hours later I come upon the man again, minus horse and cow: he is wandering round among the shops on his errands. I follow him to the saddler's—saddler and harness-maker Vogt is also a glazier, and deals in leather as well. This merchant of many parts offers to serve me first, but I explain that I must look at a saddle, and some glass, and a trifle of leather first, I am in no hurry. So he turns to the elfin countryman.

The two are old acquaintances.

"So here's you come to town?"

"Ay, that's the way of it."

And so on through the whole rigmarole; wind and weather, and the state of the roads; wife and children getting on as usual; season and crops; river's fallen so much the last week; butchers' prices; hard times nowadays, etc. Then they begin trying the leather, pinching and feeling and bending it about and talking it over. And when at last a strip is cut off and weighed, the mannikin finds it a marvel, sure, that ever it could weigh so much! Reckon it at a round figure, those little bits of weights aren't worth counting! And the two of them argue and split over this for a good solid while, as is right and proper. When at last it comes to paying for the goods, a fantastic leather purse is brought to light, a thing out of a fairy tale. Slowly and cautiously the heavy fist draws forth the coins, one skilling after another; both parties count the money over again and again, then the mannikin closes his purse with an anxious movement; that is all he has!

"Why, you've coin and paper too; I saw a note in there."

"Nay, I'll not break the note."

More reckoning and arguing—a long business this; each gives way a little, they split the difference—and the deal is over.

"And a terrible heap to pay for a bit of leather," says the purchaser. And the dealer answers:

"Nay, you've got it at a bargain. But don't forget me next time you're in town."

Towards evening I meet the mannikin once more, driving home again after his venture into the world. The cow has been left behind at the butcher's. There are parcels and sacks in the cart, but the little man himself jogs along behind, the leather seat of his breeches stretching to a triangle at every step. And whether for thoughtlessness, or an overweight of thought after all these doings and dealings, he wears a rolled-up strip of sole leather like a ring about one arm.

So money has flowed into the town once more; a peasant has come in and sold his cow, and spent the price of it again in goods. The event is noticed everywhere at once: the town's three lawyers notice it, the three little local papers notice it; money is circulating more freely of late. Unproductive—but it helps the town to live.

Every week the little local papers advertise town properties for sale; every week a list is issued by the authorities of houses to be sold in liquidation of the unpaid tax. What then? Ah, but mark how many properties come on the market that way! The barren, rocky valley with its great river cannot feed this moribund town; a cow now and again is not enough. And so it is that the properties are given up, the Swiss-pattern houses, the dwellings and shelters. Out Vestland way, if ever a house in one of the little towns should chance to come up for sale, it is a great event; the inhabitants flock together on the quay to talk it over. Here, in our little town beyond all hope, it occasions no remark when another wearied hand leaves hold of what it had. My turn now—'twill be another's before long. And none finds it worth while sorrowing much for that.

Engineer Lassen came to my lodging and said:

"Put on your cap and come with me to the station to fetch a trunk."

"No," said I. "I'm not going to do that."

"Not going to...."

"No. There's a porter at the hotel for that sort of thing. Let him earn the money."

It was quite enough. The engineer was very young; he looked at me and said nothing. But, being obstinate by nature, he would not give up at once; he changed his tone.

"I'd rather have you," he said. "I've a reason for it, and I wish you would."

"That's a different matter. Then I will."

I put on my cap, and I am ready; he walks on ahead, and I follow behind. Ten minutes waiting at the station, and the train comes in. It consists of three toy carriages, and a few passengers tumble out. In the rear carriage is a lady trying to alight; the engineer hurries to assist her.

I paid no great heed to what was happening. The lady was veiled and wore gloves; a light coat she handed to her escort. She seemed embarrassed at first, and said only a few words in a low voice, but he was quite the reverse, talking loudly and freely all the time. And, when he begged her to take off her veil, she grew bolder, and did as he said.

"Do you know me now?" she said. And suddenly I pricked up my ears; it was Fru Falkenberg's voice. I turned round and looked her in the face.

It is no easy matter to be old and done with and behave as such. The moment I realized who it was standing there I could think of nothing but my age-worn self, and how to stand and bow with ease and respect. Now, I had among my possessions a blouse, and breeches of brown corduroy such as labourers wear in the south; an excellent, well-looking suit, and new. But, alas! I had not put it on today. And the lack of it at that moment irked me. I was down-hearted at the thought. And, while the two stood there talking, I fell to wondering why the engineer had wanted me so particularly to come with him to the station. Could it be for the matter of a few skilling to the porter? Or was it to show off with a servant at his heels? Or had he thought that Fruen would be pleased to have some one she knew in attendance? If the last, then he was greatly mistaken; Fruen started in evident displeasure at finding me here, where she had thought, perhaps, to be safely concealed. I heard the engineer say: "I've got a man here, he'll take your luggage down. Have you the ticket?" But I made no sign of greeting. I turned away.

And afterwards I triumphed over him in my miserable soul, thinking how annoyed she would be with him for his want of tact. He brought up with him a man who had been in her employ when she had a home; but that man had some delicacy of feeling, he turned away, pretending not to know her! Lord knows what the woman found to run after in this tight-waisted youth with the heavy contours behind.

There are fewer people on the platform now; the little toy waggons are rolled away and shunted about to build another train; at last we are left with the whole place to ourselves. Fruen and the engineer stand talking. What has she come for? Heaven knows! Young Lovelace, perhaps, has had a spasm of longing and wants her again. Or is she come of her own accord to tell him what has happened, and ask his advice? Like as not the end of it will be they fix things up and get married some day. Mr. Hugo Lassen is, of course, a chivalrous gentleman, and she his one and only love. And then comes the time when she should walk on roses and live happily ever after!

"No, really, it would never do!" he exclaims, with a laugh. "If you won't be my aunt, then you'll have to be my cousin."

"S-sh!" whispers Fruen. "Can't you get rid of that man there?"

Whereupon the engineer comes up to me with the luggage

receipt in his hand, and in his lordliest manner, as an Inspector of Waterways addressing a gang of lumbermen, he says:

"Bring this along to the hotel."

"Very good," I answered, touching my cap.

I carried down the trunk, thinking as I went. He had actually invited her to pass as his aunt! Visibly older she might be than he; still, here again he had shown himself wanting in tact. I would not have said such a thing myself. I would have declared to all and sundry: "Behold, here is come a bright angel to visit King Hugo; see how young and beautiful she is; mark the slow, heavy turn of her grey eyes; ay, a weighty glance! But there is a shimmer of sea-fire in her hair—I love her! Mark her, too, when she speaks, a mouth good and fine, and with ever and again a little helpless look and smile. I am King Hugo this day, and she is my love!"

The trunk was no heavier than many another burden, but there were bronzed iron bands round, and one of them tore a hole in my blouse at the back. So I thanked my stars I had not worn my better one.

VII

Some days passed. I was growing tired of my empty occupation, which consisted in doing nothing but loaf about the place. I went to the foreman of the gang and asked him to take me on as a lumberman, but he refused.

These gentlemen of the proletariat think a good deal of themselves; they look down on farm-workers, and will have nothing to do with them. They are ever on the move, going from one waterway to another, drawing their wages in cash, and spending a fair part of the same in drink. Then, too, they are more popular among the girls. It is the same with men working on the roads or railways, with all factory-hands; even the mechanic is looked down upon, and as for the farm-hand, he is a very slave!

Now, I knew I could be pretty sure of a place in the gang any day if I cared to ask the engineer. But, in the first place, I had no wish to be further indebted to him, and in the second, I might be sure that if I did, my friends the lumbermen would make my life a misery until I had gone through all the trouble of making myself respected for my deserts. And that might take longer than I cared about.

And then one day the engineer came to me with instructions

that I was to observe with care. He spoke politely and sensibly this time:

"We've had no rain for a long time now; the river's getting steadily lower, and the logs are piling up on the way down. I want you to tell the man above and the one below to be extra careful about their work just now, and you yourself, of course, will do the same."

"We're sure to get rain before long," I said, for the sake of saying something.

"That may be," he answered, with the intense earnestness of youth, "but I must act all the same as if there were never to be rain again. Now remember every word I've said. I can't be everywhere at once myself, more especially now that I've a visitor."

I answered him with a face as serious as his own that I would do my very best.

So I was still bound to my idling occupation after all, and wandered up and down the river as before with my boat-hook and my rations. For my own satisfaction I cleared away bigger and bigger jams unaided, sang to myself as if I were a whole gang, and worked hard enough for many men; also I carried the new instructions to Grindhusen, and frightened him properly.

But then came the rain.

And now the sticks went dancing down through channel and rapids, like huge, pale serpents hurrying, hurrying on, now head, now tail in air.

Easy days these for my engineer!

For myself, I was ill at ease in the town and in my lodging there. I had a little room to myself, but one could hear every sound in the place, and there was little rest or comfort. Moreover, I found myself outdone in everything by the young lumbermen who lodged there.

I patroled the river-bank regularly those days, though there was little or nothing for me to do there. I would steal away and sit in hiding under an over-hanging rock, hugging the thought of how I was old, and forsaken by all; in the evenings I wrote many letters to people I knew, just to have some one to talk to; but I did not send the letters.

Joyless days were these. My chief pleasure was to go about noticing every little trifle in the town, wherever it might be, and thinking a little upon each.

But was my engineer so free from care? I began to doubt it.

Why was he no longer to be seen out early and late with this new cousin of his? He would even stop another young lady on the bridge and pass the time of day—a thing he had not done this fortnight gone. I had seen him with Fru Falkenberg once or twice; she looked so young and prettily dressed, and happy—a little reckless, laughing out loud. That's what it's like when a woman first steps aside, I thought to myself; but to-morrow or the day after it may be different! And when I saw her again later on I was annoyed with her; there was something overbold about her dress and manner, the old charm and sweetness were gone. Where was the tenderness now in her eyes? Nothing but bravado! And furiously I told myself that her eyes shone like a pair of lamps at the door of a music hall.

By the look of things the couple had begun to weary of each other, since he had taken to going out alone, and she spend much of her time sitting looking out of the window in the hotel. And this, no doubt, was why stout Captain Bror made his appearance once again; his mission was perhaps to bring jollity and mirth to others besides himself. And this jovial lump of deformity certainly did his best; his guffaws of laughter rang through the little town one whole night long. Then his leave expired, and he had to go back to drill and duty—Fru Falkenberg and her Hugo were left to themselves once more.

One day, while I was in a shop, I heard that there had been some slight difference of opinion between Engineer Lassen and his cousin. A commercial traveller was telling the shopkeeper all about it. But so great was the general respect for the wealthy engineer throughout the town that the shopman would hardly believe the story, and questioned the scandal-monger doubtingly.

"It must have been in fun, I'm sure. Did you hear it yourself? When was it?"

The traveller himself did not dare to make more of it.

"My room's next to his," he said, "so I couldn't help hearing it last night. They were arguing; I don't say it was a quarrel—lord, no! as delicate as could be. She only said he was different now from what he had been; that he'd changed somehow. And he said it wasn't his fault, he couldn't do as he liked here in town. Then she asked him to get rid of somebody she didn't like—one of his men, a lumberman, I suppose. And he promised he would."

"Well, there you are—just nothing at all," said the shopkeeper.

But the traveller had heard more, I fancy, than he cared to say. I could tell as much by his looks.

And had I not noticed myself how the engineer had changed? He had talked out loud so cheerfully at the station that first day; now he could be obstinately silent when he did go so far as to take Fruen for a walk down to the bridge. I could see well enough how

142

they stood looking each their separate ways. Lord God in heaven, but love is a fleeting thing!

All went well enough at first. She said, no doubt, that it was quite a nice little place, with a great big river and the rapids, and so strange to hear the roar of the waters all the time; and here was a real little town with streets and people in—"And then you here, too!" And he of course, would answer: "Yes, and you!" Oh, they were everything to each other at first! But then they grew weary of good things; they took too much—took love in handfuls, such was their foolishness. And more and more clearly he realized that things were getting awry; the town was such a little place, and this cousin of his a stranger—he could not keep on being her attendant squire for ever. No, they must ease off a little gradually; now and then, perhaps—only occasionally, of course—it would be as well to have their meals at different times. If not, some of those commercial travellers would be getting ideas into their heads about the loving cousins. Remember, in a little place like this—and she ... how could she understand it? A little place—yes, but surely it was no smaller now than it had been at first? No, no, my friend, it is you that have changed!

There had been plenty of rain, and the timber was coming down beautifully. Nevertheless, the engineer took to going off on little trips up or down the river. It seemed as if he were glad to get away; he looked worried and miserable altogether now.

One day he asked me to go up and tell Grindhusen to come in to town. Was it Grindhusen, I wondered, that was to be dismissed? But Fruen had never so much as set eyes on Grindhusen since she came; what could he have done to offend her?

I fetched Grindhusen in accordingly. He went up to the hotel at once to report, and the engineer put on his things and went out with him. They set out up the river and disappeared.

Later in the day Grindhusen came to my lodging, and was ready enough to tell, but I asked him nothing. In the evening the lumberman gave him Brændevin, and the spirit loosened his tongue. What about this cousin, or something, engineer has got with him? How much longer was she going to stay? As to this, nobody could say; and, anyhow, why shouldn't she stay? "'Tis naught but fooling and trouble with such-like cousin business," Grindhusen declared. "Why couldn't he bring along the girl he's going to marry?—and I told him so to his face."

"You told him?" asked one of the men.

"Ay, I did that. You may not know it, but engineer and I we sit there talking as it might be me and you," said Grindhusen, looking mighty big and proud. "What do you suppose he sent to fetch me

143

for? You'd never guess if you sat there all night. Why, he sent for me just to have a talk over things. Not that there's anything new or strange about that; he's done the same before now; but, anyhow, that's what it was."

"What'd he want to talk to you about?" asked one.

Grindhusen swelled, and was not to be drawn at once. "Eh, I'm not such a fool, but I know how to talk with a man. And it's not my way to be contrary neither. 'You know a thing or two, Grindhusen,' says the Inspector, 'and there's two Kroner for you,' says he. Ay, that's what he said. And if you don't believe me, why, here's the money, and you can see. There!"

"But what was it all about?" asked several voices at once.

"He'd better not say, if you ask me," I said.

It struck me that the engineer must have been miserable and desperate when he sent me to fetch Grindhusen. He was so little used to trouble that the moment anything went wrong he felt the need of some one to confide in. And now when he was going about day after day, thoroughly disheartened and full of pity for himself, as if he wanted to know how miserable he was at being checked in his play. This sportsman, with his figure moulded in the wrong place, was a travesty of youth, a Spartan in tears. What sort of upbringing could his have been?

Ah, well, if he had been an old man I had found reason and excuse for him enough; if the truth were known, it was perhaps but hatred of his youth that moved me now. Who can say? But I know I looked upon him as a travesty, a caricature.

Grindhusen stared at me when I had spoken my few words; the others, too, looked wonderingly.

"I'll not say, but it might be better not," said Grindhusen submissively.

But the men were not to be put off.

"And why shouldn't he tell? We're not going to let it go farther."

"No, that we shan't," said another. "But you might be one of that sort yourself and go telling tales to the Inspector."

Grindhusen took courage at this, and said:

"I'll say what I like, so don't you trouble yourself! Tell just as much as I please. For I'm saying no more than's true. And in case you'd care to know, I can tell you the Inspector's got a word to say to you very soon. Ay, that he has, or hearing goes for nothing. So you've no call to be anyway stuck up yourself. And as for me telling or not telling things, I'm saying never a thing but what's the truth. Just remember that. And if you knew as much as I do, she's nothing but a plague and a burden to him all the time, and won't let him out of her sight. D'you call that cousins, going on like that?"

"Nay, surely; nay, surely!" said the men encouragingly.

"What d'you think he sent for me about? Ay, there's the pretty fellow he sent up with the message! But there'll be a message for him one of these days: I gathered as much from the Inspector himself. I'll say no more than that. And as for me telling things, here's Inspector's been like a father to me, and I'd be a stock and a stone to say otherwise. 'I'm all upset and worried these days, Grindhusen,' says he to me. 'And what's a man to do; can you tell me that now?' 'No,' says I, 'but Inspector knows himself,' says I. Those very words I said. 'I wish to Heaven I did,' says he again. 'But it's all these wretched women,' says he. 'If it's women,' says I, 'why, there's no doing anything with them,' says I. 'No, indeed, you're right there!' says he. 'The only way's to give them what they were made for, and a good round slap on the backside into the bargain,' says I. 'By Heaven, I believe you're right there, Grindhusen,' says the Inspector, and he brightened up no end. I've never seen a man so brightened up and cheerful just for a word or so. It was a sight to see. And you can take and drown me if it isn't gospel truth every single bit I've said. I sat there just as I'm sitting now, and Inspector as it might be there...."

And Grindhusen rambled on.

Next morning early, before it was fairly light, Engineer Lassen stopped me on the street. It was only half-past three. I was all fitted out for a tramp up the river, with my boat-hook and a store of food. Grindhusen was having a drinking-bout in town, and I was going to do his beat as well as my own. That would take me right up to the top of the hills, and I had packed a double stock of food accordingly.

The engineer was evidently coming down from a party somewhere; he was laughing and talking loudly with a couple of other men, all of them more or less drunk.

"Go on ahead a bit," he said to the others. And then, turning to me, he asked: "Where are you off to?"

I told him what I had in mind.

"H'm! I don't know about that," said he. "No, I think you'd better not. Grindhusen can manage all right by himself. And, besides, I'm going to inspect myself. You've no business to go off doing things like that without asking me first."

Well, he was right of course, so far as that went, and I begged his pardon. And, indeed, knowing as I did how he was set on playing the master and lording it over his men, I might have had more sense.

But begging his pardon only seemed to egg him on; he felt deeply injured, and grew quite excited over it.

"I'll have no more of this!" he said. "My men are here to carry out my orders; that's all they've got to do. I took you on to give you a chance, not because I'd any use for you myself. And I've no use for you now, anyhow."

I stood there staring at him, and said never a word.

"You can come round to the office today and get your wages," he went on. And then he turned to go.

So I was the one to be dismissed! Now I understood what Grindhusen had meant with his hints about me. Fru Falkenberg, no doubt, had come to hate the sight of me by now, reminding her, as it must, of her home, and so she had got him to turn me off. But hadn't I been the very one to show delicacy of feeling towards her at the station, turning away instead of recognizing her? Had I ever so much as lifted my cap to her when I passed her in the street? Surely I had been considerate enough to deserve consideration in return?

And now—here was this young engineer turning me off at a moment's notice, and that with unnecessary vehemence. I saw it all in my mind: he had been worrying himself for days over this dismissal, shirking it all the time, until at last he managed to screw his courage up by drinking hard all night. Was I doing him an injustice? It might be so; and I tried to combat the thought myself. Once more I called to mind that he was young and I was old, and my heart no doubt, full of envy on that account. So I gave him no sarcastic answer now, but simply said:

"Ay, well, then, I can unpack the things I was taking along."

But the engineer was anxious to make the most of his chance now he was fairly started; he dragged in the old story about the time he'd wanted me to go and fetch a trunk.

"When I give an order, I don't expect the man to turn round and say no, he won't. I'm not used to that sort of thing. And as there's no knowing it may not occur again, you'd better go."

"Well and good," said I.

I saw a figure in a white dress at a window in the hotel, and fancied it must be Fru Falkenberg watching us, so I said no more.

But then the engineer seemed suddenly to remember that he couldn't get rid of me once and for all on the spot; he would have to see me again to settle up. So he changed his tone and said: "Well, anyhow, come up sometime to-day and get your money. Have you thought over how much it ought to be?"

"No. That'll be for engineer himself to decide."

"Well, well," he said in a kindlier voice, "after all, you've been a good man to have, I will say that for you. But, for various reasons—and it's not only for myself: you know what women—that is, I mean the ladies—"

Oh, but he was young indeed. He stopped at nothing.

"Well—good morning!" He nodded abruptly, and turned away.

But the day proved all too short for me; I went up into the woods, and stayed roaming about there all by myself so long that I didn't get to the office to draw my money. Well, there was no hurry; I had plenty of time.

What was I to do now?

I had not cared much for the little town before, but now it began to interest me; I would gladly have stayed on a while. There were complications arising between two people whom I had been following attentively for some weeks past; something fresh might happen any moment now, there was no saying. I thought of going as apprentice to a blacksmith, just for the sake of staying in the place, but then, if I did, I should be tied to the smithy all day and hampered in my movements altogether; apart from which, the apprenticeship would take too many years of my life. And years were the thing I least of all could spare.

So I let the days pass, one after another; the weather changed round again to dry, sunny days. I stayed on at the lodging-house, mended my clothes, and got some new ones made at a shop. One of the maids in the house came up one evening and offered to do some mending for me, but I was more in the mood for fooling, and showed her how well I managed the work myself.

"Look at that patch, there, now—and that!" After a while a man came up the stairs and tried the door. "Open, you within!" he said.

"It's Henrik, one of the lumbermen," said the girl.

"Is he your sweetheart?" I asked.

"No, indeed, I should think not," she answered. "I'd rather go without than have a fellow like him."

"Open the door, d'you hear!" cried the man outside. But the girl was not frightened in the least. "Let him stay outside," she said. And we let him stay outside. But that door of mine bent inwards in a great curve every now and then, when he pushed his hardest.

At last, when we'd finished making fun about my needlework and her sweethearts, I had to go out and see the passage was clear before she would venture downstairs. But there was no man there.

It was late now; I went down to the parlour for a bit, and there was Grindhusen drinking with some of the gang. "There he is!" said one of them, as I came in. It was Henrik who spoke; he was trying to

147

get his mates against me. Grindhusen, too, sided with the rest of them, and tried all he could to annoy me.

Poor Grindhusen! He was stale-drunk all the time now, and couldn't get clear of it. He had had another meeting with Engineer Lassen; they had walked up the river as before and sat talking for an hour, and when Grindhusen came back he showed a new two-Kroner piece he'd got. Then he went on the drink again, and gabbled about being in the engineer's confidence. This evening, too, he was all high-and-mightiness, not to be outdone by anybody.

"Come in and sit down," he said to me.

But one or two of the other men demurred; they would have nothing to do with me. And at this Grindhusen changed front; for sheer devilment he fell to again about the engineer and his cousin, knowing it would annoy me.

"Well, has he turned you off?" he asked, with a side glance at the others, as if to bid them watch what was coming.

"Yes," said I.

"Aha! I knew all about it days ago, but I never said a word. I don't mind saying I knew about it before any other single soul in the world of us here, but did I ever breathe a word of it? Inspector he says to me: 'I want to ask you something, Grindhusen,' says he, 'and that is, if you'll come down and work in the town instead of the man I've got there now. I want to get rid of him,' says he. 'Why, as to that,' says I, 'it's just as Inspector's pleased to command.' That was my very words, and neither more nor less. But did I ever breathe a syllable?"

"Has he turned you off?" asked one of the other men then.

"Yes," I answered.

"But as for that cousin of his," Grindhusen went on, "he asked me about her, too. Ay, Inspector, he asks my advice about all sorts of things. And now, this last time we were up the river together, he slapped his knee when he talked of her. So there. And you can guess for yourselves till tomorrow morning if you like. Everything of the best to eat and drink and every way, and costing a heap of money each week; but she stays on and on. Fie and for shame, say I, and I mean it too."

But now it seemed as if the scale had turned in my favour at the news of my dismissal; some of the men perhaps felt sorry for me, others were glad to learn that I was going. One of them offered me a drink from his own bottle, and called to the maid for "another glass—a clean one, you understand!" Even Henrik no longer bore me any grudge, but drank with me and was friendly enough. And we sat there gossiping over our glasses quite a while.

"But you'd better go up and see about that money of yours,"

said Grindhusen. "For from what I've heard, I don't fancy you'll get the Inspector to come down here with it after you. He said as much. 'There's money owing to him,' that was what he said, 'but if he thinks I'm going to run after him with it, you can tell him it's here,' he said."

VIII

But the engineer did come down after me, as it turned out, though it was queer it should be so. Anyhow, it was a triumph I had not sought, and I cared nothing for it.

He came to the lodging-house to see me, and said: "I want you to come back with me, if you please, and get your money. And there's a letter come for you by the post."

When we stepped into the office, Fru Falkenberg was there. I was taken aback at finding her there. I made a bow and stood over by the door.

"Sit down, won't you?" said the engineer, going to the table for my letter. "Here you are. No, sit down and read your letter while I'm reckoning up your pay."

And Fru Falkenberg herself motioned me to a chair.

Now, what were they looking so anxious about? And what was the meaning of this sudden politeness and "Won't you sit down?" and all the rest? I had not to wait long to find out: the letter was from Captain Falkenberg.

"Here, you can use this," said Fruen very obligingly, handing me a letter-opener.

A simple, ordinary letter, nothing more; indeed, it began almost jestingly: I had run away from Øvrebø before he knew I was going, and hadn't even waited for my money. If I imagined he was in difficulties and would not be able to pay me before the harvest was in—if that was why I had left in such a hurry, why, he hoped I had found out I was mistaken. And now he would be very glad if I would come back and work for him if I wasn't fixed up elsewhere. The house and outbuildings wanted painting, then there would be the harvesting, and, after that, he would like to have me for work among the timber. Everything looking well here, fields nice and tall, meadows nice and thick. Glad to hear as soon as you can in answer to this,—Yours, FALKENBERG.

The engineer had finished his reckoning. He turned on his chair and looked over at the wall. Then, as if suddenly remembering something, he turned sharply to the table again. Nervousness, that was all. Fruen stood looking at her rings, but I had a feeling she was stealthily watching me all the time—thoroughly nervous, the pair of them!

Then said the engineer:

"Oh, by the way, I noticed your letter was from Captain Falkenberg. How are things going there? I knew the writing at once."

"Would you like to read the letter?" I said promptly, offering it as I spoke.

"No—oh no. Thanks, all the same. Not in the least. I was only...."

But he took the letter, all the same. And Fruen came across to him and stood looking over his shoulder as he read.

"H'm!" said the engineer, with a nod. "Everything going on nicely, it seems. Thanks." And he held out the letter to give it back.

Fruen's manner was different. She took the letter from him and began studying it herself. Her hand shook a little.

"Well, now about the money," said the engineer. "Here you are; that's what I make it. I hope you're satisfied all right?"

"Yes, thank you," said I.

He seemed relieved to find that Captain Falkenberg's letter was only about myself and made no mention of anyone else. And again he tried to soften down my dismissal.

"Well, well," he said. "But if you should happen to be in these parts any time, you know where to find me. We've all but finished now for this year—there's been too much drought just lately."

Fruen was still holding the letter. Then I saw she had finished reading, for her eyes never moved; but she stood there, staring at the letter, thinking. What was in her mind, I wondered?

The engineer glanced at her impatiently.

"Are you learning it by heart?" he said, with a half-smile. "Come, dear, he's waiting."

"Oh, I beg your pardon," said Fruen quickly. "I forgot." And she handed me the letter.

"So it seems," observed the engineer.

I bowed, and went out.

On a summer evening the bridge is crowded with people out walking—school teachers and tradespeople, young girls and children. I watch my time when it is getting late, and the bridge is deserted; then I can lounge over that way myself, and stay for an hour or so in the midst of the roar. No need to do anything really but listen; only my brain is so over-rested with idleness and good sound sleep, it finds no end of things to busy itself about. Last evening I determined in all seriousness to go to Fru Falkenberg and say:

"Go away from here, Frue; leave by the first train that goes." Today I have been calling myself a fool for entertaining such a ridiculous thought, and set in its place another: "Get out of this yourself, my good man, by the first train that goes. Are you her equal, her adviser? Very well, then; see that what you do is not too utterly at variance with what you are!"

And this evening I am still treating myself as I deserve. I fall to humming a little tune, but can scarcely hear it myself! the sound is crushed to death in the roar of the water. "That's right," I say to myself scornfully. "You ought always to stand by a deafening foss when you feel like humming a tune." And I laugh at myself again. With suchlike childish fancies do I pass the time.

The noise of the rapids anywhere inland is as useful to the ear as the noise of breakers on the shore. But the voice of the breakers is louder and fainter by turns. The roar of waters in a river-bed is like an audible fog, a monotony of sound beyond reason, contrary to all sense, a miracle of idiocy. "What is the time, do you know?" "Yes, isn't it?" "Day or night?" "Yes!" As if some one had laid a stone on six keys of an organ, and walked off and left it there.

With such childish fancies do I while away the time.

"Godaften!" says Fru Falkenberg, and there she is beside me.

I hardly felt surprised; it was almost as if I had expected her. After her behaviour with her husband's letter, she might well go a little farther.

Now I could think two ways about her coming: either she had turned thoroughly sentimental at being reminded so directly of her home once more, or she wanted to make her engineer jealous; he might perhaps be watching us from his window that very moment, and I had been sent for to go back to Øvrebø. Possibly she was thoroughly calculating, and had been trying to work on his jealousy even yesterday, when she studied the letter so attentively.

It seemed, however, that none of my clever theories was to be confirmed. It was me she wanted to see, and that only to make a sort of apology for getting me dismissed. That she should ever care about such a trifle! Was she so incapable of thinking seriously that she could not see what a miserable position she herself was in? What in the devil's name had she to do with my affairs?

I had thought to say a brief word or so and point to the train, but something made me gentle, as if I were dealing with an irresponsible, a child.

"You'll be going back to Øvrebø now, I suppose?" she said. "And I thought I'd like.... H'm!... You're sorry to be leaving here,

151

perhaps? No? No, no, of course not. But I must tell you something: It was I that got you dismissed."

"It doesn't matter."

"No, no. Only, I wanted to tell you. Now that you're going back to Øvrebø. You can understand it was a little unpleasant for me at times to...."

She checked herself.

"To have me about the place. Yes, it would be unpleasant."

"To see you here. A little unpleasant; I mean, because you knew about me before. So I asked the engineer if he couldn't send you away. Not that he wanted to himself, you understand. Quite the reverse, in fact, but he did at last. I'm glad you're going back to Øvrebø."

"So?" said I. "But when Fruen comes home again surely it will be just as unpleasant to see me then?"

"Home?" she repeated. "I'm not going home."

Pause. She had frowned as she spoke. But now she nodded, and even smiled a little, and turned to go.

"Well, well, you'll pardon me, then, I know," she said.

"Have you any objection to my going back to Captain Falkenberg?" I asked.

She stopped, and looked me full in the face. Now, what was the right thing here? Three times she had spoken of Øvrebø. Was it with the idea that I might put in a word for her if opportunity offered, when I got back there? Or was she unwilling to ask of me as a favour not to go?

"No, no, indeed I've not!" she answered. "Go there, by all means."

And she turned and left me.

Neither sentimental nor calculating, as far as I could see. But she might well have been both. And what had I gained by my attempt at a confidential tone? I should have known better than to try, whether she stayed here or went elsewhere. What business was it of mine? 'Twas her affair.

You're playing and pretending, I said to myself. All very well to say she's literature and no more, but that withered soul of yours showed good signs of life when she was kind to you and began looking at you with those two eyes of hers. I'm disappointed; I'm ashamed of you, and to-morrow you go!

But I did not go.

And true it is that I went about spying and listening everywhere for anything I could learn of Fru Falkenberg; and then at times, ay, many a night, I would call myself to account for that same thing, and torture myself with self-contempt. From early morning I thought of her: is she awake yet? Has she slept well? Will she be going back home to-day? And at the same time all sorts of ideas came into my head. I might perhaps get work at the hotel where she was staying. Or I might write home for some clothes, turn gentleman myself, and go and stay at that same hotel. This last, of course, would at once have cut the ground from under my feet and left me farther removed from her than ever, but it was the one that appealed to me most of all, fool that I was. I had begun to make friends with the hotel porter, already, merely because he lived nearer to her than I. He was a big, strong fellow, who went up to the station every day to meet the trains and pick up a commercial traveller once a fortnight. He could give me no news; I did not ply him with questions, nor even lead him on to tell me things of his own accord; and, besides, he was far from intelligent. But he lived under the same roof with Fruen—ah yes, that he did. And one day it came about that this acquaintance of mine with the hotel porter brought me a piece of valuable information about Fru Falkenberg, and that from her own lips.

So they were not all equally fruitless, those days in the little town.

One morning I came back with the porter from the station; he had picked up a traveller with a heap of luggage, and had to take horse and cart to fetch the heavy grey trunks.

I had helped him to get them loaded up at the station, and now, as we pulled up at the hotel, he said: "You might lend a hand getting these things in; I'll stand you a bottle of beer this evening."

So we carried in the trunks together. They were to be taken up at once to the big luggage-room upstairs; the owner was waiting for them. It was an easy job for the two of us big, strong fellows both.

We had got them up all but one—that was still in the cart—when the porter was called back upstairs; the traveller was giving him instructions about something or other. Meantime, I went out, and waited in the passage; I did not belong to the place, and did not want to be seen hanging about on the stairs by myself.

Just then the door of Engineer Lassen's office opened, and he and Fru Falkenberg came out. They looked as if they had just got up; they had no hats on; just going down to breakfast, no doubt. Now, whether they did not notice me, or took me for the porter standing there, they went on with what they had been saying.

"Quite so," says the engineer. "And it won't be any different. I can't see what you've got to feel lonely about."

"Oh, you know well enough!" she answered.

"No, I don't, and I do think you might be a little more cheerful."

"You wouldn't like it if I were. You'd rather have me stay as I am, miserable and wretched, because you don't care for me any more."

He stopped on the stairs abruptly. "Really, I think you must be mad," he said.

"I dare say I am," she answered.

How poorly she held her own in a quarrel! It was always so with her. Why could she not be careful of her words, and answer so as to wound him, crush him altogether?

He stood with one hand on the stair-rail and said:

"So you think it pleases me to have things going on like this? I tell you it hurts me desperately—has done for a long time past."

"And me," she answered. "But now I'll have no more of it."

"Oh, indeed! You've said that before. You said it only a week ago."

"Well, I am going now."

He looked up at her.

"Going away?"

"Yes. Very soon."

But he saw that he had betrayed himself in grasping so eagerly, delightedly, at the suggestion, and tried now to smooth it over.

"There, there!" he said. "Be a nice sensible cousin now, and don't talk about going away."

"I am going," she said, and, slipping past him, went down the stairs by herself. He followed after.

Then the porter came out and we went down together. The last box was smaller than the others. I asked him to carry it up himself, pretending I had hurt my hand. I helped him to get it on his back, and went off home. Now I could go away the following day.

That afternoon Grindhusen, too, was dismissed. The engineer had sent for him, given him a severe talking to for doing no work and staying in town and getting drunk; in a word, his services were no longer needed.

I thought to myself: It was strangely sudden, this new burst of courage on the part of the engineer. He was so young, he had needed some one to back him up and agree to everything he said; now, however, seeing that a certain troublesome cousin was going away, he had no further need of comfort there. Or was my withered soul doing him an injustice?

Grindhusen was greatly distressed. He had reckoned on staying in town all the summer, as general handyman to the Inspector himself; but all hope of that was gone now. The Inspector was no longer as good as a father to him. And Grindhusen bore the disappointment badly. When they came to settle up, the Inspector had been going to deduct the two-Kroner pieces he had given him, saying they had only been meant as payment in advance. Grindhusen sat in the general room at the lodging-house and told us all about it, adding that the Inspector was pretty mean in the matter of wages after all. At this, one of the men burst out laughing, and said:

"No; did he, though? He didn't take them back, really?"

"Nay," said Grindhusen. "He didn't dare take off more than the one."

There was more laughter at this, and some one else asked:

"No, really? Which one was it? Did he knock off the first two-Kroner or the second? Ha, ha, ha! That's the best I've heard for a long time."

But Grindhusen did not laugh; he grew more and more sullen and despairing. What was he to do now? Farm labourers for the season's work would have been taken on everywhere by now, and here he was. He asked me where I was going, and when I told him, he begged me to put in a word for him with the Captain, and see if I couldn't get him taken on there for the summer. Meantime, he would stay on in the town, and wait till he heard from me.

But I knew there would soon be an end of Grindhusen's money if he stayed on in the town. The end of it was, I took him along with me, as the best thing to be done. He had been a smart hand at paint-work once, had Grindhusen; I remembered how he had done up old Gunhild's cottage on the island. He could come and help me now, for the time being; later on, we would surely find something else for him to do; there would be plenty of field-work in the course of the summer where he might be useful.

The 16th July found me back at Øvrebø. I remember dates more and more distinctly now, partly by reason of my getting old and acquiring the intensified interest of senility in such things, partly because of being a labourer, and obliged to keep account of my working days. But an old man may keep his dates in mind and forget all about far more important things. Up to now, for instance, I have forgotten to mention that the letter I had from Captain Falkenberg was addressed to me care of Engineer Lassen. Well and good. But the point appeared significant: the Captain, then, had ascertained whom I was working for. And it came into my mind that possibly the Captain was also aware of who else had been in the care of Engineer Lassen that summer!

The Captain was still away on duty when I arrived; he would be back in a week. As it was, Grindhusen was very well received; Nils was quite pleased to find I had brought my mate along, and

155

refused to let me keep him to help with the painting, but sent him off on his own responsibility to work in the turnip and potato fields. There was no end of work—weeding and thinning out—and Nils was already in the thick of the hay-making.

He was the same splendid, earnest farmer as ever. At the first rest, while the horses were feeding, he took me out over the ground to look at the crops. Everything was doing well; but it had been a late spring that year, and the cat's-tail was barely forming as yet, while the clover had just begun to show bloom. The last rain had beaten down a lot of the first-year grass, and it could not pick up again, so Nils had put on the mowing-machine.

We walked back home through waving grass and corn; there was a whispering in the winter rye and the stout six-rowed barley. Nils, who had not forgotten his schooling, called to mind that beautiful line of Bjørnson's:

"Beginning like a whisper in the corn one summer day."

"Time to get the horses out again," said Nils, stepping out a little. And waving his hand once more out over the fields, he said: "What a harvest we'll have this year if we can only get it safely in!"

So Grindhusen went off to work in the fields, and I fell to on the painting. I started with the barn, and all that was to be red; then I did over the flagstaff and the summer-house down among the lilacs with the first coat of oil. The house itself I meant to leave till the last. It was built in good old-fashioned country style, with rich, heavy woodwork and a carved border, à la grecque, above the doorway. It was yellow as it was, and a new lot of yellow paint had come in to do with this time. I took upon myself, however, to send the yellow back, and get another colour in exchange. In my judgment the house ought to be stone-grey, with doors and window-frames and verge-boards white. But that would be for the Captain to decide.

But though every one on the place was as nice as could be, and the cook in authority lenient, and Ragnhild as bright-eyed as ever, we all felt it dull with the master and mistress away. All save Grindhusen, honest fellow, who was quite content. Decent work and good food soon set him up again, and in a few days he was happy and waxing fat. His one anxiety was lest the Captain should turn him off when he came home. But no such thing—Grindhusen was allowed to stay.

156

IX

The Captain arrived.

I was giving the barn its second coat; at the sound of his voice I came down from the ladder. He bade me welcome.

"Running away from your money like that!" he said. And I fancied he looked at me with some suspicion as he asked: "What did you do that for?"

I answered simply that I had no idea of presuming to make him a present of my work; the money could stand over, that was all.

He brightened up at that.

"Yes, yes, of course. Well, I'm very glad you came. We must have the flagstaff white, I suppose?"

I did not dare tell him at once all I wanted done in white, but simply said:

"Yes. I've got hold of some white paint."

"Have you, though? That's good. You've brought another man up with you, I hear?"

"Yes. I don't know what Captain thinks...."

"He can stay. Nils has got him to work out in the fields already. And anyhow, you all seem to do as you like with me," he added jestingly. "And you've been working with the lumbermen, have you?"

"Yes."

"Hardly the sort of thing for you, was it?" Then, as if anxious not to seem curious about my work with Engineer Lassen, he broke off abruptly and said: "When are you going to start painting the house?"

"I thought of beginning this afternoon. It'll need scraping a bit here and there."

"Good. And if you find the woodwork loose anywhere, you can put in a nail or so at the same time. Have you had a look at the fields?"

"Yes."

"Everything's looking very nice. You men did good work last spring. Do no harm now if we had a little rain for the upper lands."

"Grindhusen and I passed lots of places on the way up that needed rain more than here. It's clay bottom here, and far up in the hills."

"That's true. How did you know that, by the way?"

"I looked about when I was here in the spring," I answered, "and I did a little digging here and there. I'd an idea you'd be wanting to have water laid on to the house some time or other, so I went prospecting a bit."

157

"Water laid on? Well, yes, I did think of it at one time, but....
Yes, I was going to have it done some years back; but I couldn't get
everything done at once, and then it was held up. And just now I
shall want the money for other things."

A wrinkle showed between his eyes for a moment; he stood
looking down—in thought.

"Well, well, that thousand dozen battens ought to do it, and
leave something over," he said suddenly. "Water? It would have to
be laid on to the outbuildings as well. A whole system of pipes."

"There'd be no rock-work though, no blasting."

"Eh? Oh, well, we'll see. What was I going to say? Did you
have a good time down there in the town? Not a big place, but you
do see more people there. And the railway brings visitors now and
again, no doubt."

"Aha," I thought to myself, "he knows well enough what
visitor came to stay with Engineer Lassen this summer!" I answered
that I did not care much for the place—which was perfectly true.

"No, really?"

He seemed to find something to ponder over in that; he stared
straight in front of him, whistling softly to himself. Then he walked
away.

The Captain was in good spirits; he had been more
communicative than ever before; he nodded to me as he went off.
Just as of old he was now—quick and determined, taking an interest
in his affairs once more, and sober as water. I felt cheered myself to
see him so. He was no wastrel; he had had a spell of foolishness and
dissipation, but it needed only his own resolution to put an end to
that. An oar in the water looks broken to the eye, but it is whole.

It set in to rain, and I had to stop work on the painting. Nils
had been lucky enough to get in all the hay that was cut; we got to
work now on the potatoes, all hands out in the fields at once, with
the women folk from the house as well.

Meanwhile the Captain stayed indoors all alone; it was dull
enough; now and again he would touch the keys of Fruen's piano.
He came out once or twice to where we were at work, and he carried
no umbrella, but let himself get drenched to the skin.

"Grand weather for the crops!" he would say; or again, "Looks
like being an extra special harvest this year!" But when he went back
to the house there was only himself and loneliness to meet him.
"We're better off ourselves than he is now," said Nils.

So we worked away at the potatoes, and when they were done
there were the turnips. And by the time we were through with them
the weather began to clear. Ideal weather, all that one could wish
for. Nils and I were as proud of it all as if we owned the place.

And now the haymaking began in earnest: the maids were out, spreading in the wake of the machine, and Grindhusen was set to work with a scythe in the corners and awkward parts where the machine could not go. And I got out my stone-grey paint and set about the house.

The Captain came up. "What colour's that you've got here?" he asked.

What could I say to that? I was nervous, I know, but my greatest fear was lest I should not be allowed to paint it grey after all. As it was, I said:

"Oh, it's only some ... I don't know ... it doesn't matter what we put on for the first coat...."

That saved me for the time being, at any rate. The Captain said no more about it then.

When I had done the house all grey, and doors and windows white, I went down to the summer-house and did that the same. But it turned out horrible to look at; the yellow underneath showed through and made it a ghastly colour. The flagstaff I took down and painted a clean white. Then I put in a spell of field-work with Nils and was haymaking for some days. Early in August it was.

Now, when I went back to my painting again I had settled in my mind to start on the house as early as possible, so as to be well on the way with it before the Captain was up—too far, if I could manage it, to go back! I started at three in the morning; there was a heavy dew, and I had to rub the woodwork over with a bit of sack. I worked away for an hour, and then had coffee, then on again till eight. I knew the Captain would be getting up then, so I went off to help Nils for an hour and be out of the way. I had done as much as I wanted, and my idea now was to give the Captain time to get over the shock of my grey, in case he should have got up in an irritable mood.

After breakfast I went back to work, and stood there on my ladder painting away, as innocently as could be, when the Captain came up.

"Are you doing it over with grey again?" he called up.

"Godmorgen! Yes. I don't know if...."

"Now what's the meaning of all this? Come down off that ladder at once!"

I clambered down. But I was not anxious now. I had thought out something to say that I fancied would prove effective at the right moment—unless my judgment was altogether at fault.

I tried first of all to make out it didn't matter really what colour we used for the second time either, but the Captain cut me short here and said:

159

"Nonsense! Yellow on top of that grey will look like mud; you can see that for yourself, surely."

"Well, then, we might give it two coats of yellow," I suggested.

"Four coats of paint? No, thank you! And all that white you've been wasting! It's ever so much dearer than the yellow."

This was perfectly true, and the very argument I had been fearing all along. I answered now straight-forwardly:

"Let me paint it grey."

"What?"

"It would look better. There's something about the house ... and with the green of the woods behind ... the style of the place is...."

"Is grey, you mean?" He swung off impatiently a few steps and came back again.

And then I faced him, more innocently than ever, with an inspiration surely sent from above:

"Now I remember! Yes.... I've always seen it grey in my mind, ever since one day—it was Fruen that said so...."

I was watching him closely; he gave a great start and stared at me wide-eyed for a moment; then he took out his handkerchief and began fidgeting with it at one eye as if to get out a speck or something.

"Indeed!" he said. "Did she say so?"

"Yes, I'm almost sure it was that. It's a long time back now, but...."

"Oh, nonsense!" he broke out abruptly, and strode away. I heard him clearing his throat—hard—as he crossed the courtyard behind.

I stood there limply for a while, feeling anything but comfortable myself. I dared not go on with the painting now, and risk making him angry again. I went round to the back and put in an hour cutting firewood. When I came round again, the Captain looked out from an open window upstairs and called down:

"You may as well go on with it now you've got so far. I don't know what possessed you, I'm sure. But get on with it now."

The window had been open before, but he slammed it to and I went on with the work.

A week passed. I spent my time between painting and haymaking. Grindhusen was good enough at hoeing potatoes and using a rake here and there, but not of much account when it came to loading hay. Nils himself was a first-rate hand, and a glutton for work.

I gave the house a third coat, and the delicate grey, picked out with white, made the place look nobler altogether. One afternoon I was at work, the Captain came walking up from the road. He watched me for a bit, then took out his handkerchief as if the heat troubled him, and said:

"Yes, better go on with it now you've got so far. I must say she wasn't far wrong about the colour. All nonsense though, really! H'm!"

I made no answer. The Captain used his handkerchief again and said:

"Hot again today—puh! What was I going to say? ... yes, it doesn't look so bad after all. No, she was right—that is, I mean, you were right about the colour. I was looking at it from down there just now, and it makes quite a handsome place. And anyhow, it's too late to alter it now."

"I thought so too," I said. "It suits the house."

"Yes, yes, it suits the house, as it were. And what was it she said about the woods behind—my wife, I mean? The background, or something?"

"It's a long time ago now, but I'm almost sure...."

"Yes, yes, never mind. I must say I never thought it would turn out like that—turn out so well. Will you have enough white, though, to finish?"

"Well ... yes, I sent back the yellow and got some white instead."

The Captain smiled, shook his head, and walked away. So I had been right after all!

Haymaking took up all my time now till it was done, but Nils lent me a hand in return, painting at the summer-house in the evening. Even Grindhusen joined in and took a brush. He wasn't much of a painter, he said, but he reckoned he could be trusted to paint a bit of a wall. Grindhusen was picking up fast.

At last the buildings were finished; hardly recognizable, they were, in their new finery. And when we'd cleaned up a bit in the shrubbery and the little park—this was our own idea—the whole place looked different altogether. And the Captain thanked us specially for what we'd done.

We started on the rye then, and at the same time the autumn rain set in; but we worked away all we knew, and there came a spell of sunshine in between whiles. There were big fields of thick, heavy rye, and big fields again of oats and barley, not yet ripe. It was a rich landscape to work in. The clover was seeding, but the turnips were somewhat behindhand. A good soaking would put them right, said Nils.

The Captain sent me up to the post from time to time; once he gave me a letter for his wife. A whole bundle of letters there were, to

161

different people, and hers in the middle. It was addressed care of her mother in Kristianssand. When I came back in the evening and took in the incoming post, the Captain's first words were: "You posted the letters all right?"

"Yes," I said.

Time went on. On wet days, when there was little we could do out of doors, the Captain wanted me to paint a bit here and there about the house inside. He showed me some fine enamels he had got in, and said:

"Now here's the staircase to begin with. I want that white, and I've ordered a dark red stair-carpet to put down. Then there'll be doors and windows. But I want all this done as soon as possible really; it's been left too long as it is."

I quite agreed that this was a good idea of the Captain's. He had lived carelessly enough for years past now, never troubling about the look of his house; now he had begun to take an interest in it again; it was a sort of reawakening. He took me over the place, upstairs and down, and showed me what was to be done. I noticed the pictures and sculpture in the rooms; there was a big marble lion, and paintings by Askevold and the famous Dahl. Heirlooms, I supposed they would be. Fruen's room upstairs looked just as if she were at home, with all sorts of little trifles neatly in their places, and clothes hanging still on the pegs. It was a fine old house, with moulded ceilings, and some of the walls done in costly style, but the paint-work everywhere was faded or flaking off. The staircase was broad and easy, with seats, and a mahogany handrail.

I was painting indoors one day when the Captain came in.

"It's harvest-time, I know, but this indoor work's important too. My wife will be back soon. I don't know what we're to do, really! I'd like to have the place thoroughly cleaned up."

So that letter was asking her to come back! I thought to myself. But then, again, it was some days since he had written, and I had been to the post several times myself, after, but no answer had come. I knew Fruen's writing. I had seen it six years before. But the Captain thought perhaps that he had only to say "Come," and she would obey. Well, well, he might be right; she was taking a little time to get ready, that was all.... How was I to know?

The painting had grown so important now, that the Captain went up himself to the clearing and got Lars to come down and help with the field-work in my place. Nils was by no means pleased with the exchange, for Lars was not over willing under orders on the place where he had been in charge himself in days gone by.

But there was no such need of hurry about the painting, as it turned out. The Captain sent the lad up twice to the post, but I watched for him on the way back both times, and found he had no letter from Fruen. Perhaps she was not coming after all! Ay, it might be as bad as that. Or she felt herself in a false position, and was too proud to say yes because her husband called. It might be that.

But the paint was on and had time to dry; the red stair-carpet came and was laid down with brass rods; the staircase looked wonderfully fine; wonderfully fine, too, were the doors and windows in the rooms upstairs. But Fruen did not come—no.

We got through with the rye, and set to work in good time on the barley; but Fruen did not come. The Captain went out and gazed down the road, whistling to himself; he was looking thinner now. Often and often he would come out to where we were at work, and keep with us, looking on all the time without a word. But if Nils happened to ask him anything, he did not start as if his thoughts had been elsewhere, but was quick and ready as could be. He did not seem dejected, and as for looking thin, that was perhaps because he had got Nils to cut his hair.

Then I was sent up to the post again, and this time there was a letter. Fruen's hand, and postmarked Kristianssand. I hurried back, laid the letter in among the rest of the post, and handed the whole bundle to the Captain outside the house. He took it with a careless word of thanks, showing no eagerness to see what there was; he was used to being disappointed.

"Corn coming in everywhere, I suppose?" he asked casually, glancing at the letters one after another. "What was the road like? All right?" While I was telling him, he came upon Fruen's letter, and at once packing up the whole bundle together, he turned to me with a sudden intensified interest in other people's crops and the state of the roads. Keeping himself well in hand; he was not going to show feeling openly. He nodded as he walked off, and said "Thank you" once more.

Next day the Captain came out and washed and greased the carriage himself. But it was two days more before he used it. We were sitting at supper one evening when the Captain came into the kitchen and said he wanted some one to drive him to the station tomorrow. He could have driven himself, but he was going to fetch his wife, who was coming home from abroad, and he would have to take the landau in case it rained. Nils decided, then, that Grindhusen had better drive, he being the one who could best be spared.

The rest of us went on with our field-work while they were away. There was plenty to do; besides the rye and barley not yet in, there were still potatoes to hoe and turnips to see to. But Ragnhild and the dairymaid both lent a hand; all youth and energy they were.

It might have been pleasant enough to work side by side with my old mate Lars Falkenberg once more, but he and Nils could not get on together, and instead of cheerful comradeship, a gloomy silence hung over the fields. Lars seemed to have got over his late ill-will towards me in some degree, but he was short and sullen with us all on account of Nils.

At last Nils decided that Lars should take the pair of chestnuts and get to work on the autumn ploughing. Lars was offended, and said crossly: No. He'd never heard of doing things that way before, he said, starting to plough your land before you'd got the harvest off it. "That may be," said Nils, "but I'll find you land that has been reaped enough to keep you going."

There were more words over that. Lars found everything all wrong somehow at Øvrebø. In the old days he used to do his work and sing songs after for the company at the house; now, it was all a mess and a muddle, and no sense in any way of doing things. Ploughing, indeed! Not if he knew it.

"You don't know what you're talking about," said Nils. "Nowadays you'll see folk ploughing between the corn-poles and the hay-frames."

"I've not seen it yet," said Lars. "But it seems you've seen a lot. Of all the silly goats...."

But the end of it was that Lars gave way, Nils being head man there, and went on ploughing till the Captain came home.

It crossed my mind that I had left some washing behind with Emma when I went away, before. But I judged it best not to go up to the clearing after it now, while Lars was in his present mood.

X

The Captain and his wife came next day. Nils and I had talked over whether to hoist the flag; I dared not myself, but Nils was less cautious, and said we must. So there it was, flapping broad and free from its white staff.

I was close at hand when the carriage drove up and they got out. Fruen walked out far across the courtyard, looked at the house, and clapped her hands. I heard her, too, loud in wonder as she entered the hall—at sight of the stairs, no doubt, and the new red carpet.

Grindhusen had no sooner got the horses in than he came up to me, all agape with astonishment over something, and drew me aside to talk.

"There must be something wrong," he said. "That's not Fru Falkenberg, surely? Is she married to him—the Captain, I mean?"

"Why, yes, Grindhusen, the Captain's wife is married to the Captain. What makes you ask?"

"But it's that cousin girl! I'll stake my life on it if it's not the very same one. The Inspector's cousin that was there."

"Not a bit of it, Grindhusen. But it might be her sister."

"But I'll stake my life on it. I saw her with him myself I don't know how many times."

"Well, well, she may be his cousin as far as that goes, but what's it to do with us?"

"I saw it the moment she got out of the train. And she looked at me, too, and gave a start. I could see her breathing quickly after. Don't come telling me.... But I can't make out.... Is she from here?"

"Was Fruen pleased, or did she look unhappy?" I asked.

"Nay, I don't know. Yes, I think she was." Grindhusen shook his head, still marvelling how this could be the Captain's wife. "You must have seen her with the Inspector yourself," he said. "Didn't you recognize her again?"

"Was she pleased, did you say?"

"Pleased? Why, yes, I suppose so. I don't know. They talked such a lot of queer stuff the pair of them, driving home—began at the station, the minute she got out. There was a whole lot I couldn't make out at all. 'I don't know what to say,' said she, 'but I beg you so earnestly to forgive me for it all.' 'And so do I,' says he. Now did you ever hear such a thing? And they were both of them crying, I believe, in the carriage after. 'I've had the place painted and done up a bit,' said the Captain. 'Have you?' says she. And then he went on talking about all her things, and how they were still there and never been touched. I don't know what things he meant, but he thought she'd find everything still in its place, he said. Did you ever hear the like? 'All your things,' he said. And then he went on about somebody Elisabet, and said he never gave her a thought, and never had, I think he said. And she cried like anything at that, and was all upset. But she didn't say a word about being abroad, as the Captain said. No, I'll stake my life she'd come from the Inspector."

I began to fear I had made a grave mistake in bringing Grindhusen to Øvrebø. It was done now, but I wished it undone. And I told Grindhusen himself as much, and that pretty plainly.

"Fruen here's the mistress of the place, and good and kind as could be to every one, and the Captain as well, remember that. But you'll find yourself whipped out of here, and at once, if you go gossiping and telling tales. Take my advice and be careful. You've got a good job here, with good pay and decent food. Think of that, and keep quiet while you're here."

"Yes, yes, you're right," said Grindhusen meekly enough. "I don't say a word; only, that she's the very image of that cousin down there. And did I ever say more than that? I don't know what you've got to make such a fuss about, and as for that, maybe she's a bit fairer than the cousin. I won't swear it's the same sort of hair. And I never said it was. But if you want to know what I thought, I'll tell you straight out. I was thinking she was too good to be that cousin girl. That was my very thought. 'Twould be a shame for her to be cousin to a fellow like that, and I can't think how anybody ever could. I'm not thinking about the money now; you know as well as I do I'm not the man to make a fuss over losing a two-Kroner piece, no more than you yourself, but it was a mean thing to do, all the same, giving me the money one day and taking it back the next. Ay, that it was. I say no more than that. But I don't know what's the matter with you lately, flying out the least word a man says. And what have I said, anyway? A mean lot, that he was; paid me two Kroner a day and find my own food, and always niggling and haggling over every little thing. I've had enough of your talk anyhow, but I'll tell you what was my very thought, if you want to know...."

But all his flow of talk did not avail to hide the fact that he had recognized Fruen at once, and was still convinced that he was right.

All things in order now, the Captain and Fruen at home, bright days and a rich harvest. What more could any wish for?

Fruen greets me with a kindly glance, and says:

"The place looks different altogether after the way you've painted it so nicely. The Captain's ever so pleased."

She seemed calmer now than when I had seen her last, on the stairs of the hotel in the town. She did not start and breathe quickly at sight of me as she had with Grindhusen, and that could only mean she was not displeased at seeing me again! So I thought to myself, and was glad to think so. But why had she not left off that unsteady glance, that flutter of the eyes, she had fallen into of late? If I were the Captain, now, I would speak to her about it. And her complexion, too, was not what it had been. There were some curious little spots about the temples. But what matter? She was no less pretty for that.

"I'm afraid, though," she went on, "it wasn't my idea at all with the lovely grey for the house. You must have made a mistake in thinking I said so."

"Well, then, I can't make it out. But, anyhow, it's no matter; the Captain himself decided to have it."

"The staircase is simply splendid, and so are the rooms upstairs. It's twice as bright as before...."

'Twas Fruen herself was trying to be twice as bright and

"Why, yes, Grindhusen, the Captain's wife is married twice as good as before." I knew that well enough. And she fancied she owed me these little marks of kindliness, for something or other. Well and good, but now it was enough. Best let it be.

Autumn drawing on, the scent of the jasmine all importunate down in the shrubbery, and red and yellow showing up long since on the wooded hills. Not a soul in the place but is glad to have Fruen at home again; the flag, too, does its part. 'Tis like a Sunday; the maids have put clean aprons on, fresh from the ironing.

In the evening I went down by the little stone steps to the shrubbery and sat there a while. The jasmines were pouring out waves of perfume after the heat of the day. After awhile Nils came down, looking for me.

"No visitors here now," says Nils. "And no high goings-on at nights. Have you heard anything of that sort at night now, since the Captain first came back?"

"No."

"And that's full ten weeks ago now. What d'you say if I tore off this thing now?" And he pointed to his temperance badge. "Captain's given up drinking, here's Fruen home again, and no call to be unfriendly anyway to either of them."

He handed me a knife, and I cut the badge away.

We talked for a bit about the farm-work—Nils thought of nothing else. "We'll have most of the corn under shelter by tomorrow night," he says. "And thank goodness for that! Then we'll sow the winter rye. Queer thing, isn't it? Here's Lars went on year after year sowing by machine, and thought it good enough. Not if I know it! We'll sow ours by hand."

"But why?"

"On land like ours! Now just take the man over there, for instance; he sowed by machine three weeks ago and some's come up and some not. No. The machine goes too deep in the soil."

"H'm! Don't the jasmines smell fine tonight?"

"Yes. There's been a big difference with the barley and oats these last few days. Getting on time for bed, though, now!"

He got up, but I did not move. "Looks like being fine again tomorrow," says Nils, glancing at the sky. And then he went on about the grass in the garden; worth cutting, he said it was.

"You going to stay down here long?" he asked suddenly.

"Yes, for a bit; why not? Oh, well, perhaps I'd better go up too."

167

Nils walked off a few paces, then came back again.

"Better not stay here any longer," he said. "Come along up here with me."

"Think so?" I said, and rose at once. Evidently Nils had something in his mind, and had come down here on purpose to fetch me.

Had he found me out? But what was there to find out?

Did I know myself what I had gone down to the shrubbery for? I remember now that I lay face downwards, chewing a stalk of grass. There was light in a certain upstairs window of the house. I was looking at that. And that was all.

"Not being inquisitive now, but what's the matter?" I asked.

"Nothing," said Nils. "The girls said you were down here, so I just came along. Why, what else?"

So the maids had found me out, I thought to myself, and was ill pleased at the thought. Ragnhild it must be, a devil of a girl, sharp as a needle; she must have said a lot more than Nils was willing to confess. And what if Fruen herself had seen me from the window!

I resolved now to be cold and indifferent as ice henceforward all the days of my life.

Ragnhild is properly in clover. The thick stair carpet muffles every step; she can run upstairs whenever she pleases and slip down again in a moment without a sound.

"I can't make it out about Fruen," says Ragnhild.

"Here she's come back, and ought to be happy and good tempered as could be, and instead she's all tears and frowning. I heard the Captain telling her today: 'Now do be a little reasonable, Lovise,' he said. 'I'm sorry, I won't do it any more,' says Fruen; and then she cried because she'd been unreasonable. But that about never doing it any more—she's said that now every day since she came back, but she's done it again, all the same. Poor dear, she'd a toothache today; she was simply crying out with the pain...."

"Go and get on with the potatoes, Ragnhild," said Nils quickly. "We've no time for gossiping now."

We'd all of us our field-work now; there was much to be done. Nils was afraid the corn would spoil if he left it too long at the poles; better to get it in as it was. Well and good; but that meant threshing the worst of it at once, and spreading the grain over the floor of every shed and outhouse. Even in our own big living-room there was a large layer of corn drying on the floor. Any more irons in the fire? Ay, indeed, and all the while hot and waiting. Bad weather has set in, and all the work ought to be done at once. When we've finished threshing, there's the fresh straw to be cut up and salted down in bins to keep it from rotting. That all? Not by a long way:

168

irons enough still glowing hot. Grindhusen and the maids are pulling potatoes. Nils snatches the precious time after a couple of dry days to sow a patch of rye and send the lad over it with the harrow. Lars Falkenberg is still ploughing; he has given way altogether and turned out a fine ploughman since the Captain and Fruen came back. When the corn-land's too soft he ploughs the meadows; then, when sun and wind have dried things a bit, he goes on to the corn-land again.

The work goes on steadily and well; in the afternoon the Captain himself comes out to lend a hand. The last load of corn in being brought in.

Captain Falkenberg is no child at the work, big and strong he is, and with the right knack of it. See him loading up oats from the drying-frames: his second load now.

Just then Fruen comes along down the road, and crosses over to where we are at work. Her eyes are bright. She seems pleased to watch her husband loading up corn.

"Signe Arbejdet!"[13] she says.

"Thanks," says the Captain.

"That's what we used to say in Nordland."

"What?"

"That's what we used to say in Nordland."

"Oh yes."

The Captain is busy with his work, and in the rustle of the straw he does not always hear what she says, but has to look up and ask again, and this annoys them both.

"Are the oats ripe?" she asks.

"Yes, thank goodness!"

"But not dry, I suppose?"

"Eh? I can't hear what you say."

"Oh, I didn't say anything."

A long, uncomfortable silence after that. The Captain tries once or twice with a good-humoured word, but gets no answer.

"So you're out on a round of inspection," he says jestingly. "Have you seen how the potatoes are getting on?"

"No," she answers. "But I'll go over there, by all means, if you can't bear the sight of me here."

It was too dreadful to hear them going on like this. I must have frowned unconsciously—shown some such feeling. Then, suddenly remembering that for certain reasons I was to be cold as ice, I frowned the more.

Freun looked straight at me and said:

---

[13] "A blessing on the work."

169

"What are you scowling at?"

"Scowling, eh?" says the Captain, joining in, with a forced laugh.

Fruen takes him up on the instant.

"Ah! you managed to hear that time!"

"Really, Lovise...."

Fruen's eyes dimmed suddenly; she stood a moment then ran, stooping forward, round behind the frames, and sobbed.

The Captain went over to her. "What is it, Lovise, tell me?"

"Oh, nothing, nothing! Go away."

She was sick; we could hear it. And moaning and saying: "Heaven help me!"

"My wife's not very well just now," says the Captain to me. "We can't make out what it is."

"There's sickness in the neighbourhood," I suggested, for something to say. "Sort of autumn fever. I heard about it up at the post office."

"Is there, though? Why, there you are, Lovise," he calls out. "There's some sort of fever about, it seems. That's all it is."

Fruen made no answer.

We went on loading up, and Fruen moved farther and farther away as we came up. At last the frames were cleared, and she stood there guiltily, very pale after her trouble.

"Shall I see you back to the house?" asked the Captain.

"No, thank you, I'd rather not," she answered, walking away.

The Captain stayed out and worked with us till evening.

So here was everything gone wrong again. Oh, but it was hard for them both!

And it was not just a little matter that could be got over by a little give and take on either side, as folk say; no, it was a thing insuperable, a trouble rooted deep. And now it had come to mutiny, no less: Fruen had taken to locking her door at night. Ragnhild had heard the Captain, highly offended, talking to her through the wall.

But that evening the Captain had demanded to speak with her in her room before she went to bed. Fruen agreed, and there was a further scene. Each was willing and anxious, no doubt, to set matters right, but it was hopeless now; it was too late. We sat in the kitchen, Nils and I, listening to Ragnhild's story. I had never seen Nils look so miserable before.

"If things go wrong again now, it's all over," he said. "I thought to myself last summer that perhaps a good, sound thrashing would do her good. But that was just foolishness, I can see now. Did she talk about running away again?"

"She said something about it," answered Ragnhild. And then

she went on something like this: "It began with the Captain asking if she didn't think it was this local sickness she had got. Fruen answered it could hardly be any local sickness that had turned her against him so. 'Turned you against me?' 'Yes. Oh, I could scream sometimes. At table, for instance, the way you eat and eat....' 'Do I?' says the Captain. 'Well, I can't see there's anything very wrong in that; it's just natural. There's no rule for how much one ought to eat at a meal.' 'But to have to sit and look at you—it makes me sick. It's that that makes me ill.' 'Well, anyhow, you can't say I drink too much now,' said he. 'So it's better than it was.' 'No, indeed, it's worse!' Then says the Captain: 'Well, really, I do think you might make allowances for me a little, after I've—I mean, considering what you did yourself this summer.' 'Yes, you're right,' says Fruen, beginning to cry. 'If you knew how it hurts and plagues me night and day, thinking of that.... But I've never said a word.' 'No, I know,' says she, crying all the more. 'And I asked you myself to come back,' he said. But at that she seemed to think he was taking too much credit to himself; she stopped crying, and answered, with a toss of her head: 'Yes, and it would have been better if you'd never asked me back, if it was only to go on like this.' 'Like what?' says he. 'You've your own way in everything now. The same as before, only you don't care for anything at all. You never touch the piano, even; only go about cross and irritable all the time; there's no pleasing you with anything. And you shut your door at night and lock me out. Well and good; lock me out if you like!' 'It's you that are hard to please, if you ask me,' she said. 'There's never a night and never a morning but I'm worried out of my life lest you shall be thinking of—this summer. You've never said a word about it, you say. Oh, don't you, though! I'm never left long in peace without you throwing it in my teeth. I happened to say "Hugo" one day, by a slip of the tongue, and what did you do? You might have been nice and comforted me to help me over it, but you only scowled and said you were not Hugo. No. I knew well enough, and I was ever so sorry to have said it.' 'That's just the point,' said the Captain. 'Were you really sorry?' 'Yes, indeed,' said Fruen; 'it hurt me ever so.' 'Well, I shouldn't have thought it; you don't seem very upset about it.' 'Ah, but what about you? Haven't you anything to be sorry for?' 'You've got photos of Hugo on your piano still; I haven't seen you move them away yet, though I've shown you not once but fifty times I wished you to—yes, and begged you to do it.' 'Oh, what a fuss you make about those photos!' said she. 'Oh, don't make any mistake! I'm not asking you now. If you went and shifted them now, it would make no difference. I've begged and prayed of you fifty times before. Only, I think it would have been a little more decent if you'd burned

171

them the day you came home. But, instead of that, you've books here lying about in your room with his name in. And there's a handkerchief with his initials on, I see.' 'Oh, it's all your jealousy,' answered Fruen. 'I can't see what difference it makes. I can't kill him, as you'd like me to, and Papa and Mama say the same. After all, I've lived with him and been married to him.' 'Married to him?' 'Yes, that's what I say. It isn't every one that looks at Hugo and me the way you do.' The Captain sat a while, shaking his head. 'And it's all your own fault, really,' Fruen went on, 'the way you drove off with Elisabet that time, though I came and asked you not to go. It was then it happened. And we'd been drinking that evening. I didn't quite know what I was doing.' Still, the Captain said nothing for a while; then at last he said: 'Yes, I ought not to have gone off like that.' 'No, but you did,' said Fruen, and started crying again. 'You wouldn't hear a word. And you're always throwing it in my teeth about Hugo, but you never think of what you've done yourself.' 'There's just this difference,' says the Captain, 'that I've never lived with the lady you mention, never been married to her, as you call it.' Fruen gave a little scornful laugh. 'Never!' said the Captain, striking the table with his hand. Fruen gave a start, and sat staring at him. 'Then—I don't understand why you were always running after her and sitting out in the summer-house and lurking in corners,' said she. 'It was you that sat out in the summer-house,' he answered. 'Oh yes, it's always me,' said she. 'Never you by any chance!' 'As for my running after Elisabet,' said the Captain, 'it was solely and simply in the hopes of getting you back. You'd drifted away from me, and I wanted you.' Fruen sat thinking over that for a minute, then she sprang up and threw her arms around him and said: 'Oh, then you cared for me all the time! And I thought it was all over. You'd drifted away from me, too; it was years since. And it all seemed so hopeless. I never thought—I never knew.... And then it was me you cared for all the time! Oh, my dear, then it's all come right again.' 'Sit down,' said he. 'You seem to forget that something else has happened since.' 'Something else?' 'There you are, you've forgotten all about it. May I ask you, are you sorry enough for what's happened since?' At that Fruen turned hard again and said: 'Oh, you mean about Hugo? That's done and can't be altered.' 'That doesn't answer the question.' 'If I'm sorry enough? What about you; are you so innocent yourself?' At this the Captain got up and began walking up and down. 'The trouble is that we've no children,' said Fruen. 'I haven't a daughter that I could teach and bring up to be better than I am,' 'I've thought of that,' said the Captain, 'perhaps you're right.' Then he turned straight towards her and said: 'It's a nasty crash that's come over us, Lovise—like a landslide. But don't you think now we might set to

172

work and shift away all the wreckage that's been burying us for years, and get clear and breathe again? You might have a daughter yet!' At that Fruen got up and made as if to say something, but couldn't. 'Yes,' was all she said, and 'Yes,' she said again. 'You're tired and nervous, I know,' he said. 'But think a little over what I've said. Another time.' 'Good-night,' said she."

XI

The Captain spoke to Nils about the timber; he thought of disposing of the whole lot, or selling it standing. Nils took this to mean that he didn't like the idea of having more new folk about the place. "It looks like things are as bad as ever with him and Fruen," said Nils.

We are getting in the potatoes now, and since we are thus far there is less hurry and anxiety about the work. But there is still much to be done. The ploughing is behindhand, and Lars Falkenberg and I are both at it, field and meadow land.

Nils, queer creature that he was, began to find things intolerable at Øvrebø again, and talked of throwing up his place and going off altogether. But he couldn't bear the disgrace of leaving his service like that. Nils had his own clear notions of honour, handed down through many generations. A young man from a big farm could not behave like a lad from a cottar's holding. And then he hadn't been here long enough yet; Øvrebø had been sadly ill-managed before he came: it would take some years to bring it round again. It was only this year, when he'd had more help with the work, that he'd been able to do anything properly. But from now onward he might begin to look for some result of his work; look at this year's harvest, the fine heavy grain! The Captain, too, had looked at the crops with wonder and thankfulness—the first time for many years. There would be plenty to sell.

All things considered, then, it was senseless for Nils to think of leaving Øvrebø. But he must go home for a couple of days to his people—they lived a little way north of us. So he gave himself two days' leave as soon as the potatoes were all out of the ground. No doubt he'd good reason for going—perhaps to see his sweetheart, we thought—and when he came back he was bright and full of energy as ever, and took up work again at once.

We were sitting at dinner in the kitchen one day when out comes Fruen from the front door of the house, and goes tearing down the road, all wild and excited. Then the Captain came out,

173

calling after her: "Lovise, what is it, Lovise? Where are you going?" But Fruen only called back: "Leave me alone!"

We looked at one another. Ragnhild rose from the table; she must go after her mistress, she said.

"That's right," said Nils, calm as ever. "But go indoors first and see if she's moved those photographs."

"They're still there," said Ragnhild as she went out.

Outside, we heard the Captain telling her to go and look after her mistress.

There was no one but took thought for Fruen in her distress.

We went out to the fields again. Said Nils to me:

"She ought to take away those photos; it's not right of her to leave them there. I don't know what she can be thinking of to do it."

What do you know about it? I thought to myself. Oh, I was so clever with my knowledge of the world, and all I'd learned on my wanderings, I thought I would try him now; perhaps he was only showing off.

"I can't understand why the Captain hasn't taken and burnt them long ago," said I.

"No, that's all wrong," said Nils. "I wouldn't have done that either."

"Oh, indeed!"

"It wouldn't be for me to do it, but for her."

We walked on a little. And then Nils said a thing that showed his sound and right instinct.

"Poor lady!" he said. "She's not got over that slip of hers this summer; it's troubling her still. From all I can see, there's some people pick up again all right after a fall, and go on through life with no more than the mark of a bruise. But there's some that never get over it."

"Fruen seems to be taking it easy enough," said I, still trying him.

"How can we tell? She's been unlike herself, to my mind, ever since she's been back," he answered. "She's got to live, of course, but she's lost all harmony, perhaps. I don't know much about it, but harmony, that's what I mean. Oh yes, she can eat and laugh and sleep, no doubt, but ... I followed one such to the grave, but now...."

And at that I was no longer cold and wise, but foolish and ashamed, and only said:

"So it was that? She died, then?"

"Yes. She wished it so," said Nils. And then suddenly: "Well, you and Lars get on with the ploughing. We ought soon to be through with things now."

And we went each our separate way.

I thought to myself: a sister of his, perhaps, that had gone wrong, and he'd been home and followed her to the grave. Herregud! there are some that never get over it; it shakes them to their foundations; a revolution. All depends on whether they're coarse enough. Only the mark of a bruise, said Nils. A sudden thought came to me, and I stopped: perhaps it was not his sister, but his sweetheart.

Some association of ideas led me to think of my washing. I decided to send the lad up for it.

It was evening.

Ragnhild came to me and begged me to keep awake again; there was dreadful trouble up at the house. Ragnhild herself was greatly upset, and dared not sit anywhere now in the half-dark but upon my knees. It was always so with her; emotion made her frightened and tender—frightened and tender, yes.

"But can you be away like this? Is there any one in your place in the kitchen?" I asked.

"Yes. Cook's going to listen for the bell. You know, I side with the Captain," she declared. "I've sided with him all along."

"Oh, that's only because he's a man."

"No, it's not."

"You'd much better side with Fruen."

"You only say that because she's a woman," answered Ragnhild in her turn. "But you don't know all I do. Fruen's so unreasonable. We didn't care a bit about her, she said, and left her all to herself, whatever might happen. Did you ever hear such a thing, when I'd just gone after her. And then there's another dreadful thing...."

"I don't want to hear any more," I said.

"But I haven't been listening outside—what are you thinking of? I was there in the same room, and heard them."

"Did you? Well, well, stay here till you've calmed down a little; then we'll go and find Nils."

And so frightened and tender was Ragnhild that she threw her arms round me because I was kind to her. A strange girl!

Then we went down to Nils.

"Ragnhild thinks that somebody ought to keep awake for a bit," I said.

"Yes," said Ragnhild. "Oh, it's so dreadful—worse than ever it's been! Heaven knows what the Captain'll do! Perhaps he won't go to bed at all. Oh, she's fond of him and he's fond of her, too; only, everything's all wrong! When she went running off like that today, the Captain was standing outside the house, and said to me: 'Go and look after your mistress, Ragnhild,' and I went after her, and there

175

she was, standing behind a tree down the road, and she just stood there, crying, and smiled at me. I tried to get her to come in again, but she said we didn't care about her; it didn't matter where she went. 'The Captain sent me after you,' said I. 'Did he, though?' she asked. 'Now? Was it just now?' 'Yes,' said I. 'Wait, then,' she said, and stood quite a while. 'Take those hateful books that are lying in my room and burn them,' she said; and then: 'Oh no, I'll do it myself, but I'll ring for you after supper, and then you must come up at once.' 'I will,' said I, and then I got her to come in."

"And you know," said Ragnhild suddenly, "she's going to have a child."

We looked at one another. Nils' face grew, as it were, veiled beneath a film of something indistinct. All expression faded, the eyes asleep. But why should it affect him so? For the sake of saying something, I turned to Ragnhild and asked:

"Fruen was going to ring for you, you said?"

"Yes, and so she did. There was something she wanted to tell the Captain, but she was afraid, and wanted to have me there. 'Light a candle and pick up all this host of buttons I've upset,' she said. And then she called out to the Captain in his room. I lit the candle and began picking up buttons; dozens of them there were, all sorts. The Captain came in. 'I only wanted to tell you,' says Fruen at once, 'that it was kind of you to send Ragnhild after me to-day. Heaven bless you for that!' 'Never mind about that, my dear,' says he. 'You were nervous, you know.' 'Yes, I'm all nerves just now,' she answered, 'but I hope it'll get better in time. No, the trouble is that I haven't a daughter I could bring up to be really good. There's nothing I can do!' The Captain sat down on a chair. 'Oh yes, there is,' he said. 'Yes, you say? Oh, I know it says in that book there.... Oh, those hateful books!—Ragnhild take them away and burn them,' she says. 'No, wait, I'll tear them to bits now myself and put them in the stove here.' And then she started pulling them to pieces, taking ever so many pages at a time and throwing them in the stove. 'Don't be so excited, Lovise,' said the Captain. 'The Nunnery," she said— that was one of the books. 'But I can't go into a nunnery. There's nothing I can do. When I laugh, you think I'm laughing,' she said to the Captain, 'but I'm miserable all the time and not laughing a bit.' 'Is your toothache any better?' he asked. 'Oh, that toothache won't be better for a long time to come!' she said; 'you know that well enough.' 'No, indeed, I don't.' 'You don't know?' 'No.' 'But, heavens! can't you see what's the matter with me?' said Fruen. The Captain only looked at her and did not answer. 'I'm—oh, you said today I might have a daughter after all, don't you remember?' I happened to look up at the Captain just then...."

Ragnhild smiled and shook her head; then she went on:

"Heaven forgive me for smiling, but the Captain's face was so queer; he stood there like a sheep. 'Didn't you guess as much before?' asked Fruen. The Captain looked over at me and said: 'What's that you're doing there all this time?' 'I asked her to pick up those buttons for me,' said Fruen. 'I've finished now,' said I. 'Have you?' said Fruen, getting up. 'Let me see.' And she took the box and dropped them again all over the floor. Oh, they went rolling all over the place, under the table, under the bed and the stove! 'There, now, did you ever see such a mess?' said Fruen. But then she went off again at once talking about herself, and said again: 'But I can't understand you didn't you see I was—didn't see what was the matter with me.' Can't those buttons wait till tomorrow?' said the Captain. 'Why, yes, perhaps they can,' said Fruen. 'But then I'll be treading on them everywhere. I can't ... I'm rather afraid of stooping just now.... But, never mind, we'll leave them for now,' she said, and stroked his hand. 'Oh, my dear, my dear!' she says. But he drew his hand away. 'Oh, so you're angry with me!' she said. 'But then, why did you write and ask me to come back?' 'My dear Lovise, we're not alone here,' he says. 'But surely you must know what made you write?' 'I suppose it was because I hoped things would come right again.' 'And they didn't?' 'Well, no!' 'But what was in your mind when you wrote? Were you thinking of me? Did you want me again? I can't make out what was in your mind.' 'Ragnhild's finished, I see,' said the Captain. 'Good-night, Ragnhild!'"

"And then you came away?"

"Yes, but I dare not go far because of Fruen. You may be sure it wasn't nice for her when I was out of the room, so I had to be somewhere at hand. And if the Captain had come and found me and said anything, I'd have told him straight out I wasn't going farther away with Fruen in the state she was. As it happened, he didn't come at all, but they began again in there. 'I know what you're thinking of,' said Fruen—'that perhaps it's not ... it wouldn't be your child. Oh yes, indeed it might be so! But, God knows, I can't find words this moment to make you forgive me!' she said, all crying. 'Oh, my dear, forgive me, forgive me!' said Fruen, and went down on her knees on the floor. 'You've seen what I did with the books, and that handkerchief with the initials on—I burnt that before, and the books, you know....' 'Yes, and—here's another handkerchief with the same initials on—' says the Captain. 'Oh, heavens! yes, you're ever so considerate, Lovise.' Fruen was all upset at that. 'I'm sorry you should have seen it,' she said. 'It must be one I brought back with me when I came home. I haven't looked through my things properly since. But does it really matter so very much? Surely—' 'Oh no,' said he. 'And if you'd only listen to me,' she went on, I'm almost certain it's you that ... I mean, that the child is yours. Why should it not be? Oh, I don't know how to say it!' 'Sit down again,' said the Captain. But Fruen must have misunderstood; she got up and said: 'There you are! You won't listen to me. Really, I can't make out why you ever wrote to me at all. You might just as well have left me alone.' Then the Captain said something about being in prison; if a man grew up in a prison yard, he said, and you take him out, he'll long to be back in his prison yard again, he said. It was something like that, anyway. 'Yes, but I was with Papa and Mama, and they weren't hard like you; they said I had been married to him, and weren't unkind to me at all. It isn't every one that looks at things like you do,' 'You don't want that candle alight now Ragnhild's gone, do you?' said the Captain. 'It looks so out of place to have it burning there beside the lamp—as if it were ashamed.' 'Ashamed of me,' she says quickly. 'Oh yes, that was what you meant. But you've been to blame as well.' 'Don't misunderstand me,' he says. 'I know I've been to blame. But that doesn't make your part any better.' 'Oh, you think not? Well, of all the.... So yours doesn't count, then?' 'Yes, I say I've been to blame, not in the way you mean, but in other ways—in old things and new.' 'Oh, indeed!' 'Yes, but I don't come home bringing the fruits of it under my heart to you.' 'No,' says Fruen, 'but you know it was you all along that wouldn't ... that didn't want us to have children. And I didn't want it, either, but you ought to have known better. And they said the same thing at home. If only I'd had a daughter....' 'Oh, don't let's go over all that again,' says the Captain—he called it something or other—a romance, I think it was. 'But it's true,' says Fruen, 'and I can't think how you can deny it.' 'I'm not denying anything. Do sit down, now, Lovise, and listen to me. All this about having children, and a daughter to bring up and so on, it's something you've picked up lately. And, you snatched at the idea at once, to save yourself. But you never said a word about wanting children before—not that I ever heard.' 'Yes, but you ought to have known better.' 'There again, that's something you've heard, something new. But it doesn't matter: quite possibly things might have been different if we'd had children. I can see that myself now, but now it's too late, more's the pity. And here you are now—like that....' 'Oh, heavens, yes! But I tell you it may be yours after all—I don't know.... Oh!...' 'Mine? said the Captain, shaking his head. 'Well, the mother should be the one to know. But in this case, it seems, she doesn't. The woman I'm married to doesn't know—or do you?' But Fruen did not answer. 'Do you know? I ask you!' Oh, but again she could not answer, only slipped down to the floor again and cried. Really, I don't know—but perhaps I'm on her side after all; it was dreadful for her, poor thing. And then I was just going to knock at the door and go in, but then the Captain went on again. 'You can't say it,' he said. 'But that's an answer in itself, and plain enough.' 'I can't say more,' said Fruen. She was still crying. 'I'm fond of you for lots of things, Lovise,' says the Captain, 'and one of them's because you're truthful.' 'Thank you,' she says. 'They haven't taught you to lie as yet. Get up, now.' And he helped her up himself, and set her in the chair. But it was pitiful to see her crying so. 'Don't cry, now,' he says. 'I want to ask you something. Shall we wait and see what it's like when it comes—what sort of eyes it has, and so on?' 'Oh, heaven bless you, yes, if you would! Oh, my dear, God bless you, God bless you.' 'And I'll try to bear with things as they are. It's an aching misery all the time, but I'll try. And I've been to blame as well.' 'God bless you, God bless you!' she said again. 'And you,' he said. 'And now good-night until tomorrow.' Then Fruen leaned down over the table and cried and cried so dreadfully. 'What are you crying for now?' he asked. 'You're going,' she said. 'Oh, I was afraid of you before, but now I can't bear to be without you. Couldn't you stay a little?' 'Stay here, with you, now?' he asked. 'Oh no, I didn't mean ... it wasn't that ... only, it's so lonely. I didn't mean....' 'No,' said the Captain. 'You can understand I don't feel like staying any longer now. Ring for the maid!'"

"And then I had to run," Ragnhild concluded.

Said Nils, after a while: "Have they gone to bed now?"

Ragnhild could not say. Yes. Perhaps. Anyhow, Cook was there in case. "But, only think of it, how dreadful! I don't suppose Fruen can sleep."

"You'd better go and see if there's anything you can do."

"Yes," said Ragnhild, getting up. "But I side with the Captain after all, and no mistake, whatever you say. Yes, that I do."

"It's none so easy to know what's right."

"Only think of letting that engineer creature.... How she ever could, I don't know! And then to go down and stay with him there, after, as she did; what a thing to do! And she's all those handkerchiefs of his, ever so many, and a lot of her own are gone; I suppose they used each other's anyhow. Lived with him, she said! And she with a husband of her own!"

XII

The Captain has done as he said about the timber; there's a cracking and crashing in the woods already. And a mild autumn, too, with no frost in the ground as yet to stop the ploughing; Nils grasps at the time like a miser, to save as much as possible next spring.

Now comes the question whether Grindhusen and I are to work on the timber. It crosses my mind that I had intended really to go off for a tramp up in the hills and over the moors while the berries were there; what about that journey now? And another thing, Grindhusen was no longer worth his keep as a wood-cutter; he could hold one end of a saw, but that was about all he was good for now.

No, for Grindhusen was changed somehow; devil knows how it had come about. He had not grown bald at all; his hair was there, and thick and red as ever. But he had picked up a deal at Øvrebø, and went about bursting with health and good feeding; well off here? He had sent good sums of money home to his family all that summer and autumn, and was full of praise for Captain and Freun, who paid such good wages and treated their folk so well. Not like the Inspector, that weighed and counted every miserable Skilling, and then, as true as God's in heaven, go and take off two Kroner that he'd given as clear as could be ... ugh! He, Grindhusen, was not the man to make a fuss about a wretched two Kroner, as long as it was a matter of any sense or reason, but to go and take it off like that—fy Fan! Would you ever find the Captain doing such a thing?

But Grindhusen was grown so cautious now, and wouldn't even get properly angry with any one. Even yet, perhaps, he might go back and work for the Inspector on the river at two Kroner a day, and humbly agree with all his master said. Age, time, had overtaken him.

It overtakes us all.

Said the Captain:

"That water-supply you spoke about—is it too late to do anything with it this year?"

"Yes," I answered.

The Captain nodded and walked away.

I ploughed one day more, then the Captain came to me again. He was out and about everywhere these days, working hard, keeping an eye on everything. He gave himself barely time for a proper meal, but was out again at once, in the fields, the barn, the cattle-sheds, or up in the woods where the men were at work.

"You'd better get to work on that water-supply," he said. "The ground's workable still, and may stay so for a long time yet. What help will you want?"

"Grindhusen can help," I said. "But...."

"Yes, and Lars. What were you going to say?"

180

"The frost may set in any day now."

"Well, and then it may snow and soften the ground again. We're not frost-bound here every year," said the Captain. "You'd better take a few extra hands, and set some of them to digging, the rest to the masonry work. You've done all this before, I think you said?"

"Yes."

"And I've spoken to Nils myself," he said, with a smile. "So you'll have no trouble in that way. You can put the horses in now."

So bravely cheerful he was, I could not help feeling the same, and wanted to begin at once; I hurried back with the horses, almost at a run. The Captain seemed quite eager about this water-supply, now that the place looked so nice with its new paint, and after the fine harvest we'd had. And now he was cutting a thousand dozen battens in the woods, to pay off his debts and leave something over!

So I went off up the rising ground, and found the old place I had marked down long before for the reservoir, took the depth down to the house, pacing and measuring this way and that. There was a streamlet came down from the hillside far above, with such a depth and fall that it never froze in winter; the thing would be to build a small stone reservoir here, with openings at the sides for the overflow in autumn and spring. Oh, but they should have their water-supply at Øvrebø! As for the masonry work, we could break out our stone on the site itself; there was layer on layer of granite there.

By noon next day we were hard at work, Lars Falkenberg digging the trench for the pipe-line, Grindhusen and I getting stone. We were both well used to this work from the days when we had been road-making together at Skreia.

Well and good.

We worked four days; then it was Sunday. I remember that Sunday, the sky clear and far, the leaves all fallen in the woods, and the hillside showing only its calm winter green; smoke rose from the chimney up in the clearing. Lars had borrowed a horse and cart that afternoon to drive in to the station; he had killed a pig and was sending it in to town. He was to fetch letters for the Captain on the way back.

It occurred to me that this evening would be a good time to send the lad up to the clearing for my washing: Lars was away, and no one could take offence at that washing business now.

Oh yes, I said to myself, you're very careful to do what's right and proper, sending the lad up to fetch that washing. But you'll find it isn't that at all. Right and proper, indeed; you're getting old, that's what it is.

I bore with this reproach for an hour. Then—well, it was all nonsense, like as not, and here was a lovely evening, and Sunday into the bargain, nothing to do, no one to talk to down here.... Getting old, was I? Afraid of the walk uphill?

And I went up myself.

Early next morning Lars Falkenberg came over again. He drew me aside, as he had done once before, and with the same intent: I had been up to the clearing yesterday, it seemed; it was to be the last time, and would I please to make no mistake about that!

"It was the last of my washing, anyhow," I said.

"Oh, you and your washing! As if I couldn't have brought along your miserable shirt a hundred times since you've been here!"

Now, by what sort of magic had he got to know of my little walk up there already? Ragnhild, of course, at her old tricks again—it could be no one else. There was no doing anything with that girl.

But now, as it happened, Nils was at hand this time, as he had been the time before. He came strolling over innocently from the kitchen, and in a moment Lars's anger was turned upon him instead.

"Here's the other scarecrow coming up, too," says Lars, "and he's a long sight worse than you."

"What's that you say?" said Nils.

"What's that you say!" retorted Lars. "You go home and rinse your mouth with a mixture or something, and see if you can talk plain," said he.

Nils stopped short at this, and came up to see what it was all about.

"I don't know what you're talking about," said he.

"No, of course not. You don't know anything that's any sense. But you know all about ploughing in standing crops, don't you? There's not many can beat you at that."

But here Nils grew angry for once, and his cheeks paled.

"What an utter fool you are, Lars! Can't you keep your mouth shut with that nonsense?"

"Fool, eh? Hark at the silly goat!" said Lars, turning to me. "Thinks himself mighty fine, doesn't he? 'Utter'" he says—and goes white about it. "I've been more years than you at Øvrebø, and asked in to sing up at the house of an evening more than once, let me tell you. But things have changed since then, and what have we got instead? You remember," he said, turning to me, "what it was like in the old days. It was Lars here and Lars there, and I never heard but the work got done all right. And after me it was Albert, that was here for eighteen months. But then you, Nils, came along, and now it's toil and moil and ploughing and carting manure day and night, till a man's worn to a thread with it all."

Nils and I could not help laughing at this. And Lars was in no way offended; he seemed quite pleased at having said something funny, and, forgetting his ill-will, joined in the laugh himself.

"Yes, I say it straight out," said he. "And if it wasn't for you being a friendly sort between whiles—no, friendly I won't say, but someways decent and to get on with after a fashion ... if it wasn't for that...."

"Well, what then?"

Lars was getting more and more good humoured. "Oh," he said, with a laugh, "I could just pick you up and stuff you down in your own long boots."

"Like to feel my arm?" said Nils.

"What's going on here?" asked the Captain, coming up. It was only six o'clock, but he was out and about already.

"Nothing," said Lars and Nils as well.

"How's the reservoir getting on?" asked the Captain. This was to me, but before I could answer he turned to Nils. "I shall want the boy to drive me to the station," he said. "I'm going to Christiania."

Grindhusen and I went off to our work on the reservoir, and Lars to his digging. But a shadow seemed to have fallen over us all.

Grindhusen himself said openly: "Pity the Captain's going away."

I thought so, too. But he was obliged to go in on business, no doubt. There were the crops as well as the timber to be sold. But why should he start at that hour of the day? He couldn't catch the early train in any case. Had there been trouble again? Was he anxious to be out of the way before Fruen got up?

Trouble there was, often enough.

It had gone so far by this time that the Captain and Fruen hardly spoke to one another, and whenever they did exchange a word it was in a careless tone, and looking all the other way. Now and again the Captain would look his wife properly in the face, and say she ought to be out more in the lovely air; and once when she was outside he asked if she wouldn't come in and play a little. But this, perhaps, was only to keep up appearances, no more.

It was pitiful to see.

Fruen was quiet and nice. Now and again she would stand outside on the steps looking out towards the hills; so soft her features were, and her reddish yellow hair. But it was dull for her now—no visitors, no music and entertaining, nothing but sorrow and shame.

The Captain had promised to bear with things as they were,

and surely he was bearing all he could. But he could do no more. Disaster had come to the home, and the best will in the world could not shoulder it off. If Fruen happened to be hasty, as she might now and then, and forgot to be grateful, the Captain would look down at the floor, and it would not be long before he put on his hat and went out. All the maids knew about it, and I had seen it myself once or twice. He never forgot what she had done—how could he?—though he could keep from speaking of it. But could he keep from speaking of it when she forgot herself and said:

"You know I'm not well just now; you know I can't walk far like I used to!"

"S—sh, Lovise!" he would say, with a frown. And then the mischief was there as bad as ever.

"Oh, of course you must bring that up again!"

"No, indeed! It's you that brought it up yourself. You've lost all sense of modesty, I think; you seem to have no shame left."

"Oh, I wish I'd never come back at all! I was better off at home!"

"Yes, or living with that puppy, I dare say."

"You said he'd helped you once yourself. And I often wish I were back there with him again. Hugo's a great deal better than you are."

She was all irresponsible in her words, going, perhaps, further than she meant. But she was changed out of knowledge to us all, and spoiled and shameless now. Fru Falkenberg shameless! Nay, perhaps not; who could say? Yet she was not ashamed to come out in the kitchen of an evening and say nice things to Nils about how young and strong he was. I was jealous again, no doubt, and envied Nils for his youth, for I thought to myself: Is every one gone mad? Surely we older ones are far to be preferred! Was it his innocence that attracted her? Or was she merely trying to keep up her spirits a little—trying to be younger than she was? But then one day she came up to the reservoir where Grindhusen and I were at work, and sat watching us for a while. It was easy work then for half an hour; the granite turned pliable, and yielded to our will; we built away like giants. Oh, but Fruen sat there irresponsible as ever, letting her eyes play this way and that. Why could she not rid herself of this new habit of hers? Her eyes were too earnest for such playing; it did not suit her. I thought to myself, either she was trying to make up for her foolishness towards Nils by favouring us in turn, or starting a new game altogether—which would it be? I could not make it out, and as for Grindhusen, he saw nothing in it at all, but only said, when Fruen had gone: "Eh, she's a strange, kind-hearted soul, is

Fruen. Almost like a mother. Only fancy going and feeling if the water wasn't too cold for us!"

One day, when I was standing by the kitchen entrance, she said:

"Do you remember the old days here—when you first came?"

She had never once spoken of this till now, and I did not know what to say. I stammered out: Yes, I remembered.

"You drove me down to the Vicarage once," she said.

Then I half fancied that perhaps she was not disinclined to talk to me and occupy her mind a little; I felt I must help her, make it easier for her. And perhaps I was a little touched myself at the thought.

"Yes," I said, "I remember. It was a glorious drive. But Fruen must have found it cold towards the last."

"It was you that must have felt cold," she answered. "You lent me your own rug from the box. Oh, you poor thing!"

I was even more moved at this, and foolish ideas came into my head. Ah, then she had not forgotten me! The few years that had passed since then had not made so much difference in me after all!

"Fruen must be mistaken about the rug, I think," said I. "But I remember we stopped at a cottage to eat, and the woman made coffee, and you gave me things yourself."

As I spoke, I leaned up against the fence, with my arms round a post. Perhaps this somehow offended her, looking as if I expected her to stand gossiping there with me. And then I had said, "We stopped at a cottage," as if we had been equals. It was a bad mistake on my part, of course, but I had got a little out of hand after all these vagabond months.

I stood up straight again the moment I saw she was displeased, but it was too late. She was just as kind as ever, but she had grown suspicious and easily hurt with all her trouble, and found rudeness in what was merely awkwardness of mine.

"Well, well," she said, "I hope you find yourself as comfortable now at Øvrebø as before."

And she nodded and walked away.

Some days passed. The Captain had not come back, but he had sent a post card, with a kind message, to Fruen: he hoped to be home again next week. He was also sending pipes, taps, and cement for the water supply.

Fruen showed me that card. "Here," she said, "the Captain has sent these things for your work. You had better get them down from the station."

We stood there together, looking at the card; mid-day it was, and we were just outside the house. I can't say how it was, but I was standing there quite close to her, with my head bent in towards hers, and it made me feel happy all through. When she had finished reading she looked up at me. No play of her eyes now; but she must have caught some expression in my face, for she looked at me still. Did she feel my presence as I felt hers? Those two heavy eyes raised towards mine and held there were loaded to the brim with love. She could not be responsible for her actions now. There was a pathological depth in her glance, an influence from far within, from the life she bore under her heart. Her breath came heavily, her face flushed dark all over, then she swung round and walked slowly away.

There I stood, with the card in my hand. Had she given it to me? Had I taken it?

"Your card," I said. "Shall I...."

She held out her hand without looking round, and walked on.

This little episode occupied my mind a great deal for some days. Ought I to have gone after her when she walked away? Oh, I might have tried, might have made the attempt—her door was not far off. Pathological? But what had she brought me the card for at all? She could have told me by word of mouth what there was to say. I called to mind how six years before we had stood in just that same way reading a telegram the Captain had sent her. Did she find pleasure in situations of that sort, and go out of her way to seek them?

Next time I saw her there was no trace of any embarassment in her manner—she was kind and cold. So I had to let it drop altogether. And, anyhow, what did I want with her at all? No, indeed!

Some visitors came to see her one day—a neighbour's wife, with her daughter. They had heard, no doubt, that the Captain was away, and thought she might be glad of a little society; or perhaps they had come out of curiosity. They were well received; Fru Falkenberg was amiable as ever, and even played the piano for them. When they left, she went with them down to the road, talking sensibly of practical affairs, though she might well have had other things in her head than coops and killing pigs. Oh, she was full of kindly interest in it all! "Come again soon—or you, at any rate, Sofie...." "Thanks, thanks. But aren't you ever coming over to us at Nedrebø?" "Oh, I? Of course—yes. I'd walk down with you now if it weren't so late." "Well, tomorrow, then?" "Yes, perhaps I might come over tomorrow.—Oh, is that you?" This was to Ragnhild, who had come down with a shawl. "Oh, what an idea!—did you think I should catch cold?"

Altogether things were looking brighter now at Øvrebø; we no

186

longer felt that shadow of uneasiness over us all. Grindhusen and I worked away at our famous reservoir, and Lars was getting on farther every day with his trench. Seeing the Captain was away, I wanted to make the most of the time, and perhaps have the work nearly done by the time he came back; it would be a grand thing if we could get it finished altogether! He would be all the better for a pleasant little surprise, for—yes, there had been something of a scene the night before he left. Some new reminder, no doubt, of the trouble that had come upon his house; a book, perhaps, still unburnt, lying about in Fruen's room. He had ended up by saying: "Anyhow, I'm cutting timber now to pay it off. And the harvest we've got in means a lot of money. So I hope the Lord will forgive me—as I do Him. Good-night, Lovise."

When we had laid the last stone of the reservoir, and cement over all, I went down with Grindhusen to help Lars with the trench—we took a section each. The work went on easily and with a will—here and there a stone had to be blasted out, or a tree felled up in the woods; but the trench moved steadily upwards, until we had a long black line from the house to the reservoir itself. Then we went back again and dug it out to the proper depth. This was no ornamental work, but a trench—an underground resting place for some pipes that were to be buried on the spot. All we were concerned with was to get down below the reach of frost, and that before the frost itself came to hinder us. Already it was coating the fields at night. Nils himself left all else now, and came to lend a hand.

But masonry and digging trenches are but work for the hands; my brain in its idleness was busy all the while with every conceivable idea. As often as I thought of that episode with the post card, it sent, as it were, a glow all through me. Why should I think any more about it? No, of course not. And I had not followed her to the door after all.

But there she stood, and you there. Her breath came towards you—a taste of flesh. Out of a darkness she was, nay, not of earth. And her eyes—did you mark her eyes?

And each time something in me turned at the thought—a nausea. A meaningless succession of names poured in upon me, places of wild and tender sound, whence she might be: Uganda, Antananarivo, Honolulu, Venezuela, Atacama. Verse? Colours? I knew not what to do with the words.

XIII

Fruen has ordered the carriage to drive her to the station.

No sign of haste in her manner; she gives orders to the cook about packing up some food for the journey, and when Nils asks which carriage he is to take, she thinks for a moment, and decides to take the landau and pair.

So she went away. Nils himself drove for her.

They came back the same evening; they had turned back when half-way out.

Had Fruen forgotten something? She ordered fresh horses, and another hamper of food; she was going off again at once. Nils was uneasy, and said so; it was almost night, they would be driving in the dark; but Fruen repeated her order. Meantime, she sat indoors and waited; she had not forgotten anything; she did nothing now but sit staring before her. Ragnhild went in and asked if there was anything she could do. No, thank you. Fruen sat bowed forward as if weighted down by some deadly grief.

The carriage was ready, and Fruen came out.

Seeing Nils himself ready to drive again, she took pity on him, and said she would have Grindhusen to drive this time. And she sat on the steps till he came.

Then they drove off. It was a fine evening, and nice and cool for the horses.

"She's past making out now," said Nils. "I can't think what's come to her. I'd no idea of anything, when suddenly she taps at the window and says turn back. We were about half-way there. But never a word of starting out again at once."

"But she must have forgotten something, surely?"

"Ragnhild says no. She was indoors, and I thought for a moment of those photograph things, if she was going to burn them; but they're still there. No, she didn't do a single thing while she was back."

We walked across the courtyard together.

"No," Nils went on, "Fruen's in a bad way; she's lost all harmony for everything. Where's she going off to now, do you think? Heaven knows; she doesn't seem to be altogether sure of it herself. When we stopped to breathe the horses, she said something about being in such a hurry, and having to be in different places at once—and then she ought not really to be away from home at all. 'Best for Fruen not to hurry about anything,' I said, 'but just keep quiet.' But you know how she is nowadays; there's no saying a word to her. She just looked at her watch and said go on again."

"Was this on the way to the station?"

"No, on the way back. She was quite excited, I thought."

"Perhaps the Captain sent for her?"

Nils shook his head. "No. But perhaps—Lord knows. What was I going to say—it's—tomorrow's Sunday, isn't it?"

"Yes; what then?"

"Oh, nothing. I was only thinking I'd use the day off to mark out firewood for the winter. I've been thinking of that a long while. And it's easier now than when the snow's about."

Always thinking of his work, was Nils. He took a pride in it, and was anxious now, moreover, to show his gratitude for the Captain's having raised his wages since the harvest.

It is Sunday.

I walked up to have a look at the trench and the reservoir; a few more good days now, and we should have the pipes laid down. I was quite excited about it myself, and could hardly wait for tomorrow's working-day to begin again. The Captain had not interfered in the arrangements, not with a single word, but left all to me, so that it was no light matter to me if the frost came now and upset it all.

When I got back, there was the landau outside the house—the horses had been taken out. Grindhusen would about have had time to get back, I thought; but why had he pulled up in front of the steps to the house?

I went into the kitchen. The maids came towards me; Fruen was in the carriage, they said; 'she had come back once again. She had just been to the station, but now she was going there again. Could I make out what was the matter with her, now?

"Nervous, I expect," said I. "Where's Nils?"

"Up in the woods. Said he'd be away some time. There's only us here now, and we can't say more to her than we have."

"And where's Grindhusen?"

"Changing the horses again. And Fruen's sitting there in the carriage and won't get out. You go and speak to her."

"Oh, well, there's no great harm in her driving about a bit. Don't worry about that."

I went out to the carriage, my heart beating fast. How miserable and desperate she must be! I opened the carriage door, and asked respectfully if Fruen would let me drive this time.

She looked me calmly in the face. "No. What for?" she said.

"Grindhusen might be a little done up, perhaps—I don't know...."

"He promised to drive," she said. "And he's not done up. Isn't he nearly ready?"

"I can't see him," I answered.

189

"Shut the door again, and tell him to come," she commanded, wrapping herself more closely as she spoke.

I went over to the stables. Grindhusen was harnessing a fresh pair of horses.

"What's all this?" I asked. "Going off again, are you?"

"Yes—that is, I thought so," said Grindhusen, stopping for a moment as if in doubt.

"It looks queer. Where's Fruen going to, do you know?"

"No. She wanted to drive back again last night as soon as we got to the station, but I told her that it was too much for either of us to drive back then. So she slept at the hotel. But this morning it was home again, if you please. And now she wants to go to the station again, she says. I don't know, I'm sure...."

Grindhusen goes on harnessing up.

"Fruen said you were to make haste," I said.

"All right, I'm coming. But these girths are the very devil."

"Aren't you too tired to drive all that way again now?"

"No. You know well enough I can manage it all right. And she's given me good money, too. Extra."

"Did she, though?"

"Ay, that she did. But she's a queer sort, is Fruen."

Then said I: "I don't think you ought to go off again now."

Grindhusen stopped short. "You think so? Well, now, I dare say you're right."

Just then came Fruen's voice from outside—she had come right over to the stable door.

"Aren't you ready yet? How much longer am I to sit waiting?"

"Ready this minute," answered Grindhusen, and turned to again, busier than ever. "It was only these girths."

Fruen went back to the carriage. She ran, and the thick fur coat she had on was too heavy for her, she had to balance with her arms. It was pitiful to see; like a hen trying to escape across the barnyard, and flapping its wings to help.

I went over to the carriage again, politely, even humbly. I took off my cap, and begged Fruen to give up this new journey.

"You are not driving me!" she answered.

"No. But if Fruen would only give it up and stay at home...."

At this she was offended; she stared at me, looked me up and down, and said:

"Excuse me, but this is no business of yours. Because I got you dismissed once...."

"No, no, it's not that!" I cried desperately, and could say no more. When she took it that way I was helpless.

Just for one moment a wave of fury came over me; I had only

190

to put out my arms and I could lift her out of the carriage altogether, this child, this pitiful hen! My arms must have twitched at the thought, for she gave a sudden frightened start, and shifted in her seat. Then all at once the reaction took me; I turned foolish and soft, and tried once more:

"It'll be so dismal for us all here if you go. Do let us try if we can't hit on something between us to pass the time for you! I can read a little, reading aloud, and there's Lars can sing. Perhaps I might tell stories—tell of something or other. Here's Grindhusen coming; won't you let me tell him you're not going after all?"

She softened at this, and sat thinking for a little. Then she said:

"You must be making a mistake altogether, I think. I am going to the station to meet the Captain. He didn't come the first day, or yesterday either, but he's sure to come some time. I'm driving over to meet him."

"Oh!"

"There you are. Now go. Is Grindhusen there?"

It was like a slap in the face for me. She was right; it sounded so natural—oh, I had made a fool of myself again!

"Yes, here he is," I answered. There was no more to be said.

And I put on my cap again, and helped Grindhusen myself with the harness. So confused and shamed was I that I did not even ask pardon, but only fretted this way and that way seeing to buckles and straps.

"You are driving then, Grindhusen?" called Fruen from the carriage.

"Me? Yes, surely," he answered.

Fruen pulled the door to with a bang, and the carriage drove off.

"Has she gone?" asked the maids, clasping their hands.

"Gone—yes, of course. She's going to meet her husband."

I strolled up to the reservoir again. Grindhusen away meant one man less; why, then, the rest of us must work so much the harder.

But I had already come to realize that Fru Falkenberg had only silenced me with a false excuse when she declared she was going to meet her husband. What matter? The horses were rested; they had done no work the days Nils had been helping us with the trench. But I had been a fool. I could have got up on the box myself without asking leave. Well, and what then? Why, then at least any later follies would have had to pass by way of me, more or less, and I might have stopped them. He, he! infatuated old fool! Fruen knew what she was doing, no doubt; she wanted to pay off old scores, and

191

be away when her husband came home. She was all indecision, would and would not, would and would not, all the time; but the idea was there. And I, simple soul—I had not set out a-wandering on purpose to attend to the particular interests of married folk in love or out of it. 'Twas their affair! Fru Falkenberg had changed for the worse. There was no denying it; she had suffered damage, and was thoroughly spoiled now; it hardly mattered any longer what she did. Ay, and she had taken to lying as well. First, music-hall tricks with her eyes, then on till it got to lying. A white lie today, tomorrow a blacker one, each leading to another. And what of it? Life could afford to waste her, to throw her away.

We put in three days' work at the trench; only a few feet left now. There might be three degrees of frost now at nights, but it did not stop us; we went steadily on. Grindhusen had come back, and was set to tunnelling under the kitchen where the pipes were to go; but the stable and cowshed was more important, and I did the underground work for these myself. Nils and Lars ran the last bit of trech up meanwhile, the last bit of way to the reservoir.

Today, at last, I questioned Grindhusen about Fruen.

"So you didn't bring Fruen back with you again this last time?"

"No. She went off by train."

"Off to her husband, I suppose?"

But Grindhusen has turned cautious with me; these two days past he has said never a word, and now he only answers vaguely:

"Ay, that would be it, no doubt. Ay, surely, yes. Why, you might reckon that out yourself, she would. Her own husband and all...."

"I thought perhaps she might have been going up to her own people at Kristianssand."

"Why, that might be," says Grindhusen, thinking this a better way. "Lord, yes, that would be it, of course Just for a visit, like. Well, well, she'll be home again soon, for sure."

"Did she tell you so?"

"Why, 'twas so I made out. And the Captain's not home himself yet, anyway. Eh, but she's a rare openhanded one, she is. 'Here's something for food and drink for yourself and the horses,' she says. 'And here's a little extra,' she says again. Eh, but there's never her like!"

But to the maids, with whom he felt less fear, Grindhusen had said it didn't look as if they'd be seeing Fruen back again at all. She had been asking him all the way, he said, about Engineer Lassen; she must have gone off to him after all. And, surely, she'd be well enough with him, a man with any amount of money and grand style and all.

Then came another card for Fruen from the Captain, this time only to say would she please send Nils to meet him at the station on Friday, and be sure to bring his fur coat. The post card had been delayed—it was Thursday already. And this time it was fortunate, really, that Ragnhild happened to look at the post card and see what it said.

We stayed sitting in Nils's room, talking about the Captain—what he would say when he got back, and what we should say, or if we ought to say anything at all. All three of the maids were present at this council. Fruen would have had plenty of time to get to Kristiania herself by the day the Captain had written his card; she had not, it seemed—she had gone somewhere else. It was more than pitiful altogether.

Said Nils:

"Didn't she leave a note or anything when she went?"

But no, there was nothing. Ragnhild, however, had done a thing on her own responsibility which perhaps she ought not to have done—she had taken the photos from the piano and thrown them in the stove. "Was it wrong, now?"

"No, no, Ragnhild! No!"

She told us, also, that she had been through Fruen's wardrobe and sorted out all handkerchiefs that were not hers. Oh, she had found lots of things up in her room—a bag with Engineer Lassen's initials worked on, a book with his full name in, some sweets in an envelope with his writing—and she had burnt it all.

A strange girl, Ragnhild—yes! Was there ever such an instinct as hers? It was like the devil turned monk. Ragnhild, who made such use herself of the thick red stair-carpet and the keyholes everywhere!

It suited me and my work well enough that the Captain had not ordered the carriage before; we had got the trench finished now all the way up, and I could manage without Nils for laying the pipes. I should want all hands, though, when it came to filling in again. It was rain again now, by the way; mild weather, many degrees of warmth.

It was well for me, no doubt, these days that I had this work of mine to occupy my thoughts as keenly as it did; it kept away many a fancy that would surely otherwise have plagued me. Now and again I would clench my fists as a spasm of pain came over me; and when I was all alone up at the reservoir I could sometimes cry aloud up at the woods. But there was no possibility of my getting away. And where should I go if I did?

193

The Captain arrived.

He went all through the house at once—into the parlour, out into the kitchen, then to the rooms upstairs—in his fur coat and overboots.

"Where's Fruen?" he asked.

"Fruen went to meet Captain," answered Ragnhild. "We thought she'd be coming back now as well."

The Captain's head bowed forward a little. Then cautiously he began questioning.

"You mean she drove with Nils to the station? Stupid of me not to have looked about while I was there!"

"No," said Ragnhild; "it was Sunday Fruen went."

At this the Captain pulled himself together. "Sunday?" he said. "Then she must have been going to meet me in Kristiania. H'm! We've managed to miss each other somehow. I had to make another little journey yesterday, out to Drammen—no, Frederikstad, I mean. Get me something to eat, will you?"

"Værsaagod, it's already laid."

"It was the day before yesterday, by the way, I went out there. Well, well, she'll have had a little outing, anyhow. And how's everything going on? Are the men at work on the trench?"

"They've finished it, I think."

The Captain went in, and Ragnhild came running at once to tell us what he had said, that we might know what to go by now, and not make things worse.

Later in the day he came out to where we were at work, greeted us cheerily, in military fashion, and was surprised to find the pipes already laid; we had begun filling in now.

"Splendid!" he said. "You fellows are quicker at your work than I am."

He went off by himself up to the reservoir. When he came back his eyes were not so keen; he looked a little weary. Maybe he had been sitting there alone and thinking of many things. He stood watching us now with one hand to his chin. After a little he said to Nils:

"I've sold the timber now."

"Captain's got a good price for it, maybe?"

"Yes, a good price. But I've been all this time about it. You've been quicker here."

"There are more of us here," I said. "Four of us some times."

And at that he tried to jest. "Yes," he said; "I know you're an expensive man to have about the place!"

But there was no jest in his face; his smile was hardly a smile at all. The weakness had gripped him now in earnest. After a little, he sat down on a stone we had just got out, all over fresh clay as it was, and watched us.

I took up my spade and went up, thinking of his clothes.

"Hadn't I better scrape the stone a bit clean?"

"No, it doesn't matter," he said.

But he got up all the same, and let me clean it a little.

It was then that Ragnhild came running up to us, following the line of the trench. She had something in her hand—a paper. And she was running, running. The Captain sat watching her.

"It's only a telegram!" she said breathlessly. "It came on by messenger."

The Captain got up and strode quickly a few paces forward toward this telegram that had come. Then he tore it open and read.

We could see at once it must be something important. The Captain gave a great gasp. Then he began walking down, running down, towards the house. A little way off he turned round and called to Nils:

"The carriage at once! I must go to the station!"

Then he ran on again.

So the Captain went away again. He had only been home a few hours.

Ragnhild told us of his terrible haste and worry, poor man; he was getting into the carriage without his fur coat, and would have left the food behind him that was packed all ready. And the telegram that had come was lying all open on the stairs.

"Accident," it said. "Your wife.—Chief of Police." What was all this?

"I thought as much," said Ragnhild, "when they sent it on by messenger." Her voice was strange, and she turned away. "Something serious, I dare say," she said.

"No, no!" said I, reading and reading again. "Look, it's not so very bad! Hear what it says. 'Request you come at once—accident to your wife.'"

It was an express telegram from the little town, the little dead town. Yes, that was it—a town with a roar of sound through it, and a long bridge, and foaming waters; all cries there died as they were uttered—none could hear. And there were no birds.

But all the maids spoke now in changed voices; 'twas nothing but misery amongst us now; I had to appear steady and confident myself, to reassure them. Fruen might have had a fall, perhaps, she was not as active of late. But she could, perhaps, have got up again and walked on almost as well as ever—just a little bleeding.... Oh, they were so quick with their telegrams, these police folk!

"No, no!" said Ragnhild. "You know well enough that when the Chief of Police sends a telegram it's pretty sure to mean Fruen's been found dead somewhere! Oh, I can't—I can't—can't bear it!"

Miserable days! I worked away, harder than ever, but as a man in his sleep, without interest or pleasure. Would the Captain never come?

Three days later he came—quietly and alone. The body had been sent to Kristianssand; he had only come back to fetch some clothes, then he was going on there himself, to the funeral.

He was home this time for an hour at most, then off again to catch the early train. I did not even see him myself, being out at work.

Ragnhild asked if he had seen Fruen alive.

He looked at her and frowned.

But the girl would not give up; she begged him, for Heaven's sake, to say. And the two other maids stood just behind, as desperate as she.

Then the Captain answered, but in a low voice as if to himself:

"She had been dead some days when I got there. It was an accident; she had tried to cross the river and the ice would not bear. No, no, there was no ice, but the stones were slippery. There was ice as well, though."

Then the maids began moaning and crying; but this was more than he could stand. He got up from the chair where he was sitting, cleared his throat hard, and said:

"There, there, it's all right, girls, go along now. Ragnhild, a minute." And then to Ragnhild, when the others had gone: "What was I going to say, now? You haven't moved some photos, have you, that were on the piano here? I can't make out what's happened to them."

Then Ragnhild spoke up well and with spirit—and may Heaven bless her for the lie!

"I? No, indeed, 'twas Fruen herself one day."

"Oh? Well, well. I only wondered how it was they had gone."

Relieved—relieved the Captain was to hear it.

As he was leaving he told Ragnhild to say I was not to go away from Øvrebø till he returned.

XIV

No, I didn't go away.

I worked on, tramped through the weariest days of my life to their end, and finished laying the pipes. It was a bit of a change for us all on the place the first time we could draw water from a tap, and we were none the worse for something new to talk about for a while.

Lars Falkenberg had left us. He and I had got rid of all disagreement between us at the last, and were as we had been in the old days when we were mates and tramped the roads together.

He was better off than many another, was Lars; light of heart and empty of head; and thereto unconscionably sound and strong. True, there would be no more singing up at the house for him now or ever after, but he seemed to have grown a trifle doubtful of his voice himself the last few years, and contented himself now for the most part with the things he had sung—once upon a time—at dances and gentlefolk's parties. No, Lars Falkenberg was none so badly off. He'd his own little holding, with keep for two cows and a pig; and a wife and children he had as well.

But what were Grindhusen and I to turn our hands to now? I could go off wandering anywhere, but Grindhusen, good soul, was no wanderer. All he could do was to stay on at one place and work till he was dismissed. And when the stern decision came, he was so upset that he could not take it easily, but felt he was being specially hardly used. Then after a while he grew confident again, and full of a childlike trust—not in himself, but in Fate, in Providence—sat down resignedly, and said: "Ay, well, 'twill be all right, let's hope, with God's help."

But he was happy enough. He settled down with marvellous ease at whatever place he came to, and could stay there till he died if it rested with himself. Home he need not go; the children were grown up now, and his wife never troubled him. No, this red-haired old sinner of former days—all he needed now was a place, and work.

"Where are you going after this?" he asked me.

"A long way, up in the hills, to Trovatn, to a forest."

He did not believe me in the least, but he answered quickly and evasively:

"Ay, I dare say, yes."

After we had finished the pipes, Nils sent Grindhusen and myself up cutting wood till the Captain returned. We cut up and stacked the top-ends the woodmen had left; neat and steady work it was.

"We'll be turned off, both of us," said Grindhusen. "When Captain comes, eh?"

"You might get work here for the winter," I said. "A thousand dozen battens means a lot of small stuff left over that you could saw up for a reasonable wage."

"Well, talk to the Captain about it," he said.

And the hope of regular work for the winter made this man a contented soul. He could manage well enough. No, Grindhusen had nothing much to trouble about.

But then there was myself. And I felt but little worth or use to myself now, Heaven help me!

That Sunday I wandered restlessly about. I was waiting for the Captain; he was to be back today. To make sure of things as far as I could, I went for a long walk up along the stream that fed our reservoir. I wanted to have another look at the two little waters up the hillside—"the sources of the Nile."

Coming down on the way back, I met Lars Falkenberg; he was going home. The full moon was just coming up, red and huge, and turned things light all round. A touch of snow and frost there was, too; it was easy breathing. Lars was in a friendly mood: he had been drinking Brændevin somewhere, and talked a great deal. But I was not altogether pleased at meeting him.

I had stood there long up on the wooded hillside, listening to the soughing of earth and sky, and there was nothing else to hear. Then there might come a faint little rustling, a curled and shrunken leaf rolling and rustling down over the frozen branches. It was like the sound of a little spring. Then the soughing of earth and sky again. A gentleness came over me; a mute was set on all my strings.

Lars Falkenberg wanted to know where I had been and where I was going. Reservoir? A senseless business that reservoir thing. As if people couldn't carry water for themselves. The Captain went in too much for these new-fangled inventions and ploughing over standing crops and such-like; he'd find himself landed one day. A rich harvest, they said. Ho, yes, but they never troubled to think what it must cost, with machines for this and that, and a pack of men to every machine again. What mustn't it have cost, now, for Grindhusen and me that summer! And then himself this autumn. In the old days it had been music and plenty at Øvrebø, and some of us had been asked into the parlour to sing. "I'll say no more," said Lars. "And now there's hardly a sizeable stick of timber left in the woods."

"A few years' time and it'll be as thick as ever."

"A few years! A many years, you mean. No, it's not enough to go about being Captain and commanding—brrrr! and there it is! And he's not even spokesman for the neighbours now, and you

198

never see folk coming up now to ask him what he'd say was best to do in this or that...."

"Did you see the Captain down below? Had he come back yet?" I broke in.

"He's just come back. Looked like a skeleton, he did. What was I going to say?... When are you leaving?"

"Tomorrow," I said.

"So soon?" Lars was all friendliness, and wishing me good luck now; he had not thought I should be going off at once.

"It's all a chance if I see you again this time," he said. "But I'll tell you this much, now: you'd do well to stop frittering your life away any more, and never staying on a place for good. And I say as much here and now, so mark my words. I dare say I haven't got on so grandly myself, but I don't know many of our likes have done better, and anyway not you. I've a roof over my head at the least, and a wife and children, and two cows—one bears autumn and one spring—and then a pig, and that's all I can say I own. So better not boast about that. But if you reckon it up, it amounts to a bit of a holding after all."

"It's all very well for you, the way you've got on," said I.

Lars is friendlier than ever after this appreciation; he wishes me no end of good, and goes on:

"There's none could get on better than yourself, for that matter. With the knack you've got for all kinds of work, and writing and figuring into the bargain. But it's your own fault. You might have done as I told you these six, seven years ago, and taken one of the other girls on the place, like I did with Emma, and settled down here for good. Then you wouldn't be going about now from place to place. But I say the same again now."

"It's too late," I answered.

"Ay, you're terribly grey. I don't know who you could reckon to get now about here. How old are you now?"

"Don't ask me!"

"Not exactly a young one, perhaps, but still—What was I going to say? Come up with me a little, and maybe I'll remember."

I walked up, and Lars went on talking all the way. He offered to put in a word for me with the Captain, so I could get a clearing like he had.

"Funny to go and forget a thing like that," he said. "It's gone clean out of my head. But come up home now. I'll be sure to hit on it again."

All friendliness he was now. But I had one or two things to do myself, and would not go farther.

"You won't see the Captain tonight, anyway."

No, but it was late. Emma would be in bed, and would only be a trouble.

"Not a bit of it," said Lars. "And if she has gone to bed, what of it? I shouldn't wonder, now, if there was a shirt of yours up there, too. Better come up and take it with you, and save Emma going all the way down herself."

But I would not go up. I ventured, however, to send a greeting to Emma this time.

"Ay, surely," said Lars. "And if so be as you haven't time to come up to my bit of a place now, why, there it is. You'll be going off first thing tomorrow, I suppose?"

It slipped my mind for the moment that I should not be able to see the Captain that evening, and I answered now that I should be leaving as early as could be.

"Well, then, I'll send Emma down with that shirt of yours at once," said Lars. "And good luck to you. And don't forget what I said."

And that was farewell to Lars.

A little farther down I slackened my pace. After all, there was no real hurry about the few things I had to pack and finish off. I turned back and walked up again a little, whistling in the moonlight. It was a fine evening, not cold at all, only a soft, obedient calm all over the woods. Half an hour passed, and then to my surprise came Emma, bringing my shirt.

Next morning neither Grindhusen nor I went to the woods. Grindhusen was uneasy.

"Did you speak to the Captain about me?" he asked.

"I haven't spoken to him."

"Oh, I know he'll turn me off now, you see! If he had any sense, he'd let me stay on to cut up all that cord-wood. But what's he know about things? It's as much as he can manage to keep a man at all."

"Why, what's this, Grindhusen? You seemed to like the Captain well enough before."

"Oh yes, you know! Yes, of course. He's good enough, I dare say. H'm! I wonder, now, if the Inspector down on the river mightn't have some little scrap of a job in my line. He's a man with plenty of money, is the Inspector."

I saw the Captain at eight o'clock, and talked with him a while; then a couple of neighbours came to call—offering sympathy in his bereavement, no doubt. The Captain looked fatigued, but he was not a broken man by any means; his manner was firm and steady enough. He spoke to me a little about a plan he had in mind for a big drying-house for hay and corn.

No more of things awry now, Øvrebø, no more emotion, no soul gone off the rails. I thought of it almost with sadness. No one to stick up impertinent photographs on the piano, but no one to play on that piano, either; dumb now, it stands, since the last note sounded. No, for Fru Falkenberg is not here now; she can do no more hurt to herself or any other. Nothing of all that used to be here now. Remains, then, to be seen if all will be flowers and joy at Øvrebø hereafter.

"If only he doesn't take to drinking again," I said to Nils.

"No, surely," he said. "And I don't believe he ever did. It was just a bit of foolery, if you ask me, his going on like that just for the time. But talking of something else—will you be coming back here in the spring?"

"No," I answered. "I shall not come again now."

Then Nils and I took leave of each other. Well I remember that man's calm and fairness of mind; I stood looking after him as he walked away across the yard. Then he turned round and said:

"Were you up in the woods yesterday? Is there snow enough for me to take a sledge up for wood?"

"Yes," I answered.

And he went off, relieved, to the stables, to harness up.

Grindhusen, too, comes along, on the way to the stable. He stops for a moment to tell me that the Captain has himself offered him work cutting wood. "'Saw up all the small stuff you can,' he said; 'keep at it for a while. I dare say we can agree all right about wages.' 'Honoured and thank you, Captain,' says I. 'Right! Go and tell Nils,' he says. Oh, but he's a grand open-handed sort, is the Captain! There's not many of his like about."

A little while after, I was sent for up to the Captain's room. He thanked me for the work I had done both indoors, and out, and went on to settle up. And that was all, really. But he kept me there a little, asking one or two things about the drying-shed, and we talked over that for a bit. Anyhow it would have to wait till after Christmas, he said. But when the time came, he'd be glad to see me back. He looked me in the face then, and went on:

"But you won't come back here again now, I suppose?"

I was taken by surprise. But I faced him squarely in return, and answered:

"No."

As I went down, I thought over what he had said. Had he seen through me, then? If so, he had shown a degree of trust in me that I was glad to think of. At least, he was a man of good feeling.

Trust me? And why should he not? Played out and done with as I was. Suffered to go about and do and be as I pleased, by virtue of my eminent incapacity for harm. Yes, that was it. And, anyhow, there was nothing to see through after all.

I went round, upstairs and down, saying good-bye to them all, to Ragnhild and the maids. Then, as I was coming in front of the house with my pack on my shoulder, the Captain called to me from the steps:

"Wait! I just thought—if you're going to the station, the lad could drive you in."

Thoughtful and considerate again! But I thanked him and declined. I was not so played out but that I could surely walk that way.

Back in my little town again. And if I have come here now, it is because the place lies on my way to Trovatn, up in the hills.

All is as it was before here now, save for thin ice on the river above and below the rapids, and snow on the ice again.

I take care to buy clothes and equipment here in the town, and, having got a good new pair of shoes, I take my old ones to the cobbler to be half-soled. The cobbler is inclined to talk, and begs me to sit down. "And where's this man from, now?" he asks. In a moment I am enveloped by the spirit of the town.

I walk up to the churchyard. Here, too, care has been taken to provide equipment for the winter. Bundles of straw have been fastened round plants and bushes; many a delicate monument is protected by a tall wooden hood. And the hoods again armoured with a coat of paint. As if some provident soul had thought: Well, now, I have this funeral monument here; with proper care it may be made to last for generations!

There is a Christmas Fair on, too, and I stroll along to see. Here are skis and toboggans, butter scoops and log chairs from the underworld, rose-coloured mittens, clothes' rollers, foxes' skins. And here are horse-dealers and drovers mingling with drunken folk from up the valley. Jews there are, too, anxious to palm off a gaudy watch or so, for all there is no money in the town. And the watches come from that country up in the Alps, where Bocklin—did not come from; where nothing and nobody ever came from.

But in the evening there is brave entertainment for all. Two dancing-halls there are, and the music is supplied by masters on the hardingfele, and wonderful music it is, to be sure. There are iron strings to it, and it utters no empty phrases, but music with a sting in its tail. It acts differently upon different people: some find it rich in national sweetness; some of us are rather constrained to grit our teeth and howl in melancholy wise. Never was stinging music delivered with more effect.

The dance goes on.

In one of the intervals the schoolmaster sings touching verses about an

> *"aged mother, worn with toil*
> *And sweating as 'twere blood...."*

But some of the wild youths insist on dancing and nothing else. What's this! Start singing, when they're standing here with the girls all ready to dance—it's not proper! The singer stops, and meets the protest in broadest dialect: What? Not proper? Why, it's by Vinje himself! Heated discussion, pro and contra, arguing and shouting. Never were verses sung with more effect.

The dance goes on.

The girls from the valley are armoured five layers thick, but who cares for that! All are used to hard work. And the dance goes on—ay, the thunder goes on. Brændevin helps things bravely along. The witches' cauldron is fairly steaming now. At three in the morning the local police force appears, and knocks on the floor with his stick. Finis. The dancers go off in the moonlight, and spread out near and far. And nine months later, the girls from the valley show proof that after all they were one layer of armour short. Never was such an effect of being one layer short.

The river is quieter now—not much of a river to look at: the winter is come upon it now. It drives the mills and works that stand on its banks, for, in spite of all, it is and will be a great river still, but it shows no life. It has shut down the lid on itself.

And the rapids have suffered, too. And I who stood watching them once and listening, and thought to myself if one lived down there in the roar of it for ever, what would one's brain be like at last? But now the rapids are dwindled, and murmur faintly. It would be shame to call it a roar. Herregud! 'tis no more than a ruin of what it was. Sunk into poverty, great rocks thrust up all down the channel, with here and there a stick of timber hung up thwart and slantwise; one could cross dry-shod by way of stick and stone.

I have done all I have to do in the town, and my pack is on my shoulders. It is Sunday, and a fine clear day.

I look in at the hotel, to see the porter; he is going with me a bit of the way up the river. The great good-hearted fellow offers to carry my things—as if I could not carry them myself.

We go up along the right bank; but the road itself lies on the left; the way we are taking is only a summer path, trodden only by the lumbermen, and with some few fresh tracks in the snow. My companion cannot make out why we do not follow the road: he was always dull of wit; but I have been up this path twice before these

203

last few days, and I am going up it once again. It is my own tracks we can see all the time.

I question him:

"That lady you told me about once—the one that was drowned—was it somewhere about here?"

"Eh? Oh, the one that fell in! Yes. Ay, it was close by here. Dreadful it was. There must have been twenty of us here, with the police, searching about."

"Dragging the channel?"

"Yes. We got out planks and ladders, but they broke through under us; we cut up all the ice in the end. Here"—he stopped suddenly—"you can see the way we went."

I can see in the dark space where the boats had moved out and broken through the ice to drag the depth; it was frozen over again now.

The porter goes on:

"We found her at last. And a mercy it was, I dare say. The river was low as it was. Gone right down at once, she had, and got stuck fast between two stones. There was no current to speak of; if it had been spring, now, she'd have travelled a long way down."

"Trying to cross to the other side, I suppose?"

"Ay. They're always getting out on the ice as soon as it comes; a nasty way it is. Somebody had been over already, but that was two days before. She just came walking down on this side where we are, and the engineer, he was coming down the road on the other side—he'd been out on his bicycle somewhere. Then they caught sight of each other and waved or made a sign or something, for they were cousins or something, both of them. Then the lady must have mistaken him somehow, the engineer says, and thought he was beckoning, for she started to come across. He shouted at her not to, but she didn't hear, and he'd got his bicycle and couldn't move, but, anyhow, some one had got across before. The engineer told the police all about how it happened, and it was written down, every word. Well, and then when she's half-way across, she goes down. A rotten piece of ice it must have been where she trod. And the engineer, he comes down like lightning on his bicycle through the town and up to the hotel and starts ringing. I never heard the like, the way he rang. 'There's someone in the river!' he cries out. 'My cousin's fallen in!' Out we went, and he came along with us. We'd ropes and boat-hooks, but that was no use. The police came soon after, and the fire brigade; they got hold of a boat up there and carried it between them till they got to us; then they got it out and started searching about with the drag. We didn't find her the first day, but the day after. Ay, a nasty business, that it was."

"And her husband came, you said. The Captain?"

"Yes, the Captain, he came. And you can reckon for yourself the state he was in. And we were all the same for that matter, all the town was. The engineer, he was out of his senses for a long while, so they told us at the hotel, and when the Captain arrived, the engineer went off inspecting up the river, just because he couldn't bear to talk any more about it."

"So the Captain didn't see him, then?"

"No. H'm! Nay, I don't know," said the porter, looking around. "No, I don't know anything about that—no."

His answer was so confused, it was evident that he did know. But it was of no importance, and I did not question him again.

"Well, thanks for coming up with me," I said, and shared a little money with him for a winter wrap or something of the sort. And I took leave of him, and wanted him to turn back.

He seemed anxious, however, to go on with me a little farther. And, to get me to agree, he suddenly confesses that the Captain had seen the engineer while he was here—yes. The porter, good foolish creature, had understood enough of the maids' gossip in the kitchen to make out that there was something wrong about the engineer and this cousin of his who had come to stay; more than this, however, he had not seen. But, as regards the meeting between the two men, it was he himself who had acted as guide to the Captain on his way up to find the engineer.

"He said he must find him, and so we went up together. And the Captain, he asked me on the way, what could there be to inspect up the river now it was frozen over? And I couldn't see myself, I told him. And so we walked up all day to about three or four in the afternoon. 'We might see if he's not in the hut here,' I said, for I'd heard the lumbermen used the place. Then the Captain wouldn't let me go on with him any farther, but told me to wait. And he walked up to the hut by himself, and went in. He'd not been in the place more than a bare couple of minutes, when out he comes, and the engineer with him. There was a word or so between them—I didn't hear; then all of a sudden the Captain flings up one arm like that, and lands out at the engineer, and down he goes. Lord! but he must have felt it pretty badly. And not content with that, he picks him up and lands out at him again as hard as before. Then he came back to me and said we'd be going home."

I grew thoughtful at this. It seemed strange that this porter, a creature who bore no grudge or ill-will to any one, should leave the engineer up there at the hut without aid. And he had shown no disapproval in his telling of the thrashing. The engineer must have been miserly with him, too, I thought, and never paid him for his

205

services, but only ordered him about and laughed at him, puppy that he was. That would be it, no doubt. And this time, perhaps, I was not misled by jealous feelings of my own.

"But the Captain—he was free with his money, if you like," said the porter at last. "I paid off all my owings with what he gave me—ay, indeed I did."

When at last I had got rid of the man, I crossed the river; the ice was firm enough. I was on the main road now. And I walked on, thinking over the porter's story. That scene at the hut—what did it amount to, after all? It merely showed that one of the two men was big and strong, the other a little, would-be sportsman heavily built behind. But the Captain was an officer—it was something of that sort, perhaps, he had been thinking. Perhaps he ought to have thought a little more in other ways while there was yet time—who can say? It was his wife! who had been drowned. The Captain might do what he pleased now; she would never come again.

But if she did, what then? She was born to her fate, no doubt. Husband and wife had tried to patch up the damage, but had failed. I remember her as she was six or seven years back. She found life dull, and fell in love a trifle here and there perhaps, even then, but she was faithful and delicate-minded. And time went on. She had no occupation, but had three maid-servants to her house; she had no children, but she had a piano. But she had no children.

And Life can afford to waste.

Mother and child it was that went down.

EPILOGUE

A wanderer plays with muted strings when he comes to fifty years. Then he plays with muted strings.

Or I might put it in this way.

If he comes too late for the harvest of berries in autumn, why, he is come too late, that is all; and if one fine day he finds he can no longer be gay and laugh all over his face in delight of life, 'tis because he is old, no doubt; blame him not for that! And there can be no doubt that it requires a certain vacuity of mind to go about feeling permanently contented with oneself and all else. But we have all our softer moments. A prisoner is being driven to the scaffold in a cart. A nail in the seat irks him; he shifts aside a little, and feels more at ease.

A Captain should not pray that God may forgive him—as he forgives his God. It is simply theatrical. A wanderer who cannot reckon every day on food and drink, clothes and boots, and house and home, feels just the right degree of privation when all these luxuries are lacking. If you cannot manage one way, why, there will be another. But if the other way should also fail, then one does not forgive one's God, but takes up the responsibility oneself. Shoulder against what comes—that is, bow to it. A trifle hard for flesh and blood, and it greys a man's hair sadly. But a wanderer thanks God for life; it was good to live!

I might put it that way.

For why these high demands on life? What have we earned? All the boxes of sweetmeats a sweet-tooth could wish for? Well and good. But have we not had the world to look upon each day, and the soughing of the woods to hear? There is nothing so grand in all the world as that voice of the woods.

There was a scent of jasmine in a shrubbery, and one I know thrilled with joy, not for the jasmine's scent but for all there was—for the light in a window, a memory, the whole of life. He was called away from the jasmines after, but he had been paid beforehand for that little mishap.

And so it is; the mere grace that we are given life at all is generous payment in advance for all the miseries of life—for every one of them.

No, do not think we have the right to more sweetmeats than we get. A wanderer's advice: no superstition. What is life's? All. But what is yours? Is fame? Oh, tell us why! A man should not so insist on what is "his." It is comical; a wanderer laughs at any one who can be so comical. I remember one who could not give up that "his." He started to lay a fire in his stove at noon, and by evening he got it to burn at last. He couldn't leave the comfortable warmth to go to bed, but sat there till other people got up, lest it should be wasted. A Norwegian writer of stage plays, it was.

I have wandered about a good deal in my time, and am grown foolish now, and out of bloom. But I do not hold the perverse belief of old men generally, that I am wiser than I was. And I hope I may never grow wise; 'tis a sign of decrepitude. If I thank God for life, it is not by virtue of any riper wisdom that has come to me with age, but because I have always taken a pleasure in life. Age gives no riper wisdom; age gives nothing but age.

I was too late for the berries this year, but I am going up that way all the same. I am allowing myself this little treat, by way of reward for having worked well this summer. And I reach my goal on the 12th of December.

It is true, no doubt, that I might have stayed down among the villages. I could have managed somehow, no doubt, as did all the others who had found it time to settle down. And Lars Falkenberg, my colleague and mate, he had urged me to take up a holding with keep for a wife and two cows and a pig. A friend's advice; vox populi. And then, why, one of the cows might be an ox to ride, a means of transport for my shivering age! But it came to naught—it came to naught! My wisdom has not come with age; here am I going up to Trovatn and the waste lands to live in a wooden hut!

What pleasure can there be in that? Ai, Lars Falkenberg, and ai, every one else, have no fear; I have a man to come up with things I need.

So I drift about and about by myself, looking after myself, living alone. I miss that seal of Bishop Pavel's. One of his descendants gave it to me, and I had it in my waistcoat pocket this summer, but, looking for it now, I find I have lost it. Well, well; but, anyhow, I have been paid in advance for that mishap, in having owned it once.

But I do not feel the want of books to read.

The 12th of December—I can keep a date in mind and carelessly forget things more important. It is only just now I remember about the books—that Captain Falkenberg and his wife had many books in their house—novels and plays—a whole bookcase full. I saw it one day when I was painting windows and doors at Øvrebø. Entire sets of authors they had, and authors' complete works—thirty books. Why the complete works? I do not know. Books—one, two, three, ten, thirty. They had come out each Christmas—novels, thirty volumes—the same novel. They read them, no doubt, the Captain and his wife; knew every time what they should find in the poets of the home; there was always such a lot about all coming right in the end. So they read them, no doubt. How should I know? Heavens, what a host of books! Two men could not shift the bookcase when I wanted to paint behind; it took three men and a cook to move it. One of the men was Grindhusen; he flushed under the weight of those poets of the home, and said: "I can't see what folk want with such a mighty crowd of books!"

Grindhusen! As if he knew anything about it! The Captain and his wife had all those books, no doubt, that none should be lacking; there they were all complete. It would make a gap to take away a single one; they were paired each with the rest, uniform poetry, the same story throughout.

An elk-hunter has been up here with me in the hut. Nothing much; and his dog was an ill-tempered brute. I was glad when he went on again. He took down my copper saucepan from the wall, and used it for his cooking, and left it black with soot.

It is not my copper saucepan, but was here in the hut, left by some one who was here before. I only rubbed it with ashes and hung it up on the wall as a weather-guide for myself. I am rubbing it up again now, for it is a good thing to have; it turns dim unfailingly when there is rain or snow coming on.

If Ragnhild had been here, now, she would have polished up that saucepan herself. But then, again, I tell myself, I would rather see to my own weather-guides; Ragnhild can find something else to do. And if this place up in the woods were our clearing, then she would have the children, and the cows, and the pig. But my copper things I prefer to do myself, Ragnhild.

I remember a lady, the mistress of a house: she did no work at all, and saw to nothing, least of all to herself. And ill she fared in the end. But six or seven years back I had never believed any one could be so delicate and lovely to another as she. I drove her once, upon a journey, and she was shy with me, although she was a lady, and above me. She blushed and looked down. And the strange thing was that she made me feel a kind of shyness myself, although I was only her servant. Only by looking at me with her two eyes when she spoke to me, she showed me treasures and beauty beyond what I knew before; I remember it still. Ay, here I sit, remembering it yet, and I shake my head and say to myself how strange it was—how strange! And then she died. And what more? Nothing more. I am still here, but she is gone. But I should not grieve at her death. I had been paid beforehand, surely, for that loss, in that she looked at me with her two eyes—a thing beyond my deserts. Ay, so it must be.

Woman—what do the sages know of woman?

I know a sage, and he wrote of woman. Wrote of woman in

thirty volumes of uniform theatre-poetry: I counted the volumes once in a big bookcase. And at last he wrote of the woman who left her own children to go in search of—the wonderful! But what, then, were the children? Oh, it was comical: a wanderer laughs at anything so comical.

What does the sage know of woman?

To begin with, he was not a sage at all till he grew old, and all he knew of woman then was from memory. But then, again, he can have no memory of her, seeing he never knew her. The man who has an aptitude for wisdom busies himself jealously with his little aptitude and nothing else; cultivates and cherishes it; holds it forth and lives for it.

We do not turn to woman for wisdom. The four wisest heads in the world, who have delivered their findings on the subject of woman, simply sat and invented her out of their own heads— octogenarians young or old they were, that rode on oxen. They knew nothing of woman in holiness, woman in sweetness, woman as an indispensable, but they wrote and wrote about her. Think of it! Without finding her.

Heaven save me from growing wise! And I will mumble the same to my last turn: Heaven save me from growing wise!

Just cold enough now for a little outing I have had in mind: the snow-peaks lie rosy in the sun, and my copper saucepan points to fair. It is eight in the morning.

Knapsack and a good stock of food, an extra lashing in my pocket in case anything should break, and a note on the table for the man with supplies in case he should come up while I am away.

Oh, but I have been showing off nicely all to myself: pretending I was going far, and needed to equip myself with care, had occasion for all my presence of mind and endurance. A man can show off like that when he is going far; but I am not. I have no errand anywhere, and nothing calls me; I am only a wanderer setting forth from a hut, and coming back to it again; it does not matter where I am.

It is quiet and empty in the woods; all things deep in snow, holding their breath as I come. At noon, looking back from a hill, I can see Trovatn far behind; white and flat it lies, a stretch of chalk, a desert of snow. After a meal I go on again, higher and higher, nearing the fjeld now, but slowly and thoughtfully, with hands in my pockets. There is no hurry; I have only to find a shelter for the night.

Later on in the afternoon I sit down again to eat, as if I needed a meal and had earned it. But it is only for something to do; my hands are idle, and my brain inclined to fancies. It gets dark early:

well to find a sheltered cleft in the hillside here; there are fallen firs enough lying about for a fire.

Such are the things I tell of now, playing with muted strings.

I was out early next morning, as soon as it began to get light. A quiet, warm snowfall came on, and there was a soughing in the air. Bad weather coming, I thought to myself; but who could have foreseen it? Neither I nor my weather-guide looked for it twenty-four hours ago.

I left my shelter and went on again over moor and heath; full day again now, and snowing. It was not the best of shelters I had found for the night: passably soft and dry, with branches of fir to lie on, and I had not felt the cold, but the smoke from my fire drifted in over me and troubled my breathing.

But now, this afternoon, I found a better place—a spacious and elegant cave with walls and roof complete. Room here for me and my fire, and the smoke went up. I nodded at this, and decided to settle down here, though it was early yet, and still quite light; I could distinctly make out the hills and valleys and rocks on a naked fjeld straight ahead some few hours' march away. But I nodded, as if I had reached my goal, and set to work gathering firewood and bedding for the night.

I felt so thoroughly at home here. It was not for nothing I nodded and took off my knapsack. "Was this the place you were making for?" I say, talking to myself in jest. "Yes," I answer.

The soughing in the air grew stronger; it was not snow that was falling now, but rain. Strange—a great wet rainfall down over the cave, over all the trees outside, and yet it was the cold Christmas month—December. A heat-wave had taken it into its head to visit us.

It rained and rained that night, and there was a soughing all through the trees outside. It was like spring; it filled my sleep at last with so rich an ease, that I slept on sound and deep till it was broad day.

Ten o'clock.

The rain had ceased, but it is still warm. I sit looking out of the cave, and listening to the bend and whisper of the trees. Then a stone breaks loose on the fjeld opposite; it butts against a rock and brings that down as well; a few faint thuds are heard. Then a rumble: I see what is happening, and the sound echoes within me; the rock loosened other rocks, an avalanche goes thundering down the mountain-side, snow and earth and boulders, leaving a smoky cloud in its wake. The stream of rubble seems in a living rage; it thrusts its way on, tearing down other masses with it—crowding, pouring, pouring, fills up a chasm in the valley—and stops. The last few boulders settle slowly into place, and then no more. The thunder over, there is silence, and within myself is only a breathing as of a slowly descending bass.

And so I sit once more, listening to the soughing of the woods. Is it the heaving of the AEgean sea, or is it the ocean current Glimma? I grow weak from just listening. Recollections of my past life rise within me, joys by the thousand, music and eyes, flowers. There is nothing more glorious than the soughing of the woods. It is like swinging, rocking—a madness: Uganda, Antananarivo, Honolulu, Atacama, Venezuela.

But it is all the years, no doubt, that make me so weak, and my nerves that join in the sounds I hear. I get up and stand by the fire to get over it; now I think of it, I feel I could talk to the fire a little, make a speech to the dying fire. I am in a fire-proof house here, and the acoustic conditions are good. H'm!

Then the cave is darkened; it is the elk-hunter again with his dog.

It begins to freeze as I trudge along homeward to my hut. The frost soon hardens the ground, moor and heath, making it easy walking. I trudge along slowly and carelessly, hands in my pockets. There is no hurry now; it matters little where I am.

www.ingramcontent.com/pod-product-compliance
Lightning Source LLC
Chambersburg PA
CBHW030447250626
47154CB00003BA/1165